Pretty

A HARLEM SITUATION

BRAD BATHGATE

The Great Persuader
P.O. Box 1100
New York N.Y. 10030
www.Poetryisalive.com

International Standard Book Number 0-9712581-1-2

© 2004 Derrick Wilson TX 6-011-277 2004

Published by **The Great Persuader Publishing**©

P.O. Box 1100
New York NY 10030
Greatpersuader@Hotmail.com
www.poetryisalive.com

This book is a work of fiction. Names, characters, places and incidents either are the product of the author's imagination or used fictitiously, and any resemblance to actual person, living or dead, events, or local is entirely coincidental.

Cover design and layout by Derrick Wilson
Printed In the United States of America

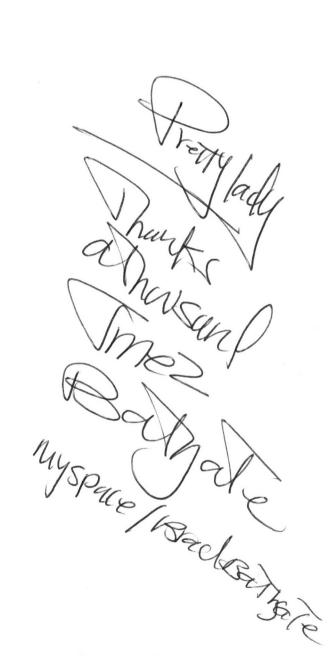

Pretty lady
Thanks a thousand
Timez
Bathgate
myspace/Blackbathgate

Most New Yorkers are bad actors...
playing crazy

Chapter 1:

.

Even at the bottom of the low, the sun shines in a pretty ugly kind of way - yet those summer days in Harlem were still sweet. That's when the hustlers got their exotic cars washed on the city sidewalks, and then drove off with their rims shining from the Armor Oil that made their tires look like they were dipped in hot grease. The merry old men wore their straw hats slightly tipped to the side, anxiously anticipating the next number as they talked trash around their game of checkers.

Once the basketball tournaments got started uptown, some of the guys would head up that way to meet some of the prettiest girls on the planet, while others would just hang out and socialize. You could catch a glimpse of motorcycles racing up and down the avenues, doing dangerous stunts and revving their engines for every girl with a big butt and a nice smile.

And there was Chuck Love, looking older than his twenty-three years. You could see it in his body language, his demeanor and the people he chose to associate with.

It was early in the afternoon when Chuck headed uptown to check out the Rucker basketball games, and since he had to pass by Mr. Ray's barbershop on the way there, he decided to stop by and say hello. The barbershop was a neighborhood watering hole that had been in the same location for years. Mr. Ray had given Chuck his first haircut and his first job - when Chuck was only nine years old he would go by the shop on Saturday mornings to sweep up.

This was an old-fashioned barbershop, where photographs

of boxing legends and a pair of ancient boxing gloves adorned the plywood walls along with a few trophies that belonged to Mr. Ray. He had been a good amateur boxer in his younger years, though he couldn't cut it as a pro. But if you wanted to talk about boxing, Mr. Ray was always ready. He could go on for hours, walking you over to his wall of fame, showing off his boxing gloves or the photos of his favorite fighters and their best attributes. Mr. Ray was tall with bushy gray hair and good eating habits that keep his skin clear and his bones in good working condition.

Today when Chuck dropped in it was general small talk as usual, until Mr. Ray asked him how was he doing in school. Chuck had mostly good news to tell, but when he came to the part about the recent drug bust on the college campus, that started Mr. Ray's mouth right off.

"Listen Chuck, anybody that needs a drug to change the way dey think, or in orda ta have a good time... can't be too bright. You got a good head on ya shouldas Chuck, an' I know that you know betta. Now all you gotta do is finish school like ya daddy wanted, an' come back ta New York wit a diploma, an' start that magazine thing that you always talkin' 'bout. Anything as long as it's sump'n bigga an' betta den de bullshit dese young dudes out here waste dey time on. Dey always thinkin' small. Not you Chuck, that's why I like you," Mr. Ray continued. Then he looked around the shop to make sure there were no children present before he went on. "Whateva you do Chuck, jus' don't mess aroun' an' end up in jail like dese bottom-shelf fools out here, somewhere makin' collect calls back home ta ya mama an' worryin' her half ta death."

"You got that right," Mr. Allen testified from the back of the shop. He was Mr. Ray's co-worker, a good-humored guy from Akron, Alabama. He and Mr. Ray were old friends and had worked together ever since their late twenties. The regular customers always enjoyed chatting and laughing with him, and there were days when some of them would just stop by the shop to sit around and laugh with Allen all day, whether or not they needed a haircut.

Mr. Ray then turned around to face Chuck and said, "You know Chuck, women always sayin' that all men are dogs... but who raised those dogs? Women!"

"Ya got that right," Allen said again.

"Every time one of those grown-ass boys get inta some kinda trouble, da first thing dey do is run to dey mama's house ta hide - dat's cause dey mama excuses all her baby's wrong-doin', and calls dat "love." Da main reason you got a bunch of grown-ass men still livin' wit dey mama, an' walkin' aroun' the apartment wit dey unda'wear on, n'shit... is cause dey mama don't know when ta let go."

"Ya got dat right!" Mr. Allen vigorously agreed. He was cutting a customer's hair and he stepped a few feet away to finish off Mr. Ray's rant, "Da apple tree knows when ta let go of da apple. If it holds on to too long, it'll get spoiled."

"Dat's right," Mr. Ray testified as if he were in church.

"Da mama lion knows when ta let the huh, huh, huh! What'cha call da baby lion?" Mr. Allen asked.

"A cub," Chuck said.

"Yeah, a cub. Da mama lion knows when ta let go of da cub. The womens, dey is da only ones dat don't know when ta let go of dese grown-ass men."

"Every time one of dey sons do sump'n wrong," Mr. Ray added, "Da mama is da first one ta run ta her boy's defense... callin' her grown-ass son her baby."

"When I wuz comin' up... my Daddy ain't play dat shit!" Allen yelled.

"Mine eitha."

Chuck stood there for some time, laughing with the older men, feeling right at home. Eventually he made his way uptown, and he was leaning up against a parked car with a couple of friends when a brand new 1985 pearl-white M3 BMW drew up and parked a few feet away from them. It was Zachary, Mr. Ray's nephew. A light-skinned man who stood almost six feet tall, he had a nice smile and a nasty disposition. He was a no-nonsense kind of guy who was "not afraid of nothin'." He had just come out after another small stint, and it was obvious from his demeanor that he was pleased to be back on the streets. It was in the way he greeted everybody with hugs and slapping fives.

Zachary was a hustler in the truest sense of the word, a player with his hands in everything. At one time he had sold drugs, but he stepped away before it cost him his life. He claimed that it was a shady business with too many bad characters involved. Once he'd left that behind, he started driving a couple of girls down to the Philadelphia strip clubs, and he was making good money off of it for a while. But when he got tired of driving up and down the turnpike he went back to playing Three Card Monte. The money was not as fast as it was with selling drugs, but it didn't come with the same kind of risk or the endless headaches.

It takes a certain kind of character to be a player like Zachary was. He had charisma as well as all the necessary skills, and he was a good talker. He kept his crew in line, and whenever you saw him, he always had an attractive girl by his side. Mr. Ray called his nephew's female friends "high-maintenance chicks," or "drama queens." But that didn't matter to Chuck, because he thought they were fine as hell. Even though Zachary and Chuck had never formally been introduced, they remembered seeing each other a couple of times back at the barbershop.

Chuck was quietly drooling over Zachary's car when he caught sight of Apple, a girl he'd been crazy about ever since high school. Back when she and Chuck were younger, they'd passed love letters and kissed once, but Apple was just too fast for him. She admired Chuck's wit and sense of humor, but she felt there wasn't anything he could do for her.

When Chuck saw Apple go by that afternoon, he quickly slid away from his boys to try and get her attention, and just at that moment Zachary was doing the same thing, but he had to jump out of his car first. They'd both seen Apple simultaneously, and just that quick, Chuck was on the right side of her and Zachary was on her left, and that's how the two men officially met. They both knew the same girl, and when Chuck realized this, it was like a dose of self-confidence for him. They took turns speaking to Apple, Chuck going first, and then they took turns introducing themselves to each other. Zachary went first this time. Then the two men began talking together, and unconsciously they stepped away from Apple. One way or another, word had gotten to Zachary that Chuck knew his way around certain parts of Kentucky, and that he was able to run guns up the highway.

"So you're Chuck?" Zachary smirked, "I heard some interesting things about you."

"Yeah, from who?" Chuck smiled back at him, non-committal.

"That ain't important," Zachary chuckled.

"Well… whateva you heard I hope it wuz good."

"Yeah, it wuz, it wuz all good!" Zachary smiled. He had his left arm folded across his chest with his right finger held up to his chin like a deep thinker. It was evident that this was an awkward moment for him, approaching Chuck without really knowing him - so to break the silence Zachary complimented Chuck on the chain that he wore around his neck. It was small, with an odd-shaped ornament hanging in the middle of it, and it was clearly inexpensive - but its symbolic value made it priceless. Chuck quickly told the story behind the chain, and then he and Zachary began to talk business.

"Listen Chuck," Zachary started calmly, "from what I unda'-stand… I heard that you're a man who can get ya hands on some joints?"

Chuck wasn't surprised that the word was getting around so fast, but he'd never expected to be approached by Zachary. He was a little apprehensive about this conversation, but he didn't want to pass up an opportunity to make some money. He cleared his throat and replied, "Yeah, that's true… any kinda guns you want, I can get 'em! I can't get no grenades n'shit. But I can get'cha semi-automatics, an' revolvas." He made sure to talk slow and throw in a little humor so he wouldn't seem too anxious about working with the big-timers.

"How difficult would it be for you to get'em up here to the city?" Zachary asked, as he rested his back against a nearby tree with his arms still crossed. The tree shaded one side of his face while the sun bounced off his gold medallion. "I know a couple of people that's been askin' aroun', plus I got these dudes on 8th Avenue that's been buggin' the hell outta me about this shit. I told'em that I know somebody, an' luckily I bumped into you. Ya know what I'm sayin'?"

"I feel you, I feel you. It wouldn't be no trouble at all. Jus' let me know when you're ready, an' we can talk… But first you gotta teach me some of those card tricks that you do," Chuck teased, feeling him out. He made lazy hand gestures, pretending to shuffle cards. "So when it's time for me to go back to school an' I need some cash… I'll be able to beat those country cats outta' dey lunch money."

Chuck's lighthearted behavior made Zachary smile - it was as if he had researched a craft that Zachary perfected, and he seemed sincere about learning it.

"What'chu know 'bout my hustle?" Zachary laughed, "That shit take years to learn. You can't jus' go an' try that shit anywhere. Somebody will try to hurt you. Ya know what I'm sayin'… That shit takes a lot of practice, word up!"

There was a slight chuckle between the two men and they got so deep into their common ground that twenty minutes passed without either of them noticing. It wasn't until Zachary turned around to ask Apple for a pen that they both realized she had moved off down the street. It was a missed opportunity for Chuck to rekindle an old flame, and when he looked around all he could see was her back disappearing.

"Damn," was all he could say, in a low voice. He wanted to run and catch up to her, but he feared embarrassing himself in the presence of his friends. By then, Zachary had gone to his car to tell the girl in the passenger's seat to hand him a pen. She let down the window and the music that she'd been gyrating her body to got a little louder. The car's leather interior smelled like new money to Chuck, and he caught himself daydreaming. He longed for a taste of the fast-paced life that Zachary wore so well.

The two men exchanged numbers, slapped five and then continued to talk while walking backwards away from each other, promising to keep in touch about their business plans.

Chuck turned around to rejoin his friends, and his college classmate Tone met him half way. He shrugged his head, gesturing toward Zachary to find out what he'd wanted, and Chuck told him that it was nothing much. He didn't want to share his plans with anyone yet, for fear that someone might try cutting in on his chance to make some money.

Chuck wanted the cars with the butter-soft leather seats, the respect on the street and the attractive women that Mr. Ray considered "high-maintenance chicks." But more then anything else he wanted the money to jumpstart his sports magazine - and all he had to do was start bringing guns from the South to the city, and build a relationship with Zachary.

Chapter 2:

Things had slowed down back at Mr. Ray's barbershop - the haircutting business was unpredictable like that. One minute there would be standing room only, then all was calm and quiet the next. The radio was playing music with brief intermissions of news. Mr. Allen had just gotten off the telephone with his wife, and he was wiping down his station while Mr. Ray took advantage of the free time to lather his own face and shave.

Just then a customer walked in, greeted Mr. Ray and began to take off his hat and jacket, telling Mr. Ray that he'd just seen his nephew hanging out uptown.

"Yeah?" Mr. Ray replied without much interest. He acknowledged the customer with a simple hello, and then continued shaving, "I'll be right wit'chu, young man."

"He wuz dressed nice," the customer grinned, "but that's Zachary for ya… He always dressed nice."

"Big deal," Mr. Ray replied. He knew Zachary was back on the streets the same way he knew when he was in jail. "I'm tired of talkin' to Zachary. He a grown-ass man… twenty-nine years old, an' he still goin' back-n-forth to jail…" Mr. Ray then turned around with the razor in his hand, waving it like a wand as he spoke, "It ain't gon' be long befo' he go back… you mark my word. I dunno what's wrong wit him. But I'll tell you what, I ain't gon' waste my time tryin' to figure him out. Every time I turn aroun' he's in some kinda trouble." Mr. Ray turned in Mr. Allen's direction, and Mr. Allen nodded his head to show that he agreed. Mr. Ray looked as if he had a bad taste in his mouth as he continued, "I dunno what's wrong wit dat boy. Maybe he like takin' showers wit other men... who knows!"

The comment caused a loud snicker from Mr. Allen. He had the biggest smile on his face when he yelled from the back of the shop, "All dese years we done worked togetha... an' you still say some of the funniest shit." He shook his head, still smiling as he continued wiping down his station.

Mr. Ray still had a little shaving cream under his nose, and he shrugged his shoulders as he repeated, "The boy knows hangin' out uptown is the wrong place for'em to be, but I ain't gon' worry. He'll be happy when somebody kill his yella ass." After he finished shaving he splashed on a little barber's lilac, and then cleaned his chair with his barber's cape.

Once Mr. Ray had started cutting the customer's hair, he began reminiscing about Zachary when he was only five years old and his mother would bring him in for a haircut. "He wuz so small, I needed to sit'em on telephone books," Mr. Ray said. "He wuz a cute little guy, but mischievous as hell! His mama would stand over me like an inspector. Followin' me aroun' the chair, gettin' huh foot crossed up in the cords. Stoppin' me to kiss Zachary, wipin' his face, an' tellin' me, 'Don't cut his baby hair!'" Mr. Ray sucked his teeth in aggravation. "That boy wouldn't sit still for shit. He'd start cryin' an' beggin' for shit he didn't want, an' soon as I finish his haircut an' put'em on the floor, he start playin' an' runnin' aroun' the shop again."

Mr. Allen stood a few feet away from Mr. Ray's chair, and it seemed like every bit of his 5'5" height could fit into his thick mustache. His Alabama accent could make the most serious situation seem humorous. "I been cuttin' hair for twenty some-odd years," he said, "an' I done seen all types of hair, an' till this very day, brotha, I's still ain't neva seen no baby hair! Somebody please tell me what that shit is?"

"It's jus' some meaningless bullshit dat some brain-washed negro done made up," Mr. Ray griped.

The customer was just sitting there between the two barbers, smiling and absorbing the barbershop harangue, forgetting all about his haircut.

"She's my own sista," Mr. Ray added, "an' I use'ta hate seein' huh come through that front door of this barba'shop."

"You ain't the only one," Mr. Allen said, "I use'ta hate cuttin' dat boy's hair when you wuzn't aroun'."

Mr. Ray went on to describe how his sister would always nitpick about the haircut before he was even finished, "It ain't how you start the haircut; I use'ta tell huh… It's how you finish. The end result is what counts… She use'ta be on one side of me, askin', 'How come this side don't look like that side?' An' afta all dat hard work she an' dat boy put me through, she ain't wanna pay me, jus' 'cause she my sista. I use'ta tell huh, 'Nancy, I got bills to pay jus' like you do.' She'd have ta pay for Zachary's haircut if she took'em somewhere else. But once she realized I wuzn't gon' put up wit huh bullshit no mo', she stopped bringin' Zachary by here. I knew dat boy wuzn't gon' amount to shit, 'cause my sista spoiled'em. She'd bring Zachary in here wit eighty-dolla tennis shoes on his feet when he wuz only ten years old!"

The customer sat there laughing, following the conversation like a spectator at a tennis match.

"Eighty dollas," Mr. Allen yelled with his croaky voice. He looked down at his shoes and said, "What ten-year-old boy need some eighty-dolla sneakas fo'? Hell I can buy two pair of shoes for that price."

"Ya ain't lyin'," Mr. Ray concurred, "She'd have dat boy dressed in all of da latest styles, wit a big-ass leatha jacket hangin' off his shoulder n'shit. Name brand jeans an' a earring in his damn ear. Right away I knew he wuz gon' be trouble. She wuz showin' more concern for dat boy's clothes an' hair instead of what wuz goin' on in his damn head. I try ta tell huh, when ya spend money on clothes wit all kinda logos goin' across da chest an' all dat otha shit, one day it's gon' be outta' style, an' den you gon' be stuck wit a buncha ugly name-brand shit! But she neva listen to me. She use'-ta tell me, 'I'ma buy my baby things we couldn't afford when we wuz growin' up.' An' I told huh dat she need'ta go an' find da man dat got huh pregnant, so he can teach dat boy how to piss standin' up! An' stop sittin' on the toilet like a little girl. But' afta I told huh dat, I ain't hear from huh since. She called it bein' mad at me... But I'll tell you what, I ain't have'ta put up wit dat bad-ass boy no mo'."

Chapter 3:

A couple of days after the two men had exchanged numbers, Zachary gave Chuck a call. Somehow Mr. Ray's name came up in the conversation, and right away Zachary jumped on his case. "That bastard is crazy! You know that, Chuck? He always somewhere preachin', brotha this an' brotha that! I don't be in the mood for that shit man. Word up I don't. That's why I only go by once in a while, jus'ta make sure everythin' is a'ight. Ya know what I'm sayin'? Afta all, he is my blood. I jus' can't take that preachin' shit, man!"

Chuck started laughing to himself, moving the phone away from his mouth and holding it against his chest to muffle his amusement. After he regained control he replied, "Nah, ya uncle is cool people."

"Yeah, he a'ight, I'm not sayin' no different, but he should be thinkin' of ways to make money. Look at me - I'm always thinkin' of ways to make some money, Chuck. Sump'n that's gon' put some cash in a muthafucka's pockets - an' my uncle don't get it! Money makes this world go 'round, baby! Not that preachin' shit he be talkin'. That's what's wrong wit dese black folks out here now, dey too damn preachy an' religious! Most people only get religion afta' dey done fucked everybody ova or backstab'em. An' the women, dey only start goin' ta church once dey ass an' titties start saggin'. When dey young an' fine, dey don't wanna hear nothin'a muthafucka gotta say."

Zachary's voice lowered suddenly, and he went on with a darker tone. "My mama wuz one of the most religious damn people I eva knew... an' when she died, she had nut'n to show for her devotion but a bunch of bills to pay." His voice began to crack as he continued. He sounded distressed and bitter, almost as if he was about to tear up. "An' when it came time to bury her, we couldn't even afford a fuckin' tombstone. Do you believe that shit? A tombstone only cost about two G's back then... an' between four adults in my famly, Chuck, we couldn't get the money togetha! That kinda money wuz hard to come by back then. Now I make damn near twice that much in one day. But from then on, I jus' promised myself I'll neva be broke again. Besides, those spiritual muthafuckas sit aroun' all day, waitin' for sump'n good to come strollin' along instead of goin' out there an' gettin' it for dey self! Fuck that man! I need money... an' I need it now. Tell God to put some cash in a muthafucka's pockets, then I'll be straight."

Although Chuck had never cared for talking on the phone, he listened in some amazement. Zachary was smart, and he was coming from an angle Chuck had never expected. Chuck didn't agree with all of what he was saying, but he felt at least he was learning something he would need to know about Zachary.

"My mother use'ta drag me an' my brotha to church two times a week plus Sundays," Zachary declared. "We wuz taught to turn the otha cheek, love thy neighbor, an' all that otha tolerable mess. An' out of all the bullshit black people went through, as far as gettin' hung, raped, beat, murdered, burned an' dcy feet chopped off and all that... nut'n neva happen to the guys that did it. God neva stepped in the picture to stop the bullshit," he cried. The whole time Zachary had been speaking, he'd sounded like a Don-slash-preacher - it was in the way he kept raising and lowering his voice.

Chuck sat there and listened, and he heard what Zachary was saying. His head swam with an electrifying current that caused the veins in his arms to sting. He took a deep breath and swallowed to suppress the need to spit. He now understood why the guys in the hood feared and respected Zachary. Many men who were big in stature could be bullish and arrogant, and they rarely had to prove what they were made of, because their size seemed to say it all. But Zachary was neither muscular nor tall - he just had a different outlook on life. Make money and live free, or die trying. Zachary refused to be humiliated, waiting for crumbs at the foot of another man's table - and Chuck could not agree more. Now he felt ready to take a chance and live on the edge, if that's what it took to get ahead.

§

It was a little after 3:00 p.m. on the following day when Chuck noticed Zachary's car stopped at a traffic light on the corner of 144th Street and Lenox Avenue, where they had agreed to meet. The calm in the city made it easier to hear the music emanating from Zachary's stereo. You could feel the bass vibrating under your feet, and Chuck knew it was Zachary by the depth of the beat. But it wasn't until the car got a little closer that he noticed there were also two young ladies riding with him. The girl in the front seat was reaching over Zachary's lap, practically in his crotch, toying with the stereo just as they pulled up.

"Wassup, yo?" Chuck said as he leaned into the car and extended his hand to shake Zachary's. He didn't bother to acknowledge the girls until the one in the front seat leaned forward and spoke.

"Hey Chucky," - her voice was soft and sweet with the sun in her smile. She was beautiful, with keen facial features and hazelnut lip-gloss that tastefully flattered her complexion. It was Apple, of course. Chuck gazed at her in amazement as she glanced over at Zachary - it was as if she was hoping for his approval. Zachary looked sideways at Chuck, and the girl in the backseat just sulked, observing them all.

Zachary was smiling with high spirits. "Wassup?" he said again. "You look like you just got hit wit a straight right hand, Chuck!" He playfully punched Chuck in the arm, then the two of them walked across the street to talk in private. The girl in the back seat didn't wait until the men were out of earshot before she leaned forward and started digging for information. "Who's that boy?" she asked.

"What boy you talkin' about?" Apple drawled lazily, disguising her envy. She didn't want Chuck, but she didn't want the other girl to say anything to him either.

"The damn boy that wuz jus' standin' here," the girl retorted. "The same boy that wuz jus' starin' you in da face while he wuz sayin' "Wassup?" to Zachary. That's what boy!"

"Oh, that boy," Apple answered, coloring in spite of herself. "That's jus' Chucky," she smiled. Even when Chuck had first noticed Apple, his glance had given her a first-class feeling, and she couldn't stop blushing. She went on to remind the girl that Chuck had gone to the same school with them. "We use'ta call'em Chubby Chucky back in the days… But'chu probly don't rememba, 'cause you neva took yo' black ass to school."

The girl in the back seat was trying to hold back a smile, but she had to have the last word. "Ah, go ta hell bitch…" she teased. "An' I do rememba him if you wanna know. He's that boy that use'-ta write you all those little poems n'shit."

Apple mused for a minute, "Yeah, he sure did write me some cute little love letters, girl." She was still blushing, but tried to look disinterested. "He wuz a real nerd back then." Apple rested back against the seat, staring into space, and the more they talked the more she remembered. "He wuz a bookworm too. The teacha's pet. But he done got a little olda now… an' he got all cute n'shit!"

"He sure did." The other girl whispered, "He jus' need to

grow some more ass in the back-pocket section," she laughed. She was still looking out the car window, watching the men walk across the street with her eyes drawn to the arch of Chuck's back. His slender build and wide shoulders appeared to give him added height.

"I'ma tell Paul," Apple teased.

"Ssshit, I don't want him. I wuz jus lookin'."

"I'm jus playin', damn, but I think he goes to college down in Kentucky, somewhere," Apple declared.

"Kentucky? What the hell he goin' to school way down there for? I heard it's way too country down there, girl." She moved a little closer to Apple and whispered, "What'chu think him an' Zachary talkin' about?"

"Who knows?" Apple carelessly replied. "Could be anythin', knowin' Zachary."

"Do you think he wanna come downtown an' work wit us…? Or maybe Zachary wanna go down to Kentucky an' run some game on those muthafuckas down south!"

"You must be crazy girl," Apple screamed, "I wouldn't go down there for a million dollas…"

"Stop the bullshit," the other girl barked, "You must be crazy ya damn self, an' you know you would go! You would do anythin' Zachary ask you to."

"No I wouldn't. I ain't goin' down there girl! Those country-ass people down there don't play around." Apple turned to face the girl. "Dey ain't throwin' my black ass in jail… or unda' it. I wouldn't go down there if my life depended on it! I'm keepin' my black ass right up here in Harlem where I belong. I rememba we went down to Cherry Hill tryin' to hustle, an' shit didn't work out, an' that bastard Zachary was bitchin' all the way up the turnpike."

The backseat girl's eyes narrowed in disbelief; she knew Apple like the back of her hand, and was certain she would do anything Zachary asked her to, or at least consider it. The girls had lived together every since they were teenagers. They would even tell the neighbors that they were sisters, and they'd said it so many times they'd almost begun to believe it themselves. That was back when Apollonia "Apple" Alcindor was three months short of turning seventeen, a young girl lost in a woman's body, and her mother Vera Alcindor had a new man, Uncle Charlie. She would tell Apple, "There's only gonna be one Miss Bitch in this house, an' if you wanna be grown before I say so... you can go find somewhere else to stay." All through her childhood, Apple remembered being introduced to one new uncle after another, and for all she knew, one of those uncles was her father. Luckily for her, the backseat girl's mother had a heart of gold; not only did she give Apple a place to stay, but she even gave her a set of keys to let her come and go as she pleased.

"I wish you could hear yaself talkin' right now!" The girl screeched in a catty, high-pitched voice. Then she put up her hand as if she was directing traffic. "No, let me put it this way - I wish I had a tape recorda, jus' so I could play the shit back an' let you hear how crazy you sound! She rested back in the seat and rolled her eyes at Apple. Her lips were tight and small, barely opening as she spoke. "All he gotta do is jus' ask you one time, an' soon as you tell'em no, he'll start lookin' at you sweet an' callin' you baby this an' baby that, an' before you know it, you be doin' whateva he say! That bastard Zachary do-not-give-a-dam-about-you! He don't give a damn about me or nobody else. All he cares about is his damn self an' makin' money. An' I can guarantee you he's tryin' to find a way to use that boy over there too." The girls were yelling back and forth, drawing casual attention from passersby. "The only reason I go downtown is 'cause I need the money, an' you know them muthafuckas downtown don't give a damn about us. It's jus' the greed in dey heart that makes dem think dey gon' wring us out and throw us away... But as soon as I save enough money, then I'm dust - an' you can have that apartment to yaself... an' jus' go on kissin' Zachary's greedy ass." The girl grabbed her handbag and jumped out of the car. She slammed the door behind her, leaving Apple sitting alone with an improbable look on her face.

§

Zachary and Chuck were in the park, sitting on the top of one of the benches, and navigating an awkward silence before they began to talk about how they would make everything happen.

Zachary was brushing off his pants, and he felt a sudden urge to share some of his personal beliefs. "Do you smoke Chuck?" he asked.

"Nah, you?"

"Nope, that shit is nasty. That's the main reason I don't like goin' to bars an' clubs. I use'ta go out all the time, but not no mo'. I hate when that smoke smell gets stuck in my clothes, then I gotta walk aroun' smellin' like cigarette butts n'shit. I spend good money on my gear, ya know what I'm sayin'?"

That afternoon Zachary had on a pair of beige tropical wool slacks that perfectly grazed the tops of his chocolate suede loafers, which looked almost edible. His short-sleeved shirt was made of raw silk, and displayed a homemade tattoo that was painful to look at.

"So why'd you ask me if I smoke?" Chuck probed.

"'Cause, I jus' want to know. To me, smokin' is a sign of weakness."

"So why didn't you ask me if I wuz scared to die or sump'n?"

"'Cause, there's different ways of bein' weak, ya know what I'm sayin'?

Chuck didn't really know, but he knew it was important to follow along. 'Do I have a weakness?' he thought to himself, and then, 'Where is Zachary goin' with this weakness shit?' But before Chuck could come up with an acceptable answer, Zachary broke his train of thought by resuming his speech.

Chuck's mind concentrated for a moment and then wandered off again; he couldn't wait to describe how he planned to move the guns from the South to the city. It would be almost too easy, because he knew his way up and down the highway with his eyes closed. He'd traveled the route many times before with his friends from college, during the holidays and summer breaks. Not only did he know the way, he knew a shortcut that would cut the ride by an hour. Kentucky was a little more than a thousand miles away, and whenever he and his friends came to the city, they would turn on the radar detector and do 80 to 100 miles an hour non-stop. It would take him about 12 hours to get to New York, 13 at most. Besides, he knew that if they took the route everybody else used, they would have to stop for tolls and get hassled by the state troopers. Sometimes they would drive the back roads, and whenever one of them got too tired, they would simply pull to the side of the highway, switch drivers and keep on moving.

"So tell me, Chucky my man, how is this thing gonna work?" Zachary finally punctured Chuck's reverie with the right question.

"Well, it's pretty simple," Chuck said. "You know I go to school down south... right? An' down there, the rules about buyin' guns are not as stric' - dey practically sell them shits ova the counta. Dey sell'em in the pawnshops an' in the regular stores. All you need is a driva's license from that state. It's the boondocks man. It's so fuckin' laid-back down there... If you want to go fishin' an' you need some worms... you can buy them shit's from a vendin' machine."

"Get the hell outta here," Zachary cackled. "You sayin' dey sell worms outta vendin' machines? Get the fuck outta here, Chucky!"

"Yup, worms in a damn vendin' machine, like it's soda or sump'n!"

"I ain't neva heard no shit like that before in my whole life Chuck, you got to be bullshittin' me!" Zachary was laughing so hard that he had to stop talking until he caught his breath.

"Nope," Chuck snickered, "you sayin' the same shit I said when I first saw it."

"Is you sayin' dey got dem shits in the machine wit the soda an' potato chips?" Zachary wrinkled his nose. "Fuck aroun' Chuck, we gon' see name-brand worms one day!"

The two men burst out laughing again, and Chuck would have never guessed that Zachary had such a sense of humor. But to get away with hustling as long as he had, it seemed like he'd need to have a funny bone somewhere.

After the laughter faded and they had sat in silence for a while, Chuck continued to describe his plans. "But like I wuz sayin' Zach, dey got crack-heads down there, jus' like we have up here, an' you know jus' like I know, they'll do anything for a hit. Chuck then stood up while Zachary went to sit. "Anyway, I can get me a couple of crackheads, pay'em or give'em a little sump'n sump'n. They'll go buy the joints, an' I can bring'em back to the city. Then we'll sell'em for twice, maybe three times what they're worth…"

"True, what kind can you get?

"Semi-automatics is what'chu want, right?"

"Chuck, man, I want whateva you can get'cha hands on, as long as it's not bullshit. But if you askin' what I really want, I'd like to get a coupla 9's. But don't get those nickel-plated shit. Them shits is too shiny an' too easy to spot, ya know what I'm sayin'. An' maybe a coupla 380's. And maybe a coupla ou-wops," he added, "Can you get ya hands on summa dose?" He was grinning like a child on Santa's lap.

Chuck looked him in his eyes with a straight face and said, "Zach, man, dey sell worms in vendin' machines."

Zachary laughed out loud, "That's right you did say that. Ok then, get me a coupla Uzi's like I said."

"The three-eighties are 120 dollas," Chuck explained, and Zachary cut him short in disbelief.

"That's all them shits cost?" he asked with eyes wide like turntables. "I been gettin' beat all this time and didn't even know it. I been payin' twice that much. I'ma get my money back, word up I am. So when you get the joints back up here… we can sell them shits in no time! If things work right Chuck, this shit'll be good. I'll chill out an' not hafta go downtown so much. Then I won't hafta be hidin' out from the police n'shit. I could leave those naggin'-ass girls uptown sometimes, an' jus make money offa this shit!"

"No doubt, no doubt." Chuck assured him. "I can get the Glock's 26 subcompact model with the 12-round clips, or the ones that hold 15 rounds, it's up to you."

Zachary listened to Chuck with his mouth half open, as if in a trance. When he had heard enough, he stopped Chuck and simply asked him what he needed. Chuck replied that all he would need was a rental car and money for the guns. Zachary decided that at the prices Chuck had named he could buy four guns of each type, and all Chuck had to do was cover the cost of gas. He kept reminding Chuck to be careful traveling down there with his money, and even more careful coming back.

"It's a simple thing to do Chuck, when you're travelin' from the South to the city wit'cha boys - but wit a car full of guns, things take on a whole new meanin'. You know that… right?" Chuck nodded his head, but Zachary looked Chuck straight in his eyes, speaking slowly and clearly, making sure Chuck didn't miss a word. "There are a few things to take into consideration Chuck. You gotta obey the speed limit at all times. You can speed when you jus' hangin' wit'cha boys, joke aroun' and stuff… that's cool. The worst thing that could happen is you might get a ticket. But when you're travelin' wit a car full of guns, across state lines… you can't be playin' aroun', Chuck… An' I don't want no damn cops knockin' on my door, askin' me do I know you. Ya got that?"

"Yeah, I got it man," Chuck assured him, nodding slowly several times.

"So how many miles do you have to travel?" Zachary switched to a lighter tone.

"About a thousand miles," Chuck replied.

"An' how fast you gonna go?"

"Most of the time we do about 75 to 95."

"Then that means… since you'll be dirty… you'll have to do

about 55 in some states an' 65 in others, plus you'll stop for gas, get sump'n to eat, an' maybe take a rest..."

"Rest? I don't need no rest, man. I mean I can rest while someone else is drivin'."

"Well, whateva," Zachary said, "As long as you get there an' back safe... But if you do decide to make a rest stop, I'd guess it should take about 17 maybe 18 hours... right?" Chuck knew that Zachary was insisting and not asking. "So if for any reason Five-O drive up next to you, you gotta stay calm!" Zachary insisted.

"I know that, Zach."

"But if the cops pull you ova... What'chu gonna do, Chuck?"

"I'ma stay calm, Zachary man! Don't worry, I got this. This shit is easy, man. Jus' trust me."

"I do trust you," Zachary said. "I wouldn't be sittin' wit'chu here right now if I didn't trust you. But if Five-O pull you ova Chuck, don't go diggin' in the glove compartment, searchin' for ya license before they even ask you. Wait until dey come an' ask you for it. An' please, please, please Chuck, make sure you don't have no dumb shit in the glove compartment, or sump'n lyin' aroun' in the car that's gonna make them muthafuckas suspicious. That's why I asked you if you smoke. You don't wanna give them any reason to search the car wit dose big-ass drug dogs, ya know what I'm sayin'? You fuck aroun' an' the police will have yo' ass hemmed up on the side of the road. An' always keep both hands on the steerin' wheel, where dey can see'em, so dem bastards don't shoot you in the back of yo' head. An' talk that college shit you learned in school. You know what I mean, don'cha." He patted Chuck on the back and looked him in his eyes. "But don't be sarcastic or nut'n... you know how to play'em, Chuck... Anyway, I hope it won't even come to any of that, an' everythin' gon' go nice an' smooth."

Zachary then reached into his front pocket, pulled out a couple of crisp hundred dollar bills and a couple of fifties, and gave them to Chuck. They talked a little longer and then started walking back toward the car. Chuck was still describing the South to Zachary, but he had Apple in the back of his mind. He felt by the way she and Zachary had interacted that there was nothing going on between them - but it was killing him not knowing for sure. Chuck thought that it would be better to raise the question indirectly, so that if he was wrong, Zachary wouldn't be offended.

Chuck stopped walking and said as casually as he could, "You know Zachary, every time I see you... you always got some real pretty girls wit'chu."

Zachary turned around and chuckled, "Yeah...true, true!"

"You know, those are some nice ladies you got chillin' wit'chu right now."

Zachary gave him a narrow look. "You're a funny dude, Chuck... you know that? Here we are tryin' to make moves... to make this money, an' you worryin' about some ass." Zachary shook his head and said, "I see where ya mind is at." Then he tapped Chuck on the chest with the back of his hand. "Those two girls is my down-for-whateva chicks... especially Apple." He was bragging to Chuck, and Chuck could only smile to hide the discomfort he felt in knowing that. "Wheneva I go downtown to hustle, Chuck, I take those two chicks wit me. Dey part of my crew.... Apple an' that girl in the backseat, Eyonna. She's the smart one. She's talkin' 'bout goin' back to college n'shit. She be countin' my money n'shit for me, sometimes."

"She looks familiar. You don't worry about her cheatin' you?"

Zachary sucked his teeth, "Man I'll bust her ass," he shook his head twice for emphasis. "Plus I done tested her already... more then once. E's got character an' a good heart like her mama. It's that damn Apple that I gotta keep my eyes on." He then stopped talking for a quick second as if remembering something. "Oh yeah," he said half to himself, "Apple told me ya'll went to school togetha."

Chuck did remember seeing Eyonna and Apple together at school and thinking they were sisters. Zachary told Chuck he would introduce him to Eyonna when they got back to the car, but Chuck said that they could do that another time. He wanted to go home, get some rest and get ready for the long ride.

"Okay," Zachary said, "that's cool... but like I wuz sayin', Apple be dressed like the young college bohemian chick, all submissive n'shit, but wit a shank right in her waist. She be ready to hurt sump'n!" He had stopped walking to demonstrate the way Apple would keep an ice pick tucked in her pants, anticipating any trouble. "I've seen times when Apple would fuck a bitch up for me, Chuck. She can talk dudes outta dey money, an' fuck up dey whips, but funny part about all of it is... the dudes be so strung out dat dey don't do shit! I love those girls Chuck. Word to my mutha, I do. But dey jus' be pissin' me off sometimes. But what the hell, I know dey got my back."

Chuck felt that Apple was a little more than just a part of Zachary's crew. She put a silly look on his face, made his heart throb and his sex hard, and maybe now that he knew Zachary, it would give him a chance to talk with her and catch up on the past.

As soon as Chuck got home, he called up Tone and they made plans to get out of the city right away.

Chapter 4:

Chuck and Tone crossed the Kentucky state line with no problem on Friday afternoon, and Chuck called Zachary to let him know that everything was cool. Since it was pretty early when they arrived, Tone wanted to cruise through the neighborhood. He was seeing a girl who didn't live too far from their campus, and he wanted to let her know he was in town. Afterwards he took Chuck to meet the girl who would be buying the guns for him, and the next day Tone stayed back while Chuck and the girl went to various stores to make the purchases. After Chuck had found all that he came for, he paid the girl and then headed back to New York around dawn the following morning.

Tone was supposed to help drive back to New York, but once he'd hooked up with his girlfriend, he reneged on his promise. Now Chuck was on the road by himself with about a thousand miles to drive, a trunk full of semi-automatic weapons, and no one to talk to. Every time he saw a state trooper, he heard Zachary's voice in his head, and every time he heard Zachary's voice, he thought about the money he would be making to start his company - so he took Zachary's advice about resting, and pulled into truck stops for catnaps.

It was around 9:00 p.m. when he arrived in Harlem, and he met with Zachary near Mr. Ray's barbershop. Zachary was hanging with a group of friends, and he stepped away to talk to Chuck. The two men walked into a nearby building along with Fly. Apparently it was Fly's job to follow Zachary around and take orders - Zachary would tell Fly what to do, and Fly would jump to it. Zachary and Chuck smiled and slapped five, and then Chuck told him that the guns were in the car. He tossed the car keys to Zachary and Zachary tossed them to Fly, who promptly left without a word. Chuck had an odd look on his face. He had never seen anyone jump to orders that way.

"You ain't gon' check an' see what I bought back?" Chuck asked.

Zachary just smiled and tapped Chuck on the shoulder. "When we wuz in the park talking the otha day, you told me to trust you, right?" Chuck nodded his head. Zachary stretched out his hands with a smile, "Well then baby, that's what I'm doing, I'm trustin' you." He slapped Chuck five again, then handed him eight hundred dollars.

'It ain't much money,' Chuck thought to himself, 'not afta that long-ass ride - but it's a start.' He appreciated the way Zachary operated, because he had been expecting to be asked to wait a day or two until the guns were sold before getting paid. Chuck would have waited - he had no choice. But he would have told Zachary that he couldn't work with him any more unless he was getting paid up front.

Zachary started counting a wad of money and laughed aloud, "You know Chuck, it looks like we might be on to sump'n good - you know that, right? You made it down there and back wit no problem at all. Yeah boy... we gon' make us some money this summa!"

"Yeah, we sure are," Chuck laughed, "we sure as hell are!"

"So Wassup... You hangin' out tonight, or what?"

Chuck covered his mouth and yawned, "Nah man, I'm beat. I drove back solo. I'm tired as hell right now. Word up I am."

"Yeah, I hear ya... But what happened to yo' man? The one

that drove down there wit'chu?"

"Zach, you know more than I do about that right now. That's my man 'n all... but he be actin' real fucked-up sometimes."

"Word... It's like that, is it?" Now let me get this straight, Chuck. You drove all the way back up here, by yaself?"

"Yeah, that ain't nut'n."

Zachary smiled and walked briskly over to Chuck. He patted him on the back two times and said, "Damn, boy. You what I call a real troopa." Then he broadly peeled off a couple of bills from his wad and said, "Man, take this papah, you deserve a extra hundred dollas. You wuz drivin' like a damn trucka." Zachary was still smiling when he patted Chuck on the back one more time. "Damn, Chuck - you drove, how many hours?"

"Fifteen."

"Damn, you a troopa." I know I wouldn't a' been able to make that shit all by myself." When Zachary had finished teasing and flattering Chuck, he told him that he was hanging out with some girls from around the way, and asked him would he like to come along.

Chuck was tempted, but this time he deferred. "I'm beat. Jus' give me a call later on durin' the week so we can make this papah."

Zachary chuckled and took a step back. "Listen to the college boy talkin' ghetto slang! We gotta stop hangin' togetha' before everybody start sayin' I'm corruptin' you!"

Chuck waved off Zachary's remark with a smile. "Forget you, man."

"Nah, I'm jus' jokin' wit'chu," Zachary said as the two men slapped five, "Your eyes are red as shit. Go home and get some sleep - I'll give you a call this week. "

After that first deal, the two men started to build a good working relationship, and Chuck went back and forth to Kentucky quite a few times. Tone would go along to help with the driving, but he was starting to get sloppy - and whatever his problem was, Chuck didn't have time to figure it out. Chuck was a driven man, and his only concern for the time being was to make as much money as he could. Everyone started to notice the difference in Chuck. His demeanor changed along with his friends and his wardrobe, and every step he took was one step closer to his goal. He'd saved up eleven thousand dollars and everything was going well, but eventually he had two narrow escapes with the law, and then one day Tone got into a scuffle with an elderly lady who'd had a little too much to drink...

Tone and Chuck had stopped at a gas station in a small quiet, town in Virginia to fill up the car, when a frizzy-haired, wiry old woman standing at the check-out counter accused Tone of stealing her lottery tickets. As it turned out she had simply misplaced them, and when she saw Tone counting his, she automatically assumed that he had stolen them. Tone had just placed his tickets in a brown bag he was carrying, when the lady ran over and snatched the bag away. Tone quickly grabbed it back, and when she came hurtling toward him he made a quick side-step, graceful as a matador, and she fell flat on her face into the soda aisle.

The irate woman struggled to get to her feet, and when she finally managed it, she started yelling at the top of her voice, "You bitch bastard, you stole my lotto tickets!"

A couple of policemen were socializing in the back of the store, and when they heard the commotion they came charging directly at Tone. Luckily, they quickly realized that the woman was drunk and had left her tickets at the counter without realizing, so they simply apologized to the men and they went about their business. Chuck didn't think twice about the incident - a blind man could have seen that the lady didn't know what she was talking about. But when the men got back on the road, Tone told Chuck that it had been a close call.

Chuck looked over at him and laughed, "What'chu talkin' 'bout Tone? Everybody knew you wuz tryin' to push up on that old lady..."

"You stupid?," Tone replied, "What the hell I want that old bitch for?" Then he reached into his bag and pulled out a five-ounce packet of crack cocaine. "This is what I'm talking about," Tone laughed. He was shaking his head and smiling. "I'm takin' this down South so me an' my girl can flip it. An' jus think... that white lady almost got my shit."

Chuck was trying to watch the road and stare incredulously at Tone at the same time, yelling, "Yo, what the fuck you doin', man?"

"Yo, chill out man - you know how much money I'ma make offa this shit, yo!" Tone protested, pocketing the packet with care.

"That lady almost had yo' shit, but'chu almost had us locked up in this bama-ass town. What'chu doin' wit that shit man? These fuckin' hicks down here don't play."

"Yo, chill man... Why you yellin' like that?"

"Yo Tone, I'm not gon' even argue wit'chu right now, 'cause I wanna get this shit this ova' wit. But that's some real foul shit you doin'. You know that, don'chu?"

"Oh what, you some kinda saint, now? You gettin' money wit Zachary, an' now you act like you too good for a nigga?"

"Shut ya Chinese ass up an' listen to me."

"I'm not Chinese. I'm Filipino an' Black. Don' get it twisted" Tone sounded almost menacing now.

"You think this shit is a joke don'chu?" Tone didn't answer. "Man, listen, when we travelin' down here, all we got on us is money, and Five-O can't do shit about that. But when you bring that shit wit'chu, it fucks everything up! An' the fucked-up part is, you seen me speeding, an' you didn't even say nut'n." Chuck rolled his eyes. "You gettin' real sloppy Tone. You know that, right? Word up you are, man."

Despite various similar incidents, the men made it to Kentucky and back safely again and again, and between the high times and the lows they continued to work together until the second close call. It was on a warm Sunday morning, and they were both bored with taking the same old route, so they decided to try the New Jersey Turnpike. The roads were fairly empty, and the sky was clear enough to see the moon and sun at the same time. Stacks of smoke came from the roadside factories outside of Newark airport, and the radio was playing country classic.

Both men were tired after partying all night, but Tone insisted on driving. Chuck gave him the car keys, settled back in the passenger seat and dozed off, and when he woke up, they were just inches away from colliding with the merging traffic. Tone had dozed off also, and the car had swerved and was scraping along the divider. Tone woke with a jolt when Chuck punched his arm, and immediately panicked, turning the steering wheel wildly so the car skidded to the right side of the highway. Luckily, both men walked away unscathed, and though the car was badly scratched it was still drivable, so they jumped back in and sped off before the police showed up.

When Chuck got back to New York and told Zachary about the incident, he laughed shortly, and then suggested that Chuck stop driving with Tone. He said that Chuck should take Apple with him instead the next time he went.

"She could put the rental car in her name," Zachary said, "an' she can help wit the driving too." Chuck looked at Zachary as if he doubted she would be willing to go.

"Trust me, Chuck," Zachary said in a mellow voice. "That girl will do whateva I tell her to do. I'll have her pick you up early in the mornin', a'ight?"

Chuck just nodded his head and said, "Cool."

Chapter 5:

t was 5:30 in the morning, the sky was a crispy dark blue, and plastic bags blew in the wind like abandoned kites. The streets were calm by New York City standards. A couple of young men were horse-playing on the corner, while a homeless old man picked up cans and added them to his shopping cart. Apple was already sitting in the car with the heater running, patiently waiting for Chuck to arrive. When he did, he thought to himself, 'Apple looks even better in the morning...' as he walked up to the car. She appeared comfortable in a grey sweat-suit and a pair of grey running shoes, and she had her hair pulled back in a bun, the way she had worn it in high school.

"You ready?" Chuck cheerfully asked her. Then he added, "Well you look like you ready."

"What'chu think?" she smiled slightly. Her feet were crossed, with her hands folded tightly together between her thighs.

Chuck appeared to be in a good mood as he rested his bags, noticing that the inside of the car had her lavender smell. Her smile relaxed him, and he thought to himself, 'This might not be such a bad ride after all...'

"I see you a mornin' person, huh?" Apple asked, as if talking in her sleep. She really didn't want to be in the car, let alone traveling down south, but Zachary had promised her that he would make it up to her when she got back to New York.

"Yeah... I am a mornin' person," Chuck smiled, "ain't you?"

Apple didn't answer. In fact, she didn't say much of anything until she had to ask for directions. Chuck tried to drag her attention away from wherever it was roaming.

"Huh... Apple," he said in a soft voice, but she didn't respond. "Hellooo, Miss Apple," he persisted.

"Yes, Chuck?" She wasn't making anything easy for him.

"Can I ask you a simple question?"

"It depends."

"It depends on what?"

"It depends on what'chu wanna ask me."

"It's jus' a simple question... nothin' personal..."

"Sure Chuck, go ahead. Why not? Go ahead an' ask me a simple question."

"This is the summa, right...?"

Apple just nodded her head and said, "Yes."

"So, why do you have the heat on?"

She didn't answer. She just started a little smile, reached over to the thermostat, and turned off the heat. "Shoot," she said softly, "It wuz cold in here..."

From that moment on, Chuck figured that if he wanted to get on Apple's good side, he needed to start by making her smile.

"You eva been down south?" he asked.

"Nope... but I been to Philly..."

"That ain't down south. It's totally different where you an' me are goin'. You'll see. So don't be surprised when total strangers talk to you, okay?"

"Why dey do that?"

"I dunno... southern hospitality, I guess! You know what we goin' down there for?"

"Yeah... well, kinda... more or less."

"It's really nut'n to worry about. Jus' drive nice an' smooth like you doin' right now. A'ight? An' when we get to where we goin', I jus' gotta make a few phone calls an' a coupla stops, an' in the mornin' we out, a'ight?"

Apple wanted to head back north as soon as possible and so

did Chuck, but after he and Zachary had talked, he'd decided that they should find a motel and stay for the night, get some rest, and then head back north in the morning.

The more miles they covered the more they talked, and Apple started to see Chuck differently. She remembered how bright he'd always been in school, and she thought that he really didn't need to be working with somebody like Zachary.

The hours and miles went by, and the further they got away from the city, the more Apple noticed how the South was a lot different from where she'd grown up. It was the refreshing air and the trees, the miles and miles of empty green land, the bluegrass and the mountains, the farms, and the farm animals that grazed the land. Then of course there was also the road-kill and the smell of skunk, and the overweight whites driving pickup trucks with rebel flags and shotguns in the back window.

Chuck was taking a turn driving when they arrived in Louisville around nine o'clock, having met with no trouble along the way. They checked into a motel right outside town, and Chuck advised Apple not to use the phone in the room - he told her it would be safer to use the ones in the lobby. He called Zachary and told him everything was all right, and then he called Tone

Tone arrived at the motel the following afternoon in a brand new, candy-apple red, 5-speed Mustang 5.0 with an engine that roared like a hungry lion. The car had only 19 miles on the dash and 220 mph on the speedometer. Basically, if that car had had wings, it would have been able to fly. Apple didn't want to wait at the motel alone, so Chuck suggested that she stay with Tone's girlfriend until they returned.

The New Yorkers followed behind the Mustang to the girl-friend's house, and as soon as they arrived in the neighborhood, Apple thought about turning right around and going home. She told Chuck that the houses looked like old-fashioned slave quarters on a plantation. There were five small, rundown houses where it seemed as if you could trip through the front door, and fall out the back. The screen doors didn't have any screens, and children from the surrounding area ran through the backyards with pampers on and no shirts, or shirts and no pampers, in grass that was over their heads.

The Kentucky heat cooked the gravel-covered roads, and the air seemed hot enough to bake a chicken. Most of the houses didn't have air conditioners, so the neighbors left their front doors open to keep cool. When Tone's girlfriend heard the cars arriving, she jumped up from a rundown couch and peeped through the curtains. Tone stormed into the house and immediately started yelling at her, so that she almost jumped out of her skin. The place was a mess, and Tone's nervous behavior made the New Yorkers very uncomfortable - not to mention the stench that emanated from the dingy carpet - none of it made being in Kentucky any easier.

Once the girl had collected her thoughts, she unenthusiastically started picking up the clothes and trash that were lying around, while the New Yorkers stood there watching her and wondering what they had gotten themselves into. Tone and the girl went to the back of the house, and he whispered to her forcefully that Apple was going to be staying for a little while, so he was relying on her to treat Apple right.

Chuck and Tone were just about to walk out the back door when Tone stopped short. "Oh, shoot! Where are my manners?" he blurted. "I forgot to introduce you two guys to my girl. Chuck an' - what's yo' name again?" he asked Apple.

By now she was being sulky and intentionally looking the other way, holding tightly to her purse. "Apple!" she spat.

"Nice name," he said with a silly grin, "like the kinda apple that you eat. Right?"

Apple didn't respond. She just gave him a nasty look as she clasped her purse against her body. "Sorry, no offense!" he said without rancor. "Apple an' Chuck, this is my girl Lazy-Ass," Tone said, giggling at his own joke. "Na, I'm jus' kiddin' - her name is Sugah. This is my baby Sugah." Tone went to kiss her, then stood behind her and lifted her hand as if she were a puppet, crooning,

"Sugah, say hey to the nice people."

A moment later Chuck and Tone left in the new car. The guys picked up a different girl to purchase the pistols for them this time. They made their rounds through the small town, buying twelve semi-automatic pistols. Chuck had five Lorcin 380's, five Glock's 9-millimeters, and two Uzi's, with ammunition for each firearm. He paid the girl and they dropped her off, and then the men headed back to the house, chatting casually as they went.

Chuck did most of the talking, about the next school year and how things would be better when he had some extra money in his pockets. He was also telling Tone to be ready to make another run in about two days. Tone agreed, but he was beginning to act edgy. Chuck didn't really notice; he was feeling a little better now that he had the guns, and he kept admiring Tone's new car, thinking that he would like to try it out. The two men pulled into a convenience store to get some soda and sandwiches for the girls, and then they walked to the front to pay for their things. There was a policeman in the store chatting with a clerk, and the two men acknowledged the officer with a simple hello. The officer responded civilly, then the men paid for their items and left the store. Chuck drove off happily, feeling out the fabulous car, and playfully teasing Tone.

"Yeah, boy. You down here gettin' paid, huh?" Chuck said loudly as he pounded on the steering wheel with excitement. "You need to stay ya ass down here an' jus' chill out."

Tone didn't say anything. He only smiled.

"This a bad-ass ride!" Chuck said. When he got to a red light, he stopped and pressed the accelerator two times to make the engine roar. The two men looked at each other and grinned, but when Chuck checked the rearview mirror he noticed a police car cruising along behind them. He nudged Tone with his elbow and told him not to look back, and Tone quickly started unbuckling his seat belt without a word. Chuck looked at him nervously, wondering why his demeanor had suddenly changed. He continued driving with both hands on the steering wheel, peeping frequently into the rearview mirror. He advised Tone to buckle his seat belt back up as they drove on for about two more miles, and then he stopped at a red light and looked full into the rearview mirror... the police car was still behind them.

"Ssssshit!" he whispered nervously, "Tone, Tone, the fuckin' cop jus' turned his lights on. What the fuck did I do?" He began to think aloud... "I stopped for the light... What did I do? Somebody musta dropped a dime on me! What the fuck'd I do...?" He repeated the question over and over. The palms of his hands began to sweat and stick to the steering wheel, while his mouth became as dry as if he'd been eating cotton.

Tone was grasping the door handle as if he were about to jump out of the car, and for a moment Chuck thought about doing the same. "What the fuck did I do?" he cried again as he pulled to the side of the road. He looked in the side-view mirror and could see the door of the police car opening. The officer's royal blue pants with gold stripes were tightly tucked into his spit-shined black boots. Chuck looked over at Tone, who still had his hand on the door handle - then he opened it slightly while reaching under the seat. They eyed each other, and Chuck thought to himself, 'I know this bastard Tone isn't reaching for a gun, and if he is, there ain't no way he gon' win no gunfight with this fuckin' hick!'

Chuck snarled at Tone, raising his voice just above a whisper, "What the fuck are you doing - put that shit back, man."

"Fuck you!" Tone yelled at him. His eyes were wide, with red veins traveling around his pupils. "That cop is out to get us..."

"Tone... Tone!" Chuck shouted again, beginning to lose control. "Put that fuckin' gun down, man!" Tone paid no attention, and the two men started tussling with each other as the police got closer to the car.

All summer long Tone had been acting strange. He would sometimes get in a funky mode during the school year, especially during finals, but this time it looked like there was something badly, irreversibly wrong.

Chapter 6:

Back at Sugah's place the girls had grown tired of waiting for the men to return, so they'd gone out for a bite to eat. When they pulled up at Sugah's house again, they saw Tone's red Mustang abandoned with the engine still running. The front of the car was badly smashed, the doors were swinging open, and the radio was blaring loudly. The police had the entire street roped off, and Sugah immediately expected the worst. Even though they had the air conditioner turned on full-blast, both girls were sweating. It looked as if there were close to fifty police cars in the street, plus a K-9 unit, and one of the officers was directing traffic under the blistering Kentucky sun. Sugah slowed to a creep to see what was going on, and the car almost came to a full stop, but Apple silently urged her to keep driving.

"Girl, don't stop an' talk to them muthafuckas," she whispered softly but forcefully, "Jus' take me back to the motel for a few minutes, at least until things calm down an' I can make some phone calls."

"Shit… I wanna know what happened," Sugah hissed anxiously.

"Fuck that! Listen to me…" Apple yelled with some bass in her voice, "You take me back to the fuckin' motel right now an' let's chill a few minutes. If we stay aroun' here, the fuckin' cops' gon' start askin' us all kinds of dumb shit, an' trust me, you do not want that."

Sugah was worried about Tone and Apple was worried about Chuck, but more then anything Apple wanted to get back to New York. If something had happened to Chuck, she probably couldn't find her way back, and even if she could, she didn't want to take that long ride by herself. When she arrived at the motel room, she sat on the bed for a few minutes thinking about what she would tell Zachary, while Sugah paced nearby, almost shaking with fright. When Apple finally got up the nerve to call Zachary she was still breathing heavily, and she started crying as soon as he picked up the phone.

"Zachary!... You bastard, I knew I shouldn't have listened to you," she cried. "You got me lost here in the fuckin' sticks, and now Chucky's missin' somewhere. I knew I shouldn't have come down here!"

Zachary frowned as he moved the receiver away from his ear and just stared at it. Once he'd realized who it must be, he sternly said, "Apple! You gotta listen to me... You gotta calm down now. Jus' calm down, baby, an' tell Zachary what's wrong."

"No, you calm down you bastard! I'm stuck out in the fuckin' boondocks! How'm I s'posed ta calm down? I knew I shouldn't have listened to you!"

"What's wrong? What are you talkin' about?"

"I'm holed up in some damn motel," she cried.

"Who you wit?"

"Some people Chucky know!" she barked. Apple's hair was messy from running her fingers through it repeatedly while Zachary kept urging her to calm down. He was so relaxed about the whole situation, he even told her to get a drink and call him back in a few minutes.

"Fuck you, Zachary!" Apple cried with her hair still all over the place, "I'm down here in the fuckin' country wit these fuckin' country people that Chuck stuck me wit. He told me he wuz goin' to take care of some business, an' while he wuz gone I went to get sump'n to eat, and when I gets back to the house the car that him an' his friend wuz in is sittin' there all banged the fuck up on the fuckin' grass, an' Chuck ain't nowhere around!

"You don't know where he is?"

"No, I just told you. All I know is, I'm out here stuck in the fuckin' country. I don't know nobody, and I don't have a fuckin' clue where I am. What the fuck am I s'posed to do, huh? What am I s'posed to do? You tell me that!"

"Apple baby, you gotta calm down. Where's the rent-it that ya'll drove down there?"

"At his friend's house, Zachary. An' I can't calm down!"

"Apple if you calm down, I'ma tell you what to do... A'ight?"

"What?"

"Jus' wait a while and go back over to the house and check things out. If circumstances don't change then, you got three choices. Drive back by yourself, take the bus back, or wait for Eyonna to come down an' ya'll can drive back together. Cool?"

Apple was a city girl, with Harlem in her veins. She was accustomed to the noise of New York, and the silence of the South made her think she was losing her hearing. Right away she decided that she wasn't going to wait for Eyonna, and she wasn't going to take the bus. If worst came to worst, she would just make that long drive by herself.

When Apple and Sugah got back to the house, the police were gone, Tone's new car was gone, and the neighbors were just sitting on the porch drinking liquor and gossiping in the nighttime heat. Apple and Sugah timidly entered the house. They crept through the backdoor, still wondering what had happened to the men. Then someone lightly tapped on the front door. Sugah jumped with fear that it might be the police, and the girls stopped in their tracks and stared at one another.

Sugah tiptoed to the front of the house, put her ear to the door, and waited for a second knock. She tensely asked who it was, and the answer came that it was the girl from the next house. Sugah barely opened the door a crack and snatched the girl by the arm, pulling her into the kitchen. She asked a thousand questions, and the neighbor started to talk in a deep southern accent.

"Gurrl… the police jus' left up outta' here 'bout a hour ago," the girl said nervously. She looked plainly horrified, with rollers in her hair and an extra large T-shirt that draped her body like a robe. This was a small town, and a car chase was big news. More than likely it would be on front page of the local newspaper in the morning. "Dey had dogs out here an' dey roped off da street," the girl continued.

"I know the cops wuz aroun' here," Sugah said with her hands on her hips, "But how come?"

"Dey say dey wuz lookin' fo' some car thieves."

"Car thieves? Girl, ain't no fuckin' car thieves 'round here! What dey gon' do wit a stolen car 'round here? Ain't no place to go!"

"Cops say who'eva stealin' dese cars, dey take'em to another city, 'cause dats where dey winds up - all smashed up an' stripped."

"Well… did they say that red car wuz stolen?" Apple stepped in to ask.

"Yup, dey say its some kinda' stolen car ring goin' on, an' who'eva stole dat car must be da leada', cause he fit da description dey got."

"So where's da car thieves now?" Sugah asked.

"Cops say dey got away… but dey still lookin fo'em. Dey say dey gon' search ova in dem woods come bright n'early in da mornin'."

Apple walked back into the living room with her hand over her mouth, "Oooh shit," she thought out loud, "Chucky wuz in a stolen car an' he didn't even know it! Damn, damn, damn." Now she had to decide what to do. Should she wait around to see if Chuck showed up, or just leave, since Chuck knew his own way around Kentucky? She wanted to call Eyonna or Zachary and let them know what was happening, but Sugah didn't have a phone.

The next-door neighbor had been gone for about two hours

when there was another knock at the back door, and Sugah went through the same cautious routine, afraid of the police. This time it was a male voice on the other side of the door. She opened it narrowly, and there was Chuck. He was covered in cobwebs from his head to his feet, and there was red dirt and mud stuck in his hair and fingernails. He was breathing heavily, and he brushed past Sugah before she could even invite him in.

"Where's Tone?" he yelled. Chuck was pulling his shirt over his head and wiping his face with it as he stormed through the small house. He was so agitated that he couldn't stand still. His eyes were blazing red, and his fists were balled up into tight knots. Neither of the girls said anything, they just kept looking at him and then at each other with puzzled expressions. As far as they knew, the two men had been together - and now that Chuck had shown up alone, Sugah became even more concerned. Apple ran to hug Chuck, pressing up against his dirty body and putting her face against his burning throat. At any other time he would have loved to hug her back, but now his mind was bent on safely getting out of town.

"WHERE THE FUCK IS TONE? Does anybody aroun' here unda'stand English, or am I jus' talkin' to myself?" Chuck was beside himself, out of control, and this scared the women.

"We don't know where he is, Chuck, we thought he wuz wit you," Sugah cried.

"Yeah… I know he ain't here, but where does he hang out at?" Chuck fired back.

Sugah shrug her shoulders and just stood there looking shocked and worried.

"Well, when you talk to'em, you tell'em I'm comin' to see'em! … A'ight?" As far as Chuck was concerned, the conversation was over.

Chapter 7:

Except for the crickets' mating calls echoing in the blue-grass air, and the buzz of the other insects that boogied madly around the only nightlight on the street, the small town was quiet again. There were still a couple of friends sitting on the porch, gossiping about the events of the day, and every now and then you could see the tips of their cigarettes get brighter as they inhaled the hearsay.

Chuck peeped out the kitchen window and figured it would be safer to leave right away. He snatched Apple by the arm, and the New Yorkers raced out the back door. Chuck dashed around to the side of the house, reached into a small hole behind some broken boards, and pulled out a military duffle bag. Then he and Apple jumped into the car and drove off. He was still wiping his face with his shirt while Apple sat quietly counting the miles, and wondering when he would say something. They had covered close to eighty miles by now, and his silence had her worried.

"Why you lookin' at me like that?" he asked her.

Apple shrugged her shoulders. "I dunno."

"I think I know what it is."

Apple shrugged her shoulders again, only this time she smiled a little.

"You wanna know why we came down here, right? Chuck continued.

"Yeah, I would like to know."

"We came to buy some guns. Gettin' guns down here is no problem, but takin'em back to the city is the hard part... That's why I kept tellin' you that you gotta drive safe. So now you know. Okay Miss Apple?" Chuck said playfully. He was still a little shaken from the car chase, but he was trying to loosen up and find some humor in the situation. He continued wiping the sweat and dirt from his face, and Apple went on looking at him.

"You a'ight?" she asked with a concerned look on her face. Chuck's candy-bar complexion had never been out of control throughout the night's chaotic events, and she found that attractive.

"Yeah, I'm a'ight... I jus' need sump'n to drink." Then he sniffed his armpit. "An' a shower, I know I'm kickin' right now."

The New Yorkers drove on in relative silence for about two hundred miles more, slowly getting tired of hearing the same songs played over and over on the stereo. Then Chuck made a clipped comment under his breath, and Apple glanced over in his direction.

"You say sump'n?" She asked.

"I said... I'ma kill that bastard Tone!"

"Why?"

"What'chu mean, why?" Chuck asked bitterly, "Why I'ma get'em?" he frowned and pursed his lips.

"Yeah, why, what he do?"

"You know what he did, you wuz in the house. You heard what that girl said. That muthafucka wuz drivin' me aroun' in a stolen car. The bastard. I'ma kill his ass, watch n'see."

Apple just stared at Chuck. There was a lot he wasn't telling her, which was obvious enough.

"You wanna know what happened?" He asked and it seemed as if Chuck was ready to talk.

"Yeah." was all she answered.

"I wuz right there, I heard it all."

Apple was puzzled, "What'chu mean, you wuz right where?"

"I wuz hidin' unda' the house the entire time. In that little-ass gap, where I grabbed the duffle bag from. An' I wuz yellin' at

Tone's girl, 'cause I figured she might know where he ran to."

"In that little bitty hole?" Apple asked in disbelief.

"Uh huh!"

"How you fit inside that little shit?"

"Easy! I kicked in the little piece of wood that wuz in front of it, then I crawled in backwards. After I got in the hole, I pushed that piece of wood back into place. I think some kinda animal wuz livin' down there, 'cause there wuz a buncha leaves an' sticks put together like a nest or sump'n. Then there wuz a kinda tunnel leadin' to the boiler... It felt like hell, it wuz so damn hot down there, Apple I thought I wuz gon' die!" Then Chuck backtracked to recount the whole story.

"I don't know what Zachary told you," he said, "but I came down here to buy a couple of guns fo' him, so we could sell'em back in the city. Zach wanted you ta come along so we could put the car in yo' name, an' you could help wit the drivin'. My partner Tone, he knows a couple of crackheads that can use dey driva's license to buy the joints fo'us."

"Oh," Apple said quietly. She wasn't surprised - this was a typical Zachary set-up, and she had walked in with her eyes open. Chuck barely noted her reaction, and continued his narrative.

"Me an' Tone went to a coupla pawnshops an' gun shops, an' we bought the joints and put'em in the duffle bag, an' then we stepped. Everything wuz goin' good until we stopped at a gas station to switch driva's. I wanted to try out Tone's new whip and he ain't have a problem wit that. We were on our way back to that girl's house when I saw a state troopa followin' us. I told Tone about it, and he started doin' some real dumb shit. So I said fuck it, an' we jetted."

Chuck went on to tell Apple how he had seen the officer walking up to the car, and waited until he was close enough to the window before taking off. "I threw the car into first gear, let off the clutch, smashed the gas to the floor, an' jetted! We raced about three miles down the parkway, an' all I could see in the rearview mirror wuz a cloud of black smoke. The cop turned on his siren an' came after us, an' in a coupla seconds he wuz right on our ass." Animated as ever, Chuck had Apple hanging on ever word. "I downshifted to fourth gear, jumped across the median, an' drove against the traffic. We wuz doin' about 90 miles an hour, an' everybody wuz honkin' dey horns an' cursin' at us. But what the fuck... I had to get us outta' there..."

Chuck paused to catch his breath, wiped his face, and then continued. "Tone, that bastard," Chuck grunted, "he puts me a bad taste in my mouth. Mr. Tough-Guy wuz so scared, you shoulda' seen'em, Apple. He had both his hands around his seatbelt, wit his feet locked straight under the dashboard. His head an' his back wuz pressed up against the seat wit his eyes wide open... I could see straight down his throat."

Apple was drinking in Chuck's description like a child hearing a bedtime story. "You so crazy, Chucky," she said softly.

"I had to say fuck it, Apple. What wuz I supposed to do? I'd gone too far to turn back, an' I'd broken jus' about every traffic law there is, plus there was all them fuckin' guns an' bullets in the car. Man, I'd spend the rest of my life in jail! He looked over at Apple and she was slowly shaking her head. "It's all about livin' life to the fullest, Apple," Chuck swaggered.

Apple was quiet, and he didn't know if she was impressed or angry at him. Then she reached over the backseat and handed him a shirt as he continued to scratch at the dirt that covered his body. She gently wiped the dust and cobwebs out of his hair, and together they decided to wait until they'd crossed the state line to get a room, find something to eat, and rest up. Then they would leave for the city early in the morning, right before the sun came up.

Without the large city buildings distracting the stars, Apple was noticing how clear they looked down here. She'd also noticed that most of the small towns they traveled through looked exactly alike, complete with identical truck stops, gas stations and supermarkets.

"You ever wonder what life would be like out here in the country?" she asked.

Chuck thought for a minute, "Quiet an' slow. Nut'n to do all day but eat an' have sex. You see how fat these rednecks are. Why do you ask? You thinkin' 'bout movin' down here to the country?

"Nah... jus' wonderin'. I'm a city girl, you know that Chuck. It's too damn quiet down here for me. I wouldn't be able to get no sleep. This slow life would drive me nuts. I need some noise. I need to know where the action is all the time."

Apple appeared at ease now. She was still wiping Chuck off as they walked into a diner to get breakfast to go. Apple ordered blueberry waffles and turkey sausages, while Chuck had his favorites, salmon croquettes and sweet potato fries. They took their food back to the motel to enjoy their meal in peace, and after they'd eaten, they both felt much better. Apple went to take a shower, and turned the bathroom area into a temporary home. Chuck went out to the car, and when he returned he noticed that Apple had left all kinds of skin softeners and body lotions lying around, and he smelled the same lavender fragrance that he's noticed when he'd first gotten into the car with her that morning.

When Apple had finished showering, she stood next to the bathroom door, putting lotion on her legs while Chuck went to take his shower. Suddenly Chuck began to sing, and Apple's face lit up with delight.

"Go on Chucky," she shouted over the shower noise. "Damn, you have a nice voice. I thought I wuz at the Apollo for a minute."

"You got jokes, huh?"

"Nah, I'm serious. You do have a nice voice."

"Yeah... you think so?

"Yeah... you do. You really do!"

"Thanks!" He said, meaning more. Chuck had always known that he had a nice voice - he'd been hearing it all his life. But the compliment sounded special coming from Apple. He'd only started singing so she could hear him. "I'd be more then happy to sing for you anytime, but I gotta do it in the bathroom, so it'll sound good. A'ight?"

"A'ight!" she answered with a strange tone in her voice. It was as if she wanted to say something else, but when he asked what was wrong, she just brushed it off. Apple had an idea the she wanted to share, but she would let it rest until the morning.

"Chucky," she sang out, "ya know I called Zachary earlier today."

"Yeah, why?"

"'Cause when I got back to that girl's house an' I saw the car all banged up on the grass... an' you wuzn't anywhere aroun'... what wuz I s'posed to do? I saw all'a those police out there, an' I panicked an' called Zachary.

"So what did Zachary say?"

"He told me I had three choices."

"He didn't ask you 'bout me?"

"Yeah."

"So, what'chu tell'em?"

"I told'em I ain't know where you at." Apple's voice was innocent and childlike as she spoke. "I'm glad you showed up Chuck, word I am! I dunno what I would'a done if you didn't."

"Well, I'm here now," Chuck swaggered, as if he felt like some kind of a super hero. "So you don't have nut'n to worry 'bout. A'ight?" After he finished showering, he got dressed in the bathroom and brushed his teeth standing next to her. Sometimes he peeped over at her, and fantasized about touching her and holding her close. He gawked at her breasts, the way they stood firm without a bra. When Apple called him "Chucky," it turned him on, and he began to wonder if he would be messing something up if they started seeing each other. "Wassup wit you an' Zachary?" he asked her as he went to sit on the bed, placing a pillow over his lap.

Apple didn't answer him. Instead she just looked over and grinned at him.

Chuck continued to check her out from the corner of his

eye, making sure to not move the pillow from his lap. Apple's butt was round and tight and a little darker then her well-toned legs, and that alone was enough to drive him insane. She sat on the bed in front of him with one leg folded under her and the other laid out easily across a pillow. Her waist and his eyes were parallel, her pubic hair was dark, faintly exposed, and Chuck wanted to kiss her thighs. He wanted to put her legs over his shoulders, tightly hold the split of her butt and gently suck her sex. She noticed that he was looking, and she gazed down at him and chuckled.

"Chuck… I ain't gon' even front. I like Zachary," she said, "I do, an' I do a lot of shit for'em too, but he don't show me no love in return." Her voice was affectionate, and for once she seemed real.

"So why do you bother wit'em?"

"I dunno… I guess 'cause there are times when he does look out for me."

Chuck felt that Zachary had to be doing something right to keep a woman like Apple hanging on a string, something that could make her do all of the silly things he asked her to do. He decided to try the direct approach, now that he was a little bolder and living in the fast lane. "Would I be comin' between sump'n wit you an' Zachary, if you an' me started seein' each other?"

"Why do you think there's sump'n goin' on between me an' Zachary?"

"Because, a coupla of weeks ago, when I met up wit'em an' you were in the car, you were all ova his lap… an' it jus' look like you were comfortable there."

"I wuz turning the radio station," Apple smiled.

Chuck knew that it was a little more than that, but instead he persisted. "But'chu still didn't answer my question. Would I be comin' between sump'n wit'chu an' Zachary? The reason I ask is 'cause it seems like there might be sump'n there, but it seems ta me like you the one startin' it." Chuck was smiling as he shrugged his shoulders and started blinking for emphasis. "I mean, that's what it looks like ta me."

Apple seductively moved a little closer to him with a gentle smile. Her T-shirt was cut at the sleeves, showing off her delicate muscles. Chuck stared at her mouth as she spoke. Her teeth and tongue teased him while her lavender body lotion enticed him, and he could only imagine how it tasted on her, and her being the first thing he tasted in the morning, and the last thing at night.

Apple wanted to touch his face, put her thumb in his mouth and let him bite it. "Chucky, you may think you like me, I dunno. You may even think you love me... Who knows what's goin' on in that crazy head of yours," Apple gently tapped him on his forehead. "It's prob'ly my face or my ass, if you ask me. But here we are... two people alone, an' the only thing standing between us is this an' that. But then again... why not?"

"Yeah, why not?" Chuck knew why not, but wanted to hear it from her.

"'Cause if we go any further, Chuck, come tomorrow things would change for the worse, between you and me."

"Change how?" He asked, speaking low and gentle. "You can call me crazy, Apple... but me jackin' off or havin' sex wit you would have the same results. A nut!" He leaned toward her, and the two were close enough to gaze into each other's eyes. He grabbed her hand and placed it over his heart as he continued to speak.

"Apple, it's more than sex... this thing I feel for you... I've been stupid for you every since high school, an' you know it. When I saw you uptown that day, when we were at the ballgame, man I can't even describe the vibrations I felt for you. I can love you forever an' ova'dose on ya spare time. Apple baby, there are two beds in here, an' I'm goin' to that one, right there, an' you stay here in this one. I need some sleep, so we can get up early an' get back to the city. But I want you to think about it. Okay? An' on the way back, I can promise you I won't say nut'n else about all this unless you bring it up."

Chuck was now in the other bed with the lights out. He was under the covers, and Apple was sitting in the dark trying to digest what he had just said. Just before she lay down he said, "But like I jus' said Apple, I won't say nut'n… unless you do. But if you do, then that means that you're at least thinkin' 'bout it. A'ight?"

"A'ight," she said

"Cool… have a goodnight, a'ight?"

"A'ight. You too."

Chapter 8:

It was around five o'clock in the morning when Apple stood by the rental car and took a deep breath, as if she could carry the southern fresh air in her lungs back to New York and exhale a new life. She knew that this would be something to talk about when she got home. They were well on their way back to the city with a tank full of gas, the car on cruise and the trunk packed with miscellaneous paraphernalia, including the duffle bag full of guns. If they were to get stopped by the police for whatever reason, they would claim to be college students heading home for a surprise visit. The two had rehearsed their alibi a couple of times while stopping to eat breakfast at a nearby diner.

They felt comfortable around each other now, laughing and joking about Chuck's car chase. He had made a clean getaway, and it was behind them now. Apple had her leg folded underneath her, the same way she'd been sitting back at the motel, and Chuck reached over and started playing with her hair. Apple didn't seem to mind; in fact she enjoyed it so much that it almost lulled her to sleep.

Chuck noticed that Apple had something on her mind before she'd actually said anything. It was the way she had stopped talking, and sat staring at the open road. They were half way through West Virginia when she told Chuck that she was thinking about something, and she could see the excitement rise in his eyes. At first he thought she was reconsidering what they'd talked about at the motel, and he blushed like a woman anticipating a marriage proposal from the man she'd longed for.

"What'chu thinkin' about?" He asked, trying to sound casual.

"Nut'n," she answered, though her body language said otherwise.

"Why you starin' into space, like you in a trance or sump'n?"

Apple took a deep breath, then reached over Chuck's lap to turn down the radio. "You can keep Zachary's guns if you want. You know that, right?" The color of her tight jeans complimented her smile, and Chuck sat there not knowing which he should admire more, her crotch or her boldness. "Chuck, listen to me. I told you that I had called Zachary when you went missin', right? An' I wuz cryin' n'shit, right? Well, Zachary knew I wuz tellin' the truth, 'cause I wuz cussin'em out. And that's sump'n I neva do. I think as long as I've known Zachary, I've probably only cussed at'em maybe once." This was true, and now she felt she had a perfect opportunity to pay Zachary back for all the neglect she'd endured in silence over the years. She felt he deserved it, and she would wear her secret like an invisible badge of honor, and share it gleefully with Eyonna when she got back to New York.

"All you have to do," she explained, "is tell Zachary that when you an' Tone got chased by the police, y'all had to run different ways. Tone had the guns when y'all ran into the woods, an' you ain't heard from'em since. Which is kinda' true… Right?"

Chuck's face went blank. He drove for a mile or two before saying anything, and Apple began to feel as if she might have shared her idea with the wrong person. So she tried another tack.

"What'chu think of Zachary? She asked. "I mean, do you really think you can trust'em?"

"He's cool people, at least he seems to be," Chuck said loyally.

"He a fuckin' low-life," Apple retorted, "a fuckin' snake! Believe me, Chuck - you'd be a fool to trust'em. And I know what

I'm talkin about."

Chuck looked at her doubtfully, wondering where that remark was coming from.

Apple repeated, "Don't trust'em Chuck! Take it from me! I've known Zachary damn near ten years, an' in all of those ten years he ain't neva been shit, an' he ain't neva gon' be shit, an' if you wanna keep those guns, you can... an' I won't say nut'n about it. A'ight?"

"Yeah, you may be right, but I live by my word Apple, an' he trusted me enough to ask me, so I'ma do what's right an' give'em his shit!"

"Oh please," she cried in frustration, "Fuck yo' word! That muthafucka Zachary do not give a damn about yo' word, or nobody else's word for that matta. How you think you met Zachary?"

"At Rucker Park. We were watchin' the games," Chuck confidently replied, "You were there. Me an' you bumped into each other that day. Rememba?"

"Helloooo," Apple taunted, "Wake-up! Why you think I wuz at that ballgame? I neva go to no stupid-ass basketball games. I don't even like basketball. Plus I got too much beef wit those jealous bitches that be hangin' out there."

"So what'chu tellin' me?" Chuck said with a guarded tone.

"I wuz there so you an' Zachary could get associated." She was now sitting on the edge of the seat, practically in Chuck's lap. "Listen to me, Zachary knew that you could get guns n'shit long before he even talked to you about it. Mr. Ray always be braggin' about you in the barba'shop, about how smart you are n'shit, wheneva Zachary be around... He be makin' Zachary jealous n'shit!" Apple reached over and gently tapped Chuck on the forehead as if she were knocking on a door. Bluntly, she said, "Chucky, listen to me! I know you been likin' me since high school, an' so does everybody else... includin' Zachary. He asked me to go walkin' by you when you wuz at the ballgame - that way he would have a reason to say sump'n to you instead of jus' walkin' up to you hisself. Zachary thinks he too cool for that shit, an' you took the bait.

Chucky... Zachary is tryin' to play you like you some kinda corn-ball, don't you get it?"

Chuck blankly stared at the white lines on the highway while toying with his mustache, with the heat of Apple eyes on his face. He felt as if his manhood was in question now. 'Muthafuckas ain't shit.' He thought to himself, 'First Tone drivin' me aroun' in a stolen car, an' now this!' His voice was low and calm as if he were about to explode. "So why'd you do it?" He asked Apple point-blank.

"What?"

"What the fuck you mean, 'what.' Why'd you come walkin' past me that day? That's what! You do everythin' Zachary ask you to ?"

"Chuck... I'm on Zachary's team, an' we look out for each other like that... sometimes, at least." Apple spoke and looked as if she were trying to convince herself of what she was saying. "It's been almost a year since I've seen you, Chuck. I knew you in school when we wuz younga, an' we didn't hafta worry about nothin' except gettin' a new pair of sneakas. But this is the streets, an' this shit is real, Chucky! An' I know you ain't no street dude. You a book dude! It wuzn't till we made this trip togetha that I started seein' the Chucky that I remainba from back in the days. That's the Chucky that I had a crush on, but didn't dare talk to 'cause of what my friends might think!" Apple placed her hand on top of his, and a thrill went from his spine to the nape of his neck. "Chuck," she said softly. "You can give Zachary his shit back an' keep on doin' business wit'em. Or you can keep those pistols for yourself, an' if you play it right... then you'll be all set."

'Who the fuck is Zachary?' Chuck thought to himself. 'He's a man the same as me, an' he bleeds the same way I do!' Chuck didn't try to figure it all out now right then. He had approximately six hundred more miles to think it through. He just drove on, enjoying the music and Apple's company.

She was still sitting pretty close to him when he told her that he had something to say, and when she leaned over to hear better, he quickly gave her a kiss on the cheek. Apple jumped back, called him a chump, and gave him an amused little love tap on the shoulder. She initiated the second kiss, and there was no doubt about it this time - there was chemistry between the two of them. They pecked once more like birds, and there was no telling how far things would have gone if Chuck didn't have to keep his eyes on the road.

Apple held his hand, and he quickly looked over at her and smiled. She moved her hand a little closer to his sex, and Chuck began to melt behind the steering wheel. Gently she caressed his crotch until she could feel him hardening through his pants. Chuck kept his eyes on the road, but grabbed her wrist, as he was about to lose control of the car. "Hold on girl," He said mischievously, "You gonna make us crash!"

Apple sighed and pulled her hand away, then placed it back on his lap. She wanted to ease his hunger. She wanted to give him oral satisfaction, and all Chuck could do was bite his bottom lip and turn up the air conditioner. Apple's index finger slowly crawled to the top of his zipper, and Chuck's leg straightened out, causing him to push down on the accelerator. His jeans were open now, exposing his erect sex, and Apple licked the palm of her hand and stroked him until beads of sweat began to gather on the tip of his nose.

She seductively sighed with fulfillment. "You a bad boy, huh, Chucky baby?"

"For you," he moaned. "For you I am!"

She wiped his nose with the bottom of his shirt, then she kissed his stomach, and his throbbing sex was next. Her mouth was warm and wet, and felt hollow and full all at the same time. Her lips and tongue surrounded his sex repeatedly as she stroked him back and fourth with her hand and mouth until he couldn't take it any more. Chuck could feel the seat of his pants dampen from the rush of perspiration as he ejaculated in her mouth, and the car swerved into the right lane. Apple grinned as she wiped off her hands and his sex with a towel she had taken from the motel. Chuck's legs had the shakes, and his elbows were still locked on the steering wheel. He playfully rested his head back, and moaned with his eyes wide open. "Apple," he sighed, baby, you can't be doin' that, you'll make us have a accident."

She was sitting with one of her legs underneath her again, and she took a sip of soda as she leaned over to kiss him. "Stick wit me, Chucky," she whispered, "You stick wit me…"

"Does this mean we'll be seein' each other more often…?"

"What'chu think," she replied.

Chuck leaned forward and kissed her on the forehead, and she smiled.

Chapter 9:

Apple and Chuck arrived in New York City around nine o'clock without any trouble, and she couldn't wait to see Eyonna. She just had to drop Chuck off, but not before they'd kissed again. He gently caressed her face and gazed into her eyes, and Apple lightly kissed the back of his hand as if he were a Mafia boss. Chuck stared at her soft skin, and in the back of his mind he wanted to say, 'Fuck it! Fuck the world an' everything in it! Let's shoot up this town, live our lives on the run, an' sleep in the backseat of this car without a care in the world.'

"I'll see you later on?" was all he said.

"Beep me." She replied. She waved goodbye as Chuck watched her drive off, with the scent of her still clinging to his top lip. He had a little pep in his step now, since things had pretty much gone all his way. He'd concluded his business, gotten away from the city, and spent some time with Apple - and he couldn't wait to see her again.

Apple was in the hallway of her building searching for her keys, and once she'd found them she began to unlock the door - but Eyonna beat her to it. She'd been lying across the couch reading, and had recognized the sound of Apple in the hall. Eyonna quickly swung the door open, and the two women stood back and eyed each other up and down before saying anything.

Apple looked just the same way she had when her mom had

kicked her out and she needed a place to stay. Even though the girls had split the rent and utilities evenly ever since Eyonna's mother had passed away, Eyonna had always behaved like Apple's big sister. Eyonna started to smile and said, "Girl, you betta get in here an' give me a hug." She reached to unfold Apple's arms, and the two women embraced as if they hadn't seen each other in years. They walked into the apartment together, grinning from ear to ear; they couldn't wait to catch up with one another. Apple did most of the talking that night, confessing her affection for Chuck. She talked about him as if he were a dream come true.

"I mean, he ain't like most of these knuckleheads I been seein'," Apple explained. "He makes me feel complete. Ya know what I'm sayin', E? The way a girl should feel."

Eyonna laughed and said, "You talk like you wuz smokin' some good shit while you wuz down there, an' you come back here still high. Or maybe it wuz that sweet country air."

Apple smiled, "Chuck is the fresh air that's got me high."

"Yeah okay," Eyonna cheerfully admitted defeat. "If you happy Apple, then I'm happy too. Jus' you be careful." Eyonna took Apple by the hand and firmly looked her in the eyes to show that she was serious. "Ya got me, Apple? Be careful. Zachary act like he don't like you, but the minute he see somebody else showin' you some attention… ain't no tellin' how he'll behave. He's one jealous sonnova bitch."

"I got you girl, don't worry about me. I can handle myself."

Before they knew it the clock said 3 a.m., and the last thing the girls remembered hearing was a bunch of gibberish they both mumbled before falling asleep, Apple on the living room floor in front of the television, and Eyonna on the couch. She had one leg draped across the cushions with the other barely touching the floor. Her mouth opened wide as she snored, inhaling and exhaling the sultry urban heat.

§

Earlier that same night, Chuck had a meeting with Zachary at an apartment building on 151st Street and Riverside Drive. The building was in the process of being renovated and the intercom's didn't work, so Chuck had to go to a pay phone, beep Zachary, and wait for him to call back. Zachary told Chuck to wait by the front entrance and he would buzz him in, so Chuck stood outside the glass door and looked into the glistening interior of Zachary's building. He could see that the hallway was long and narrow, with marble floors and futon chairs opposite the elevators. Chandeliers hung from the ceilings and large mirrors lined the hallway, and when Chuck was buzzed in and started to make his way up to Zachary's place, the speakers in the elevators were playing smooth contemporary jazz.

When Chuck got off the elevator, Zachary was waiting for him in the doorway of his apartment, and the two men were in high spirits when they caught sight of one another. Zachary hadn't known that Chuck was back in the city - he'd thought he was locked up somewhere down south - so he was actually surprised to be seeing him so soon. The last time the two men had communicated was when Chuck had first arrived in Kentucky, and the last time Zachary had heard any news was when Apple had called him in a frantic rage. The two men firmly shook hands, and Chuck handed Zachary the duffle bag.

Zachary looked at Chuck and asked with a curious tone, "What's this?"

"It's the joints," Chuck proudly replied.

"Ah, man," Zachary said cheerfully, "Chuck, man, good lookin' out!" He gently laid the bag back down, and asked Chuck to fill him in on what had happened down south. "Apple called me, an' she wuz yellin' on the phone n'shit, like you wuz dead or sump'n."

"Nah, man… I ain't dead. I'm right here!" Chuck replied with a boyish grin.

Zachary smiled, "I can see that, man!"

Chuck now had a better understanding of the kind of person he was dealing with, and all of the respect that he'd had for Zachary was slowing deteriorating. "I got sump'n to tell you Zachary, an' huh, it's not so good."

"What?" Zachary asked, still smiling, "It can't be as bad as the shit you went through while you wuz down south. Not the way Apple told it."

"It's a long story," Chuck said. Then he began to describe to Zachary the events of the trip the same way he'd told them to Apple, and he could see Zachary's facial expressions change at the high and low points of each adventurous incident. "I had to run through the woods an' hide under a house," Chuck stated. "An' that's when I lost the guns."

"How many did you lose?"

Chuck looked like an innocent child as he sheepishly replied, "Zachary man, I lost two of'em."

"Which two?"

"One of the 9's an' a 380."

Zachary grabbed the bag with one hand and moved it up and down as if he was weighing it. He frowned inquisitively as he searched through it. Then he started laughing out loud, and Chuck stood there perplexed, trying to figure out if he had missed a joke. Zachary slowly stopped laughing, but the smile was still on his face. "Chuck, did Apple suck yo' dick?"

Chuck's eyes expanded. Zachary's comment was like a one-two punch that he had never seen coming. "What?" is all he asked, only because he needed time to recover and think of something else to say.

"Nah, man, I'm jus' jokin,'" Zachary giggled. "I'm jus' kiddin' wit'chu Chuck, don't sweat that." He extended his hand to shake Chuck's. "I ain't worried 'bout two guns… That shit ain't no problem. You an' Apple made it back here safe. Y'all ain't locked up in jail or dead… an' that's what counts. Now ya'll can lay low for a day or two, then go back down there an' get me some more joints.

We can make at least twenty G's this month."

"That's cool wit me," Chuck replied. "Twenty G's is a good number. That means I'll make four G's for a jus' few days of work. Fuck it, we'll jus' fill the trunk up wit joints an' bring them shits on back to the city!"

"Word up!" Zachary said with a wide smile on his face. Then he and Chuck started laughing. "That's what I like to hear."

Chuck was still smiling confidently when Zachary's face suddenly turned cold. He hadn't appreciated hearing that Chuck had been driving around in a stolen car and didn't even know it. He put his index finger directly into Chuck's chest and calmly said, "As long as we work togetha Chucky, we can't afford ta have these kids tryin' ta diss us. Ya know what I'm sayin'?"

"Yeah…you right, you right."

We live an' die by our rep in these streets, Chuck. The minute we slack up, then somebody gon' think we soft n'shit. Ya know that, right? It's the worst, when people achieve their goal by doin' the wrong shit. Then dey make it a habit, an' dey continue doin' it. It's like a person who gets away with drivin' drunk for the first time. You get the picture?" Chuck nodded his head, agreeing. "So are you gonna take care of this, or do you want me to?"

"I can take care of it!" Chuck assured him, "I'll smack'em aroun' a little bit an' diss'em in front of his peoples n'shit."

But that wasn't what Zachary had planned. Besides, he felt that Chuck had taken too long to respond to his questions, so he volunteered to take care of it himself. "All I need to know," Zachary asked, "does Tone have any peoples livin' aroun' here in the city? An' second, do you care anything for this bastard?" Zachary didn't even give Chuck time to respond before he went on to say, "I mean, he did put yo' life in jeopardy."

Chuck simply replied, "Nope, I neva met any of his people. So you do what'chu gotta do. He ain't care about me, an' he almost messed me up. So fuck'em! Do what'chu gotta do."

Chapter 10:

Tone was known as the Asian ladies' man back at school, and he was one of the most popular guys on campus - but when he started hanging out with the hometown locals back in Louisville, he began to lose respect. His drug habit was taking its toll, and he was getting careless with his own life and others'.

Tone's thing was stealing new cars. He would go to the car dealerships around two or three in the morning, pick out a car he liked, and just take it. He knew that the silver box on the car window was not an alarm as most people thought, but a lock-box that contained the car keys. He would pry the box off the window, extract the keys, and simply drive the car off the lot. Once he found a safe place to park, he would switch the license plates and drive the car across the state line to a chop-shop, where they would dismantle it and resell the parts.

During the summer breaks, Tone stayed with a girl who lived in a historical section of Harlem, where the streets were lined with trees and flowers blossomed like baby's breath and that is where Zachary and Chuck were headed on the afternoon after Chuck had returned to New York.

Zachary was slouched back in the cab with his legs gapped opened. He was grabbing himself and boasting about how guys on the streets feared him because of his tough reputation. The cab cruised down 8th avenue and whenever they stopped at a red light, or turned a corner Zachary would point to the people he knew or blocks he once hustled on. In between, the hoards of black faces that strolled over the filthy sidewalks stood two different sects of Muslims. They were handing out flyers, while a dopefiends nodded into another lifetime. His hands were swollen like black boxing gloves and every time he looked like he was about to doze off and hit the ground, he'd jumped up and start wiping his runny nose. On the other end of the avenue stood a group of thugs and when Zachary noticed them, he tapped Chuck on the shoulder. "Pussy, pussy, pussy," he arrogantly grumbled, "all them bitches you see standin' on that corner right now Chuck, is pussy. As a matter of fact, that whole block is pussy. Back in the days when I wuz comin' up, I prob'ly fucked every bitch on that corner, an' fucked up every nigga out there. Dey fear me, Chuck. Ya know why?" Chuck didn't know what to say, so Zachary continued, using the back of his hand to tap Chuck on the chest. "'Cause big Zach don't play. That's how you got to be, Chuck. Ya got me? Like I wuz tellin' you back at the crib. You gotta step to dese kids right away! You gotta let'em know you ain't no joke!"

Chuck sat there absorbing every word Zachary uttered, with enough adrenaline flowing through his body to win the Boston marathon. When they arrived at Tone's doorstep, Zachary pushed the intercom buttons at random and claimed to be a delivery person. Once in the building, they tiptoed upstairs and Zachary quietly signaled for Chuck to wait by the stairwell. He figured that if Tone saw Chuck he wouldn't come to the door, and this way Chuck would be out of view of the hallway cameras.

Zachary was literally dressed to kill, in an all black linen outfit and a pair of expensive black suede loafers the he had purchased from Etu's Evans boutique in Harlem. His gold belt buckle matched the buckles on his shoes and his gold pinky ring perfectly. He looked like a shadow, and he planned on taking care of business and then going out to brunch with a female friend. His crew had made close to three thousand dollars the day before, and he wanted to have a good time. He was chewing a piece of gum, and he gently brushed his well-trimmed mustache with the palm of his hand, then bent from the waist and knocked two times on the door of apartment 3F with his heavy pinky ring. The noise inside the apartment suddenly stilled, and they could hear footsteps walking rapidly toward the door.

"Who is it?" The voice inside the apartment growled.

Chuck began creeping closer, ready to join in and show Zachary how serious he was - but Zachary gestured for him to stay back. Zachary went to knock again, and he could hear the clinking of the metal peephole as if someone was looking through it.

Zachary was now standing beside the door, just out of view of the peephole. He was pointing backwards with his thumb, silently asking Chuck if they were at the right apartment.

Chuck read his lips, then nodded and whispered, "Yeah!"

Zachary reached into his waist and pulled out one of the 9-millimeters that Chuck had bought back from Kentucky. The pistol had a new, oily smell to it and appeared powerful and deadly in Zachary's fair-skinned hands. He placed the pistol directly against the peephole, and Chuck's eyes widened. He was surprised to see Zachary holding the gun. He hadn't realized that this Tone situation was about to be taken to another level, and now it was too late to turn back. He'd thought that they were just going to bust into the apartment and beat Tone up, but as soon as the voice on the other side of the door growled once more, the gun blasted loudly and echoed to the top of the building. The smell of sulfur lingered in the air, and they heard some crashes and a heavy thud behind the door. The barrel of the gun was hot at the tip, and Zachary didn't want to tuck it into his waistline. He deftly wrapped it in a towel, placed it into a velvet shoe-bag, and walked off. Chuck was still standing stock-still with his ears ringing and his eyes wide as saucers, wondering if he was in the middle of a nightmare.

Zachary calmly turned the corner of the hallway, wiped his hair with his hands and whispered, "C'mon Chucky baby, shake it off." He smiled as he slowly took out a piece of chewing gum, and tucked the wrapper in his pocket as he began to chew. "Let's stcp."

Chuck couldn't believe his eyes. He turned around with his hands clutching his chest as if his heart would bust. He knew that if Tone wasn't dead, he would at least wish he was - and that meant that Chuck might be an accessory to murder. He wanted to run, but his legs wouldn't move that fast. He wanted to put his hands around Zachary's neck and choke him until his fingers touched, while asking repeatedly if he had lost his damn mind.

Zachary was already down the first flight of steps when he looked up at Chuck. He had a grin on his face as he quietly whispered, "C'mon, baby! Let's step the fuck outta' here before Five-O come!"

The neighbors in the building who were not out of town for the weekend were probably either out shopping or too afraid to go near their doors, and if they had, Zachary would have shot them too. The two men left the building and briskly walked to the corner, glancing frequently over their shoulders. Chuck was trailing slightly behind Zachary with his mouth still wide open as he sucked in the wind. They crossed the street, hailed a cab and headed southbound for about thirty blocks before jumping out to catch another, but this time Zachary calmly ordered the cabdriver to go across town. Chuck was sweating with fear; his chest burnt and his blood pulsated in his throat. Zachary was relaxing in the back seat, wiping his hair with his hands and checking out his reflection in the car window.

When the cab arrived at their destination, the two men jumped out and jogged into an abandoned building. The neighborhood was like a cold, deserted ghost-town, where crack addicts moved like zombies through the blighted cityscape. A pack of stray dogs stopped foraging through the trash in a vacant lot and warily watched the two men enter the building. The vestibule and stairwell were poorly lit, with missing steps and graffiti on the walls. Zachary swiftly moved through the building, sprinting easily over the missing stairs as Chuck awkwardly followed him, his anger slowly turning into confusion. The stench of animal urine reeked in the air, and just as Chuck was beginning to think that it was impossible for anyone to dwell in such dreadful conditions, Zachary stopped and banged two times on a dull, steel grey door. Apartment 6A was built like a vault, with three rusty durable padlocks on the door, and to Chuck's surprise, someone quickly answered the knock.

"Yeah?" queried a voice on the other side. Impatiently Zachary kicked the door and grumbled, "Open the fuckin' door, stupid!"

The occupant began undoing the locks, and when the door opened, Chuck saw that it was Fly. Before Fly could get out a word of greeting, Zachary shoved the shoe bag into his hands.

"What's this?" Fly asked.

Zachary ignored him, pushed past and walked to the other end of the apartment, leaving Fly standing there holding the shoe bag. "Lock it up for me," he ordered curtly.

"What is it?" Fly asked again.

Zachary stormed back down the hall toward him, barking, "What the fuck you think it is? Now stop askin' so many fuckin' questions an' do what I say… A'ight?"

Zachary turned around and told Chuck to come on in. Chuck had been standing in the dark hallway of the apartment, wondering if he smelt a dog. Fearfully he followed Zachary, and when he turned the corner of the apartment he saw that his suspicion had been correct. There before him stood two of the most vicious looking dogs he had ever seen in his life.

Chuck wasn't sure if it was the small size of the apartment that made them appear so huge, or whether his eyes were just playing tricks on him. The beasts weighed about 150 pounds each, with shiny jet-black coats, small brown spots above their eyes, and massive jawbones. They had large paws and muscle-bound bodies, so that they appeared bowlegged as they trotted around the apartment. They were surprisingly playful at the sound of Zachary's commands. He had ordered them to go and stand next to Chuck, to show how obedient they were, and they began sniffing around Chuck's legs and crotch as he stood there like a statue. He knew that you should never raise your hands to pet a strange dog without allowing them to sniff you first. He also figured that if the animals sensed how afraid he was, that would only make matters worse. Thick white bubbles of saliva formed in the corners of their jaws as they looked up at him. Chuck tensely kept his hands close to his sides, making sure not to make any sudden movements as the dogs walked back over to Zachary. Chuck then tried to hide his terror by making small talk.

"I would'a neva known there wuz dogs in here," he said, forcing the words from his mouth. "Dey wuzn't barkin' at the door or nut'n."

"I know," Zachary said as he rubbed the dogs, then he ordered them to go down the hall and sit by the front door. "That's how I want it, jus' in case somebody try to break in."

Chuck watched the massive beasts follow Zachary's orders, sitting down right where they were told.

"They'll let somebody in the apartment," Zachary proudly said, "but dey ain't gon' let'em out. An' if dey do get out, it ain't gon' be in one piece."

Chuck stood still, allowing his eyes to search around the dingy apartment. "What's dey names?" he asked, trying to care.

Zachary pointed at the dogs. "If you noticed, one of the dog's faces is a little darker than the other - that's the male. His name is Steak. The female is a little heavier, an' her name is Cheese. This apartment is what we use'ta call the temple. It's my private torture chamber."

Zachary's comment was unsettling, and Chuck's attention quickly switched from watching the dogs nervously, to trying to determine what his next words should be. Zachary arrogantly rubbed his hands together, then checked the back of his pants for dog hair. "Yeah, that's right, my torture chamber. This is where I use'ta keep my money an' my work. An' those big-ass dogs down there are my security guards, executioners an' garbage disposals. Dey made some of the toughest muthafuckas in the streets spill dey guts. Once dey gotta face dose dogs, dey sing jus' like birds, word up! Me an' my runner, we trained'em to eat human flesh - an' if I knew somebody wuz out there gettin' my money, we'd snatch'em right off the streets, bring'em up here an' make'em talk, then feed'em to the dogs. Apple wuz the bait."

Zachary's laugh made Chuck stutter as he asked him to repeat what he'd just said. He was hoping that he'd simply misunderstood, and when Zachary started over from the beginning, Chuck stopped him short. "Did you say Apple wuz the bait?" he asked, incredulously.

"Yeah... man," he sneered, "Why?"

"Nah... Jus' wonderin' is all."

"She would set guys up for me. When I first met you, I told you Apple is my down-for-whateva chick."

Chuck just stood there and listened with a million different thoughts running through his head. He wondered how he could have fallen for a girl like Apple, after all the awful things he'd heard about her. Yet he felt that when he'd looked into her eyes there was something there that everybody else seemed to overlook. He sensed that Apple had a beautiful spirit, and all she needed was someone to love her - and for him, that was an easy job.

"Pain is the great persuader Chuck, don't ever forget that," Zachary continued. "A muthafucka will play tough, but once you put a little pain on his ass, it's a completely different story. They'll tell you whateva you wanna know."

Chuck didn't say anything for the moment, he just absorbed this new information as well as he could. "Where yo' man at now?" he asked.

"Dead," Zachary replied a bit awkwardly. It was as if he felt uncomfortable discussing it.

"Yeah, word? I'm sorry to hear that."

"He got killed ova some bullshit... But what the hell? Ya

gotta die some kinda' way. Shit, you can't live fo'eva."

"Zachary man, speakin' of killin', you know the cops gon' be lookin' for us."

"What'chu talkin' 'bout, Chucky baby?" Zachary smiled as if nothing had happened, and this seemed to agitate Chuck even more. "You talkin' about that thing we jus' took care of?" Zachary continued. "Don't sweat that, Chucky my boy... don't sweat it!"

"What the fuck you mean, don't sweat it? Every cop in the fuckin' universe is gon' be lookin' for us now."

"But what did I jus' say?" Zachary calmly asked. He was now holding his hands up, gesturing for Chuck to back off with all the questions. "I said, Don't sweat that!"

"I think what'chu did is gon' get things all fucked up back aroun' the block. An' I don't wanna be on no America's Most Wanted."

Zachary stretched out his hands and asked with some irritation, "What the hell you talkin' 'bout? You said you don't give a fuck about Tone. Don't tell me you gon' start bitchin' out on me now?"

"Nah... I ain't bitchin' out on you, an' I did tell you to do what'chu gotta do, but I didn't know..."

"You didn't know what?" Zachary asked, fixing him with a piercing look. He was waiting for Chuck to reply, but as soon as Chuck opened his mouth, Zachary asked him, "What, you sayin', you didn't know he wuz gon' get smoked? What, so you scared now?"

"Nah I ain't scared! An' that shit ain't the point... But..."

"But what?" Zachary yelled, and you could see and feel the flames flaring up in each man's eyes and voice as they traded challenges back and forth. Zachary stormed over to Chuck and stood in his face like a drill sergeant. "Man, listen up, I told you we wuz gon' take care of that muthafucka, an' you told me to go ahead an' do it. Didn't you say that? Didn't you?"

"Yeah, I did say that... But..."

"But what? What'chu thought I wuz gon' do? This is the streets man, an' I don't play. If a muthafucka wanna try an' play me, then I'ma see'em, an' I'ma do'em sump'n! An' if he try an' play any-body that's down wit me, I'ma step to'em, an' it ain't gon' be nice. Now as for you... If you wanna be down wit me an' make this money, then let's make papah an' handle our business." Zachary's eyes were broad and round, and a thick vein ran through the side of his neck. "But hey, man, if you don't wanna be down, then there's the door ...an' you know ya way home." He was now pointing towards the door, with the two dogs lying right in front of it. The two men were staring at each other with their chests heaving up and down, and finally Zachary muttered, "Don't let me stop you!"

Chuck stood there for a moment thinking it all over, and just as he turned to leave, Zachary stopped him by saying, "I dunno what'chu worried about Chuck!" He was patting his own chest with the palm of his hand, "I'm in jus' as much trouble as you are... an' you can see I ain't worried about it! So I dunno why you are." Zachary walked over to Chuck and said with a conciliatory tone, "I'm jus' tryin' ta show you the length that I'd go to protect my peo-ple. The ones that are down wit me. Ya know what I'm sayin'?" The two men were still standing face to face, and Zachary calmly put his left hand on Chuck's shoulder and looked him in the eyes. "Trust me, Chuck... You don't have shit to worry about. The cam-eras in the buildings couldn't pick us up from where we were standin'... I know that buildin' very well," he assured him. "I got this *sweet sticky thing* that lives in that same buildin', an' I go by there ta visit her every now an' then. An' I told you Chuck, as long as we down togetha, you ain't got shit to worry about... A'ight?"

Chuck took his time responding, while the apartment grew quiet and the dogs' heavy breathing fogged the air. He was trying to figure out what he'd gotten himself into, but the thought of making the money he needed to start his business was also strong in his mind.

Zachary then extended a hand to shake with Chuck, and to stop him from thinking too long. "We a'ight... right Chuck? We cool, right?"

Chuck stood still for a moment; he looked at the floor and then at the ceiling. He took a deep breath, exhaled through his nose, and then slowly nodded his head. "Yeah…we a'ight, fuck it. Let's make money!"

Zachary smiled and replied with gusto, "A'ight, cool." The two men slapped five and patted one another on the back, "Now that's what I like to hear. Let's get the hell outta' this stinkin'-ass place before we start smellin' like dog!" Zachary called for his runner to come lock the door behind them. The two men were about to exit the lobby of the building when Zachary turned around and told Chuck to wait a minute. He quickly peeped outside, looking carefully left and right, and then they cautiously walked out into the quiet street. The men strode briskly to the corner side by side, talking quietly as they went. They slapped five again and went their separate ways, but not before Zachary had yelled to Chuck that he would give him a call in about two days, to make another run.

"A'ight…" Chuck replied. He got into a cab and started counting his money again. By now, he was convinced that Zachary was all business. In the short length of time that Chuck had known Zachary, he'd had his fair share of real excitement and a taste of the fast life… Everything he had ever heard about Zachary was true.

Hiding out under the house and getting away from the cops had given Chuck something to smile about, but getting someone killed, someone he knew personally, actually brought tears to his eyes. Nevertheless, he was prepared to put his heart on ice and live this kind of life, if that's what it would take to accomplish the goals he'd set for himself. Apple crossed his mind from time to time, and he couldn't wait to see her, but more then anything else, he wanted to find out the truth behind what Zachary had said about her.

When Chuck got home his mother was gone; she had a flexible work schedule at a nearby nursing home, and often when Chuck was coming in the door, Mrs. Love was on her way out. He had thrown away the boxes that the new guns were packaged in, stashed the guns in the inside pockets of his suit jackets, and hung them back in the closet. The bullets and the clips were hidden in a pair of sneakers underneath the bed. After he'd checked the closet and seen that everything was safely stowed away, he paged Apple - and to his surprise she called right back.

"Hey Mister!" she said, happy and relieved to hear from him. "Wassup?"

"Nut'n much," Chuck replied, and although he too was pleased to hear her voice, his tone was lethargic and less enthusiastic, because Zachary's remarks kept playing at the back of his head. He wanted to ask her about it, but he didn't want it to come out the wrong way - so he simply asked her what she was doing.

"Chillin' wit E," she replied. "We jus' sittin' here talkin'." Apple put the receiver against her chest; pointed to it and whispered to Eyonna that it was Chuck. Then she walked into her room and said coyly, "I wuz hopin' you'd call."

"Yeah, is that so?" Chuck flushed as he toyed with his mustache, "Hey, I got sump'n to ask you."

"Huh oh," Apple said playfully, "Yeah Chuck, what is it now?"

"Huh oh?" he replied. "Why you say that, you got sump'n to hide?"

"Na, I ain't got nut'n ta hide!"

"You sure ain't nut'n goin' on wit you an' Zachary?"

Apple paused for a second, then playfully punched the phone as if she was hitting Chuck. "Nut'n is up wit me an' Zachary…" she said with a note of exasperation creeping into her voice. "We dated for a little while a long time ago, an' that wuz it. I told you that already. An' I thought you an' me wuz tryin to start sump'n, Chuck. So why is you askin' me this again now?"

"Nah, 'cause Zachary said some ol' slick shit about'chu today, an' it caught me off guard. It fucked my head up."

"What he say? Some ol' stupid shit I bet'cha. He's good for sayin' dumb shit!"

"Yeah, he did say some dumb shit… Bust how yo' man

asked me did you suck my dick."

"What?! That rat bastard... Zachary asked you what?" When Apple yelled out, Eyonna heard her from the back room and knew something was wrong. She called out Apple's name the way a concerned mother would, asking her if everything was okay. Apple teasingly replied, "Yes, mother dear. Everything is fine. I'm still talkin' on the phone." Then she repeated her question to Chuck.

"You heard me," Chuck replied.

"He asked did I suck ya dick?" Apple asked again in disbelief.

"Word. When I told'em that I lost two of the guns, that's what he asked me."

"An' what'chu tell'em?"

"I ain't say shit. It ain't none of his fuckin' business!" Chuck stated emphatically. "Yo, Apple, I dunno what'chu got goin' on... but don'chu be tryin' to play me like a sucker. A'ight?" When she didn't respond immediately, he asked her once more, and she finally reassured him.

"Zachary is jus' a asshole," she cried, and Chuck could sense the embarrassment in her voice. "He's jus' mad 'cause I said I thought that you wuz cute. But I told you Chuck, you betta' be careful 'bout fuckin' wit Zachary."

"I hear you, I hear you. I ain't even gonna sweat that bullshit right now. Word up I ain't!" He then changed the subject, and asked what she was doing later.

"Nut'n much... why, wassup?"

"'Cause I got some business to take care of first, an' then I wanna hook up wit'chu lata' on... if that's a'ight wit'chu."

"Sure, Chuck, that's cool wit me... You know I'm down."

"So beep me aroun' seven o'clock. A'ight?"

"Cool, seven it is." She then hung up the phone and started singing and dancing back into the living room where Eyonna was waiting.

"Look at'chu." Eyonna mock-screamed. "You all happy n'shit."

"Don't sweat that, don't sweat that," Apple playfully replied.

"What'chu so happy fo', you must be hangin' out tonight, huh?"

Apple kept dancing and teasing Eyonna by not answering her. Instead she just kept saying, "Don't sweat that, don't sweat that."

Chapter 11:

Whenever Chuck came to the city for his summer breaks and school holidays, Tone was right there. Mr. Ray knew Tone as a nice guy, though he'd never said much when he was in the shop. The regulars had found plenty to chuckle about though the first time Tone walked in with Chuck for a haircut. It was a busy Saturday afternoon, the television and the radio were playing simultaneously, and the customers were arguing amiably about the championship fight that was on that night.

"Sump'n about Hearns I jus' don't like," Mr. Ray yelled, "He's a good fighta... but to me, all he got is a right hand - an' the minute you stand in the ring wit him an' take his crap, an' show him that you ain't goin' nowhere... then right away he's ready to quit. He did it against Leonard and..."

"But Leonard is a different breed of a fighta," someone yelled from the back of the shop. "He dug a little deeper."

"He mos' certainly did," Mr. Ray said, "An' Hearns don't like to dig deep. He like to jus' come in there an' and try ta knock yo' ass out and go home. Sometimes you gotta' gamble."

As the men continued to talk, Chuck recommended to Tone that he let Mr. Ray cut his hair, though Tone was skeptical because he was very fussy about his style. Nevertheless, he went over to Mr. Ray and asked him if he knew how to cut his kind of hair.

Mr. Ray started laughing so hard that he began to cough uncontrollably, and someone had to run and get him a cup of water. Everybody in the barbershop was chuckling out loud, because they all felt Mr. Ray was the best barber on this side of the equator, and they all knew that once he regained his composure, he would have something funny to say.

"Do I know how to cut yo' kinda hair?" he asked loudly. His mouth was twisted to the side and his eyes were bulging out of his head. He wasn't upset with Tone, but he thought that he'd have to tease him a bit. "Do I know how'ta cut'cho' hair… Boy, what kinda question is that? Is you crazy?" Tone just stood there looking lost as he fumbled over his words. Mr. Ray instructed him like a teacher, "Young man, you gon'on ova there to that wall, and look at all those pictures up there… an' then you come back here an' tell me what'chu see."

Tone looked around at all the faces as the shop got quiet, till all that could be heard was the sound of the television and radio playing. He walked over to the wall and checked out some the photographs, then looked back at Mr. Ray.

"You see some white people up there on that wall don'chu?" Mr. Ray asked. "An' what kinda hair do dey have?" Tone didn't say anything - he just stood there, nervously looking at Mr. Ray. "The last time I check, dey had straight hair… right?" Mr. Ray continued. "Young man, listen, I was cuttin' hair when all of Harlem's businesses wuz run by white folks. That's all I use'ta cut was straight an' curly hair." Mr. Ray was now speaking like a minister giving a sermon. "That's when you wuz jus' a little seed, swimmin' aroun' in yo' daddy's Johnson." He rolled his eyes and pointed to the pictures again. "Do I know how to cut yo' kinda hair? Boy, I should make you stay aroun' here all day an' sweep the hair off this floor!"

As usual, everybody in the shop chuckled loudly following Mr. Ray's speech, and Tone just stood there looking baffled and embarrassed. After a few seconds, Mr. Ray started smiling and walked over to Tone, then gave him a handshake and patted him on the back to let him know that he was only teasing. Tone smiled back, only wishing that he could make himself disappear.

The afternoon after the visit to Tone's apartment, when Chuck walked into the barbershop, all the customers looked at him as if he was an ugly green monster, and he knew by the their puzzled faces that something wasn't right. But it wasn't until Mr. Ray stopped shaving one of his elderly customer to give him his condolences that Chuck's suspicions were confirmed. "Hey Chuck!" Mr. Ray said. He safely closed his straight razor and reached to shake Chuck's hand. "Damn, boy, I thought you wuz ya daddy walkin' through the door jus' now. You look jus' like him with that damn hat on ya head!" Chuck smiled wanly. "Hey Chuck, all jokin' aside," Mr. Ray continued. "I jus' wanna say I'm sorry ta hear the bad news about ya friend."

Chuck dropped his head as if he found it difficult to speak. He felt a brutal stab of conscience, and didn't know where to look.

"Are you a'right, buddy?"

Chuck nodded his head and quietly murmured, "Yeah... I'm a'right Mr. Ray, thank you."

"If you need anythin', jus' let me know. Okay, Buddy?"

Chuck nodded his head once more, and from the corner of his eye he could see someone reading the newspaper. He stared at it for a moment, because in bold letters, the headline read, "SENSE-LESS KILLING - Man shot through peephole. Many questions still unanswered."

Mr. Ray promptly finished shaving his customer, who paid with a smile. "Thank you my man," Mr. Ray said. He then helped the customer on with his jacket, patted him on the back and sent him on his way. Just before the man walked out of the shop, he stopped to check his face in the mirror. He was rubbing his cleanly shaven cheeks and chin when Mr. Ray teasingly commented, "Hey, pretty boy... keep ya hands offa ya face."

The customer turned around and started laughing. He balled up his fist like a boxer and said, "Ah, forget you, ol'-timer." Then he continued to put on his hat as he teetered out of the shop, as fast as his golden legs could carry him.

On any other day, Chuck would have enjoyed sitting in the barbershop and talking with Mr. Ray's customers. Most of them were senior citizens who gave him advice on life, or reminisced about the great days in Harlem during the late 50's and early 60's. They chatted about politics and boxers, especially Sugar Ray Robinson, as well as a long list of other famous people who had lived in Harlem back in those days. But on this particular day, Chuck's mind was somewhere far away. He didn't even realize that Mr. Ray was calling him to the back of the shop for a talk until Mr. Allen tapped him on the shoulder.

Chapter 12:

While Mr. Ray and Chuck were in the back of the barbershop talking about Tone's murder, Apple was on the other side of town fighting with Zachary. She had been on the point of paging Chuck, when Zachary drove up and got out of his car with a devious smirk on his face. Apple was standing near a corner store, and he leered at her like a sleazy John. He looked her up and down, admiring her outfit, and said, "Damn, girl, you lookin' all good n'shit! Like a model on somebody runway." He didn't even bother to ask about the trip down south, or was she busy or not when he asked her to come with him to make some quick money.

Apple had on a cream-colored linen blouse that made her skin glow from the nape of her neck to the top of her forehead. A simple wash'n'set won her compliments from every man she passed, from the minute she stepped out of her front door. The Harlem breeze ruffled her light blouse, and her perfume gave off the scent of yellow roses decorating the blue sky. She had on a pair of pastel-colored split-toe sandals that matched her bag, and peach linen slacks that flared out at the ankles, making her small frame appear slightly more substantial.

Zachary's mouth began to feel dry with excitement, and he quickly readjusted his sex to the other side so Apple couldn't see him getting aroused. He went to hug her around the waist, and she quickly put her arms up to prevent his chest from touching hers. She was refusing his advances, and that puzzled him, but it frustrated him even more. He was used to having his way with Apple, and later he would mock the way she jumped at his beckon. But when she pushed him away a second time, he became really upset, and he gave her a cold stare. He'd suddenly turned hateful and nasty, sneering, "What, I can't hug you no more?... Oh, you all that now..." He stared hard into her eyes, but continued to smile. "Apple, I know you ain't go down south an' now you tryin' to come back actin' new?"

Apple wanted to get away from Zachary and go meet Chuck. She frowned, took a deep breath and said, "Zachary... I don't feel like playin' right now. Word up I don't!" He had ruffled up her blouse and she was fixing it back. "I'm too tired to be playin', Zachary... Plus I got somewhere to go, an' you holdin' me up."

"Fuck that!" he yelled. Then he reached for her hand. "You tryin' to play me now? You betta stop buggin' out an' bring ya ass on."

Apple just sucked her teeth, so he teased her, and then grabbed her by the waist. She used all of the strength her little body could muster to push him away, and he stumbled backwards.

Zachary snickered, "You jus' said you wuz tired, but you don't look tired to me... You all jazzy n'shit. Dressed up an' smellin' good n'shit, like you goin' somewhere. Where you think you goin'?"

"'Scuse me?" she snapped. She drew herself up, giving Zachary time to explain himself, but then waved him off as the words awkwardly fell from his mouth in bits and pieces. She felt he wasn't really saying much of anything, so she simply walked away. He followed her and tried to grab her by the arm, but she swirled around to face him.

Apple folded her arms across her chest, and rested back on her heels as she flared her index finger in his face, "It ain't none of yo' fuckin' business where I'm goin', Zachary! I'm a grown-ass woman... an' though you might think you own me... you don't. So please get out my way so I can get by. Thank you."

Zachary grabbed her arm and she violently pulled it away. He shoved a roll of money in her face, and when she didn't take it, he began to get aggressive. Every time he wagged his finger in her face, she knocked it away yelling, "Keep yo' hands outta my face, Zachary. You ain't got no kids, ova here!"

Zachary continued to bait her, and instead of knocking his hand away again she slightly turned her head, hiding her face. "You need to stop actin' stupid an' bring yo' fuckin' ass on, before I make you," Zachary barked. "An' I know you don't want that!"

Apple continued to turn her head away from him, and he followed her around in circles, yelling in her face. He was barely touching the tip of her nose with his finger to aggravate her even more. Then he grabbed her by the neck, and she tried her hardest to pull away - but he was too strong for her.

"As long as I'm your source of income, you are my kid, you got that?" Zachary swaggered, "I help you pay your damn bills, an' you betta not fuckin' forget it!"

Apple was not in the mood for listening, and she was tired of Zachary's aggressive behavior. She worked her left arm away from him, and smacked him as hard as she could with her open hand. He slapped her back, causing her to fall to the ground. He was about to hit her again, but he noticed that a police car had cruised by, and was just beginning to slow down. Zachary rushed over to help Apple up. He started smiling and dusting her off, to give the impression that they were only playing.

Apple got to her feet and snatched herself away from him. "Fuck you, Zachary!" She yelled hysterically. "Fuck you!" She was searching the ground for a lost earring, and kept looking over her shoulder to see if he was coming back. "You gon' get yours… you watch… You watch an' see, you muscle-head faggot!"

Zachary tried to conceal his distress by smiling; he jumped into his car, blasted the stereo, and did a U-turn in the middle of the street. Just as he sped off, the policeman who had been watching the scene put his car in reverse. Apple was bending over to pick up

her earring when the officer honked his horn to get her attention. He
asked her if everything was okay, but she didn't respond. He asked
again, and she just continued to fix her clothing, and then walked
off in the opposite direction. The officer was now driving backwards, keeping pace with her to inquire once more if she needed
help, and she told him curtly that she was fine.

"Okay then," the officer said reluctantly, "have it your way."
He slowly drove off, and Apple limped back to the apartment to
collect her thoughts. Her ankle was sore, and Zachary had put a
burning scratch on her neck where he'd grabbed her. She was biting
her bottom lip and wiping her eyes to stop the tears from rolling in
her mouth. Apple was terribly upset, and she was determined to
make Zachary pay for roughing her up that way.

When Apple stormed into the apartment, Eyonna was in her
room, listening to the radio while getting dressed. She knew that
Apple had just walked out, and she was surprised to hear her coming back so soon. "Apple," she loudly called from the back of the
apartment. "Girl, wassup? You musta forgot sump'n, huh?"

Apple didn't answer; but rushed straight into the bathroom,
locked the door, and splashed cold water on her face. Eyonna was
hopping on one foot by the bathroom door, wearing a pair of deep
purple panties with a matching bra. She was trying to put on her
socks, and wondering why Apple wasn't saying anything.

When Apple finally came out of the bathroom, Eyonna
immediately noticed the distressed look on her face, and she started yelling, "What happed ta you, Apple? Girl, what's wrong?"

Eyonna was trying to look into her eyes, but Apple pulled
away and dashed toward her room. Eyonna followed her in a help-
less frenzy; she was upset and curious at the same time. When she
noticed the scratch on Apple's neck, she automatically assumed that
she'd been out fighting, and Eyonna wanted to find out with whom,
so that they could immediately take revenge. Eyonna kept pulling
on Apple's arm, trying to get her to come back into the living room
where the light was better, so she could see her face. Apple finally

sat down on the couch, and Eyonna checked the scar, then rushed back to the bathroom for some skin ointment. She was gently massaging Apple's neck when the truth finally came pouring out of her...

Eyonna jumped up from the couch and stepped back with her hands on her hips, saying, "What'chu mean you wuz fightin' with Zachary? He a' faggot, now...? He ain't got shit betta ta do but scratch at women, huh?" Eyonna was furious, and she was fed up with Zachary mistreating her friend. She started looking around the apartment as she listened to Apple talking. Then she briskly walked to her bedroom while Apple sat there with a towel held to her neck, and a blank stare on her face. When Eyonna returned, she was flipping through the pages of her telephone book and mumbling under her breath, "That's a'ight, I got a trick for his ass."

Apple sat there with her legs crossed and a somber look on her face, "What'chu gettin' ready ta do?" She asked.

"Nut'n," Eyonna quickly replied, "I wuz jus' lookin' for sump'n ta knock his ass in the head with... But don't worry, he gon' get jus' what he askin' for - an' that's a good ol' fashion beat-down ... You watch an' see!"

Apple was now sitting up with her back straight, watching Eyonna storm back and forth through the apartment, still flipping madly through her phone book. "E... what'chu doin'?" Apple sobbed.

"What'chu think I'm doin'? Eyonna retorted. "We gon' get somebody to stomp the fear o' God into his atheistic, high-yella ass! What type o' shit is he smokin' that makes him think he can go aroun' fuckin' people ova?"

Apple shrugged her shoulders and Eyonna went over to console her for a moment, but she was too upset to sit still. She jumped up from Apple's side and said, "If he want beef... he gon' get beef. I wuz gettin' tired o' his shit anyway." After she retrieved a couple of numbers from her phone book, she franticly searched around the apartment for the cordless telephone. Just at that moment it began to ring, and she found it wedged in between the pillows on the couch. Eyonna was breathless and upset, and had no concern for phone etiquette when she answered sharply, saying, "What."

"Why you puffin' so hard?" the voice on the other end of the phone asked.

"Yo, what the fuck you hit my friend for, you faggot?"

"Hello Eyonna. How you doin'?" the voice calmly went on.

"What the hell you mean, how am I doin'? You heard what I jus' asked you. Why you hit my girl?"

"Yo, E, it wuzn't a hit, it wuz only a little pat," the voice declared. "An' it wuz an accident, an' I'm sorry. Now can you put'cha girl on the phone for me, please? I wanna apologize, plus I got sump'n ta ask her."

"Yo, fuck you, Zachary, you punk," Eyonna yelled with bass in her voice. "An' no you can't speak to her, because I'm hangin' up. Bye." After Eyonna had hung up the phone, she started dialing one of the numbers that she had found in her phone book, while Apple just sat there, not saying anything. "I'ma get somebody ta step ta his ass," Eyonna declared. She started dialing, but Apple stopped her by quickly placing her hand over the phone. Eyonna glared at her. "Yo, what'chu doin'?"

Apple's kept her hand on the phone, and simply said, "Don't do it."

"What'chu mean, don't do it? You must like it when he's out there makin' a fool out of you… Huh?"

"No…I don't, but…"

"But what, Apple? His dick ain't that damn good!"

"But all I'm sayin' is…'

"What the hell are you sayin'? I mean damn, Apple, why you let him do the kinda dumb shit that he do to you? Now move ya hand so I can make this phone call." Eyonna snatched the phone away from Apple and started dialing again.

"E, please don't do it."

"Why not?"

"'Cause, if you get somebody ta step ta Zachary, you know it's gon' get messy, an' we gon' get caught right in the middle of that shit."

"Please," Eyonna replied with a dismissive tone, "I doubt that very much. Afta all the dirty shit Zachary been through, an' all the dirty shit that he done did to people in the streets... Muthafuckas will be happy ta see him dead. They'll prob'ly throw a damn block party for his dead ass, an' I know ezzackly the right people to do it too. They'll leave his ass dead an' stinkin'.'"

All the while the girls were talking, the phone kept ringing, and Eyonna would calmly lift up the receiver and hang it up without answering. "I bet'cha it ain't nobody but that bastard Zachary callin' here again," she said with a snort. They continued to talk until the constant ringing finally became unbearable, and Eyonna snatched the receiver up to her ear. With all the bitterness that she could muster she screamed, "What. What the hell do you want?"

The voice at the other end of the line politely asked, "Hello, can I speak to Apple, please?"

"Who is this?"

"It's me, Chuck."

"Chuck? Chuck who?" Eyonna asked.

Chuck began to explain himself, but Apple quickly took the phone from Eyonna's hand, and softly said into the receiver, "Hey baby, wassup?"

Chuck lit up at the sound of her voice. "Hey, doll-face. Wassup wit'chu? I thought that you wuz gon' beep me. What happened?"

"I wuz, Chuck, and I ain't forgot about you, but I got caught up in the mix... an' me an' E started talkin'. I hope you ain't mad at me?" she coyly asked.

Chuck smiled. "I'm heated right now..."

"Where you at?"

"Uptown... by Mr. Ray's barba'shop."

"Cool, don't go nowhere. I'ma meet you there in about a hour, okay?"

"That's cool with me," he replied. "I'll be waitin'."

Apple wiped her face and jumped up from the couch, leaving Eyonna still sitting there in a huff. Apple was walking toward the bathroom to freshen up, when she stopped at the doorway and turned around with her hands on her hips. She smirked and asked, "Girl, where you goin' tonight with those sexy unda'wear on?"

Eyonna was still upset, but Apple's cheerful behavior made her jump up from the couch and run to the opposite side of the living room. She leaned up against the wall, groped her breast and said, "I got me a hot date... So don'chu wait up... 'cause I am not comin' home tonight."

"Girl, you so silly!" Apple squealed. The friends burst out laughing, then Apple sped away to change her clothes. It only took her about twenty minutes to get ready, and then she was on her way out the door. She stopped by Eyonna's room to tell her that she was leaving, and to find out who E was going out with.

"Now it's my turn to be nosey," she teased. Apple was trying to look serious, as if she were a concerned parent inquiring about her daughter's first date. "Now jus' ezzackly who you think you goin' out wit tonight, Miss Hot Pant?."

Eyonna was looking in the mirror and brushing her hair as she bragged, "Zachary's so-called cut-buddy."

Apple suddenly got serious. She rolled her eyes and sucked her teeth, "Why him?" she asked harshly. "You only think he cute 'cause he got curly hair."

Eyonna didn't respond, instead she just twisted her lips and continued to primp in the mirror.

"He only come aroun' when he think Zachary got sump'n to give his ass," Apple continued. Eyonna shrugged her shoulders and smirked. She was leaning over her nightstand to get a closer look in the mirror, when Apple asked her again, "I mean why Eyonna, what do you see in that grimy bastard?

"Grimy?" Eyonna asked loudly. "Look who's talkin'! If he grimy then you know that bastard Zachary is the king of the grim-ies, cause he practically invented that grimy shit. An' I dunno what'chu see in him, word up I don't."

"You mean what did I use'ta see in him, an' that's old news. Zachary is so played out to me now!"

"Yeah okay, you talkin' shit right now 'cause he roughed you up, but the minute you give'em a chance to apologize, ya'll gon' be right back at it again. Watch an' see."

"No... you watch an' see," Apple retorted. "E, I am so ova him right now, that you wouldn't even believe it. Zachary is so corny to me that it ain't even funny. Word up."

"Yeah, right!"

"E, listen - rememba I told you what happened to me an' Chuck when we went down south?"

Eyonna nodded her head with a sideways look, "Yeah, I rememba."

Apple swaggered, "Well, I told Chuck that he should keep Zachary's guns for hisself."

"Yeah, well did he do it?"

Apple answered Eyonna's question with a sneaky smile.

Eyonna twisted her mouth and rolled her eyes. She slowly turned around and looked at Apple. "Why?" she asked, without a trace of a smile.

Apple just shrugged her shoulders and continued to grin like a mischievous child.

"You know what, Apple? You do some real foul shit sometimes. You know that, right? That 'splains why Zachary wuz out there tryin' to beat the shit outta you, an' then you try to act like you don't know why. But the worst part about it is, Zachary won't do too much ta you, but he'll hurt that damn boy, Chucky. An' you know as well as I do that Zachary thrives on that kinda shit... that's the type of shit that get his dick hard! Then you'll stand ova there an' pretend like you su'prised."

"Nah, E, it's not like that," Apple cried. "I really like Chucky, an' I ain't gon' let Zachary put a finger on him." Eyonna looked at Apple and rolled her eyes again. "I'm for real, E," Apple continued,

"I wuz jus' lookin' out for Chuck. That's why I told him to take what he wanted, so he can make some money for hisself... An' I jus' get tired of Zachary's shit... Besides, how he gon' find out what I did unless you tell'em?"

Eyonna continued to fix her hair and shake her head, "Apple you sound lost to me. You need to make up yo' mind, girlfriend. Because if you don't, somebody is gonna get hurt bad. !" Eyonna laid her hairbrush on the dresser, walked over to Apple and spoke right to her face, "Listen, you goin' out to meet Chuck now... right?" Apple nodded. "An' he's the guy you care about now, am I right?" Another nod. "So if you really like him, then don't try to mix business with pleasure. I know you still have feelings for Zachary, but honey, you gotta let him go and move on. You got a lot goin' for you, whetha you know it or not - but these streets ain't goin' nowhere. You can go aroun' the world an' come back, girl... an' these same damn niggas gon' still be here doin' the same bullshit!"

Apple quietly stood at the threshold of the bedroom door, weighing her odds. She shook her head uneasily as she thought about all the hard times she'd been through with Zachary.

"You right, E. You are so right," she said softly. Then she looked at her watch and realized how long she and Eyonna had been talking. "Oh, shoot! Girl, I been so busy standin' here runnin' my mouth wit'chu, you gon' make me late."

"Jus' think about what I said."

"I will." Apple promised. "I will, E. An' thank you."

"Fo' what?"

"Fo' speakin' up. I know I be doin' some dumb shit some-times, but'chu always there to tell me 'bout it."

Eyonna smiled, "You my girl, Big Apple, an' if we don't look out fo' each otha, ain't nobody else gonna do it."

Apple returned the smiled and went to hug Eyonna. They said goodbye, then Apple grabbed her bag and streaked out the door to go meet Chuck.

Chapter 13:

I t was a warm, clear night when Apple met Chuck under the neon lights at Mr. Ray's barbershop, and when they caught sight of each other, they couldn't stop trading compliments on how nice they both looked. Chuck was so excited that he reached for her hand, pulled her close, and he gave her a soft kiss on the forehead.

Apple rubbed his chest and playfully said, "Wassup, strangea... Where you been all my life?"

"No, you askin' the wrong question," he blushed, "'cause I been right here, waitin' fo' you."

Chuck had on a crispy white dress shirt and dark blue jeans, his favorite pair. Whenever he sat down, they showed off the soft cotton argyle socks that made him feel like he was walking on air. His suede lace-up shoes matched his beige linen hat and Apple's skirt so well, it seemed as if they had coordinated what they would wear before leaving home.

Apple smiled, "we make a nice-lookin' couple."

§

Apple was tired of showcasing and she wanted to try something different, so she chose an Afro-centric soul food restaurant on 96th street and Columbus Avenue. It was a place where the combination of abstract art and the aromatic scent of burning rosemary made you feel as if you were in the heart of the motherland. The restaurant was softly lit and the tables were hand-painted in bright red and deep blue patterns, and small candles were placed in bottle tops to complete the atmospheric decor. The waitress welcomed and seated the couple, then placed a pitcher of water on their table and told them she'd be back to take their orders. Apple sat across from Chuck, shamelessly gazing into his eyes and listening to what he planned on doing for the summer.

Chuck only intended to work with Zachary a little longer. "I mean, I'm not tryin' to make a career out o' this shit," he insisted. "Zachary will be nickel-n-dimin' for the rest of his life, like a lotta kids out here that I know, an' dey ain't gon' end up wit shit, an' I don't wanna be like that. I figure if I can make some real money this summa... then I can parlay it into sump'n constructive. Actually, I wanna start my own publishin' company."

While he talked, Apple sat there watching his lips move and thinking to herself, 'Maybe Eyonna wuz right, he jus' might be the one. The one that could make me settle down. No more lying. No more duckin' an' dodgin'. I would sleep betta at night, an' not be always worryin' 'bout who I'm gonna beat for a coupla dollas.'

"I have two classmates who can really write," he said, "an' they love boxin' jus' like I do, an' we plan on startin' our own boxin' magazine."

"A boxin' magazine?" Apple asked, squirming in her seat. "You like boxin', Chuck?"

"I love boxin'," he replied with his eyes shining. "Why you think I'm always in the barba'shop, arguin' wit dose old men?"

Apple grimaced, "What about all that blood an' stuff that be flyin' aroun'? Those men be gettin' dey lips busted an' dey noses broke. I dunno how dey girlfriends can handle that stuff."

"It's a hurt sport, an' that all comes wit the territory."

Apple sat with her hands locked together and a sour look on her face as if she had just tasted spoiled milk. She continued to squirm as she listened to Chuck defending everything she disliked about a sport that she felt was purely brutal.

"That's jus' it," he said with a large smile. "I wanna see boxin' back on prime time TV. I'd like to watch fights on television on those long Saturday afternoons when everybody's at home... jus' like it wuz back in the days. I'd work wit the fighters, an' write things about'em that help build up their image... make'em look good on TV, an' not like the monstas that some people make them out to be. My whole idea is to bring money back to the sport, the way Ali an' Sugar Ray Leonard did. I wanna make the average fighta a household name.

"That sounds good, an' you look so excited about it too. But that's a big plan Chuck...You think you're ready for all that responsibility?"

"Hell yeah!" He looked her in the eyes and said earnestly, "Apple, you jus' don't know how bad I want this. I'll have paparazzi snappin' dey pictures while they runnin' from crowds of fans an' screamin' women. An' those photos will be published in the magazines. Sump'n to stir up a buzz of excitement aroun' da fighter."

"Oh yeah?"

"Yeah, then hopefully these guys can start gettin' endorsements from food chains an' sportswear companies again. Then the sport won't be seen as so barbaric and bloody, but people will see the beauty an' grace in it."

Apple just shook her head and smiled, "Umph, if that's what'chu want Chuck, I hope you get it."

"Hope? Ain't no hopin', Apple baby. I am gonna get it. You think I'd be botherin' with someone like Zachary, after all the shit I hear about him in the streets, 'bout how ugly he is...? I even heard that's his nickname."

"What?"

"Pretty Ugly," Chuck quoted with a smile. "Girls say he's a pretty dude on the outside, but ugly on the inside."

Apple flashed Chuck a phony grin, "Oh yeah, I heard that too."

"But that's jus' what I got to put up wit for right now, Apple. Plus I wanna write a book about my Pop's life. My Dad wuz a real character, Apple. He'd keep shoeboxes full of money underneath the bed an' in da closet. He even hid money in the pots an' pans, an' then he put'em right back under the kitchen sink. I rememba he'd leave change lyin' aroun' the house for me ta find, an' I'd go to school the next day wit a fat knot in my pocket. I use'ta treat my boys to lunch n'shit." All the while Chuck was talking, he stared into space with dollar signs in his eyes, just like a cartoon.

Apple smirked, "Yeah, I do rememba you wuz a dressed-up nerd."

"You got jokes, huh?"

They were both laughing when Apple jumped as if she had just remembered something. She took a sip of water and asked, "Wassup wit yo' chain?"

"What chain... this one?" Chuck pulled down on the chain around his neck and looked at it as if he hadn't seen it in a while.

"I don't see no otha chain on you, Chuck," she teased.

"Oh, people always askin' me about this. As a matta of fact, you the second person ta ask me about it since I been home." Chuck held the chain between two fingers. "My fatha gave me this, when he wuz lyin' on his death bed. I know it sounds corny, but you know when you're a kid... you wanna know about everything?" Apple nodded her head. "Well, I found it in my Pop's dresser draw one day, an' he said I could have it, only if I promise to graduate high school wit honors."

"An' what happened?"

"Well, he passed before I got to the twelfth grade. But I wear it all the time, so even when I'm brushin' my teeth, or takin' a shower, or jus' chillin', I see it an' I think of him... An' that helps me keep on course." Then without saying anything, Chuck pulled out some money and started counting it underneath the table, just out of Apple's view. After he'd finished, he handed her three hundred dollars. Apple just stared at it.

"What's this for?" She asked, surprised and a little suspicious.

"Jus' some money to put in ya pocket."

"Nah, that's a'ight, Chuck. I got ma own money."

"But I want you ta have it."

"Nah, put'cha money up Mr. Big Spender, save it for all'a them big projects you tellin' me about.."

"Okay," he shrugged. Then he reached over the table to hold her hand, and she softened again and smiled. "Apple, when I go back ta school, will you come down south to visit me?" Chuck asked all at once.

Her face lightened as she snatched her hand away. "You had to be readin' my mind jus' now, Chuck."

"No… But I sure wish I could sometimes."

"I wuz jus sittin' here thinkin' about givin' this city a break," Apple mused. "I'd love to go down there and visit you, Chuck. I been thinkin' about the South every since we got back… Plus I jus' need'ta slow down a little anyway."

"Slow down, how…?" Chuck teased, "You mean gettin' married an' havin' a baby kinda slowin' down?"

"No, silly!" Apple gave him a love tap on the arm and rolled her eyes. "But seriously Chuck… I jus' need a break. I get tired of the hustle and bustle. It's funny, you ever notice how people from New York complain 'bout the noise, but when dey visit their relatives in the South, dey can't stay fo' long 'cause dey say it's too quiet?"

"Yeah, that's true. But I thought you said you like the noise?"

"I do, but I jus' get tired o' the bullshit too. I get tired of bustin' my chops for that little bit of money that I make, bein' bothered wit that damn Zachary."

Yeah, but what about E - you'd leave her? Ya'll seem like ya'll can't stand ta be apart."

"Yeah, you right about that - E's my girl. I love her ta death! We been through so much shit togetha, man. Chuck… you jus' don't even know." Apple sucked her teeth and smiled as she stared into space, remembering the good and bad times she and Eyonna had spent together. "Chuck... we been through so much, that shit is truly unbelievable. Plus Eyonna's goin' back to school this fall, an' she said she ain't gon' be bothered wit Zachary no more."

"So why don'chu go back to school too?"

"Man, Chuck, I'm not a school person... Besides I'm afraid I might flunk out."

Chuck frowned, "So don't flunk out. Jus' tell you'self that failin' ain't a option."

"Chuck, I'm not cleva like you. All I know is hustlin."

"So what? School is a hustle too, an' that street shit ain't gon' lead to nothing positive fo' you, Apple. You should come down south, stay awhile, an' see how you like it. An' if you do, then you can pack up all yo' stuff an' jus' start ova down there. Rent ain't that expensive, and you know how to drive. Hell, you can enroll in the same school I go to."

Apple softly dropped her head, and Chuck gently placed his fingers under her chin to slowly lift it back up. He looked her in the eyes, and then he leaned over and kissed her. "What's wrong, baby?"

Apple shrugged her shoulders, "Nut'n I guess."

"Well then, you shouldn't drop ya head down like that. That's a sign of a beaten fighta. They do that when they lost the will to win, an' I know you ain't like that. You a fighta, Apple! That's why I like bein' wit'chu."

Apple blushed and kissed the palm of his hand. "I jus' got sump'n on my mind, that's all. An' I dunno, Chuck. I said I'd visit you down there... but movin' down south for good is a big step."

"Apple, I don't wanna live down there for the rest of my life eitha... I'm jus' givin' you a chance to start ova. An' besides... You the Big Apple, everybody knows that." By now he had moved his chair next to hers and placed his arm around her waist. "You can do whateva you puts ya mind to. Plus you know the old sayin', Apple. If you can make it there...?"

"I'll make it anywhere," she finished the lyric with uncertainty. "But I jus' don't know, Chuck..."

Chuck firmly insisted, "Apple, you were the one tellin' me that you tired of this-n-that, an' you need a break and whateva... So at least you can give it a try. An' why do you wanna be bothered wit Zachary at all if he's treatin' you like shit. You deserve betta, Apple, an' if you let me show you, I will."

"I dunno Chuck... I'll think about it, okay?" Chuck pulled her closer and they quickly kissed. "An' I'll let you know sump'n soon... A'ight?"

After they'd gazed for a moment into each other's eyes, Chuck complimented her on how charming she looked with the candlelight dancing across her face. In the back of his mind he thought about how sweet her face smelt, her soft hair and voluptuous lips. They kissed, then laughed and kissed again. Apple was practically in his lap by now, and they had to pull themselves apart when the waiter came to take their order. Twenty minutes later he returned with their meal, and Chuck was still trying to get Apple to be more specific about her plans to come visit him.

"Soon," was all she would say.

Chuck had started moping because he didn't really believe her. When the waiter was finish laying the table, Apple called Chuck's name, so he looked and waited for her to speak - but she said nothing. He asked if everything was all right, and she just shrugged her shoulders.

"Well, what is it then?" He asked moodily.

Apple still didn't say a word, but just turned her neck and showed Chuck the place where Zachary had scratched her. Chuck stared with a puzzled look on his face. Then he reached to touch the mark, and she quickly jumped back.

"Damn...how'd that happen?"

"Zachary an' I had a fight."

"What?" His mouth hung open in pure astonishment and outrage.

"Well... I think he suspects we tryin' to play him... an' if I know Zachary... he ain't gon' let it rest."

"What'chu talkin' about?" Chuck was frustrated and confused, and Apple could see the anger kindling in his eyes.

"Jus' take it easy, Chuck."

"What he say when you saw him?" he asked. He was sitting up straight in his chair now, with the candlelight bouncing on his face, giving Apple his undivided attention. He planked his silverware on the table and stared at her oddly. Many different thoughts were running through his head, as he vividly remembered Zachary's dogs and the dingy apartment, the remark he'd made about Apple, and the way he'd taken care of Tone.

"I wuz on my way to meet you, an' I ran into'em," Apple explained, "an' me an' him got into a fight, an' that's how I got this scar on my neck…"

"So what did he say that makes you think that he thinks sump'n is up?"

"I jus neva saw him act like that towards me before."

"There's a first time for everything, Apple… Maybe he's jus' jealous. Who knows? But I'ma talk to'em about it tomorrow."

"Nah… Believe me, Chuck… sump'n is up. I neva, eva seen Zachary act like that before…"

Chuck sat there at a loss. He didn't know what he should say when he next saw Zachary - should he lie to him, or just avoid him for awhile until he could think of a good story? He slouched back in his chair with his fist on his mouth and his fear turning to bitter anger. He was still thinking in circles when he slammed the table with the palm of his hand, causing Apple to jump and their glassware to tip over. She rushed to stop the drinks from spilling on the floor, but one of the waiters hovering nearby had already beaten her to it. She quietly sat next to Chuck calling his name, but he didn't answer. She tried pulling his hand away from his face and holding it in hers, but he continued to ignore her.

"Raise up off me Apple," he said bitterly, as he snatched away from her and put his hand back up to his mouth. "What am I s'posed to do now?" He yelled. Patrons in the restaurant were looking over their shoulders at them, while Apple sat there not saying anything. "Maybe this wuz sump'n you had planned all the time, huh?" Chuck's mistrust hurt Apple's feelings, and she looked as if she was about to cry.

Apple shook her head, grabbed Chuck's hand again and softly said, "Chuck it's not like that!"

He rolled his eyes and continued to show his displeasure, looking like a cornered animal, with confusion, anger and fear all rolled into one tight ball inside of him. He spoke harshly through his teeth when he asked, "What the fuck is that supposed to mean, huh? What'chu mean, it's not like that? I told you I got plans wit Zachary... I trusted you, an' took yo' advice, an' now you tellin' me he don't believe our story... all because of some shit that you an' him been through..."

"I know, Chuck, I'm sorry," she cried.

"So what now?" He asked, still unforgiving. Apple sat there quietly, while Chuck twisted his mouth to the side and shook his head in disgust. "Damn, Apple, all that shit I went through, an' now it's all about to go right down the toilet... I wuz jus' sittin' here tellin' you 'bout all my plans, an' how I need to get some money so's I can make'em happen - an' now you tellin' me this?"

"You act like it's all my fault, Chucky."

"But damn, it wuz yo' idea. When I gave Zachary his joints the other night, I told him that story about losin' the guns, an' he acted like he didn't have no problem wit it... Now you tellin' me that he rough you up."

"He did try to fuck me up!" she yelled. She was using her index finger to pull down the collar of her shirt, fully revealing the mark on her throat. "You see this shit on my neck, don't you?" She rolled her eyes and sat back in her chair with her arms folded across her chest. The two of them sat in silence for ten minutes until Chuck calmed down. Finally he looked around, took a deep breath, and said he was sorry. Apple took her time accepting his apology, only because she had really meant well.

"Okay," Chuck sighed, "tell me everything... an' don'chu

leave nut'n out. I need ta know it all, so when I see him again, I'll know what to say. I wanna clear this shit up an' move on."

Apple had to gather her thoughts before she began to explain herself, and she felt that some wine would help. The pungent, slightly sweet drink made her lips pucker, and Chuck knew not to rush her this time. Once she'd gotten up enough courage, she began to explain the devotion she'd once felt toward Zachary, and how she'd tried so hard to please him. She described the entire fight they'd had, everything Zachary had said and done, and Chuck sat there and listened. In fact, the conversation became so absorbing that they didn't even bother to eat the rest of their meal. They sat at the table with the food packed in doggy bags as they continued to sip glasses of red wine and work things through.

Apple spoke softy when she said, "I wuz a dancer…" knowing that was a part of her past, and she couldn't do anything to change it.

Chuck sat there with his face expressionless, thinking, 'Apple wuz always a street-smart girl who looked like a woman before she was one.' He felt that she had simply been doing what she had to in order to survive, and it wasn't his place to judge her. He didn't ask where, but the way his eyebrows rose up made her feel she ought to tell him.

"If you're wonderin' where, Chuck… it wuz at some afta'-hour spots in Philly. That wuz right afta my Moms put me out the house. I needed a shoulder to cry on, an' Zachary wuz right there. He wuz a smart, pretty boy that always had money, an' I wuz so young… I moved in wit E about four months afta meetin' Zachary, but by then he already had me where he wanted me. Stupid, dependent, an' in love." Apple took a sip of wine and angrily pushed away the small wicker basket that held the cornbread. "Or at least I thought I wuz," she continued. "I didn't like the nightclub lifestyle or those bitches that I worked wit, but I did what I had to do. No girl in dey right mind would like that dancin' shit, but a lotta times dey gets stuck there, same way I did... Strippin' fo' dollas, an' some nigga is takin' ya papah. Afta a while, I called myself quittin' that shit an' cuttin' Zachary off... An' I did stop dancin'... but cuttin' Zachary off wuz another story. Wheneva we broke up, he came aroun' beggin' an' promisin' to change, and I'd accept his expensive gifts an' his apologies, an' be right there wit'em again.

"What about Eyonna, wuz she dancin' too?"

"Nah, jus' cards. Eyonna didn't come along an' hustle until lata' on, when Zachary started doin' the card game. He wuz clockin' dollas too... an' everybody wanted to be down wi'dat shit. Eyonna's Mom wuz real helpful, like my motha' shoulda been. She neva told me what I should or shouldn't do, but she wuz always there for me. She would always tell me to think big an' want more outta life... 'stead o' jus' clothes an' jewelry. She didn't know what I wuz out there doin' in the streets. I think she woulda shot me."

All the while Apple was explaining herself she had a gloomy look on her face, but when she made that remark, it was the first time she smiled. She sat there quietly for a few seconds, biting her bottom lip and shamefully shaking her head. "But none of it took the place of a man, a father in my life - an' that's what I saw in Zachary. An' once he realized that, he twisted me an' used me, an' made me feel like I needed him. An' at one point in my life, that's how I felt. I wuz young an' naïve, an' I believed everything he told me. Zachary use'ta take me to South Jersey an' Philadelphia, to protect me from those rowdy frat boys an' those dirty old men. And we would leave those clubs at five an' six in the mornin'... We wuz like some kinda vampires tryin' to make it home before the sun come up, or some low-life fugitives on the run. We'd stop at those nasty diners for breakfast, drinkin' coffee outta styrofoam cups. Most'a the time we slept the day away in some cold, damp motel, or killed time walkin' aroun' in the malls like stupid lost kids."

Apple looked up to see if she could read the expression on Chuck's face, and to her surprise, he didn't look upset. "If you're wonderin' Chuck, I neva slept wit any of those men, I didn't." Apple smirked as she mocked herself and the dire life that she had lived. She held her wineglass in the air as if she were making a toast and said, "I wuz Zachary's main squeeze, hip hip hooray! An' this wuz Zachary's poo'nany." Then she sat there quietly wiping the tears from her eyes. Chuck reached over to hug her and rub her back. Apple regained her composure, and then she continued, "I use'ta set guys up for Zachary, an' we caught a lotta kids out there too. Down in Philly. The college boys stayed broke, but the sugah daddies would trick dey whole paycheck on me an' the girls. We made it a point to catch'em out there, an' send'em home wit flat pockets, or jus' enough cash for baby pampas."

By now, Apple and Chuck had each had their fair share of the wine, and he was utterly lost in her world. Her words were slurring from the refills, and the more she talked, the less remorse Chuck felt for cheating Zachary. His hands were clenched into tight fists, and beads of sweat were rolling down his back. He was furious, and if this was part of another plan that Apple had cooked up, she was doing a fine job - because Chuck had already started thinking of ways he could kill Zachary and get away with it.

"One night all the sugah daddies were splurgin' dey tax returns and gettin' drunk," Apple reported with a deceitful smile. "An' it wuz my job to get Soda Pop back to the motel."

"Who's that?"

"Soda Pop?"

"Yeah."

"He wuz a regula. A fat, greasy muthafucka wit a Jerry curl an' a lotta cash. Me an' the girls gave him that nickname 'cause he always had gas an' needed a soda to help him burp. Anyway, I got him back to the motel that night... but he didn't wanna take off his pants. He said he got robbed like that before...." Apple sucked her teeth. "Well... he wuz in for a big surprise, 'cause he wuz gon' get jerked again. I kept beggin' Soda Pop to take his pants off, that way when he fell asleep, it would be easy fo' me to go in his pockets."

"So what happened?"

"He kept tellin' me, 'No baby, jus' let Soda Pop hit it from the back.' Apple glanced in Chuck's direction, and it was the first time he'd appeared uncomfortable. Apple shrugged her shoulder and continued, "So I jus' kept feelin' on his nuts an' talkin' nasty to'em to stall for time. I wuz hopin' Zachary would bust in the room an' get me outta' there... but he didn't. So I told that fat bastard I wuz gon' give'em some head, an' he shut up."

Apple took another sip of wine and thought about changing the subject, but she had already gone too far, and the wine was talking for her by now anyway. "I got down on my knees to undo his pants, an' I got them down around his ankles. I told Soda Pop to go sit on the bed while I freshen up. Then I ran to the bathroom an' knocked on the wall two times... to give Zachary the emergency signal... but he ain't answer. Soda Pop start yellin' from da room, askin' me what's all that noise in the bathroom. Then he started buggin' out, an' yellin' for me to hurry up before his dick go down. 'Soda pop ain't young like he use'ta be,' He kept sayin'. Then he start bangin' on the bathroom door, an' when I came out to quiet him down, he started chasin' me aroun' da room wit his pants aroun' his ankles. He wuz all outta breath; sweatin' an' puffin', an' when he finally got me cornered in that little-ass motel room, he took off his shirt, an' he had titties, jus' like a girl!"

Apple had a blank stare on her face, and her body was jerking unconsciously, as if she was in the middle of a nightmare. "Anyway, he punch me in the face an' I fell to the ground, an' he started rippin' off my clothes. I wuz tryin' to fight that big fucka off." She started to cry with real tears in her eyes. "But he wuz jus' too fat. An' I got tired of dat muthafucka hittin' me an' makin' me dizzy, so I gave in."

"That's okay Apple, you don't have to tell me no more."

Apple quickly held up her hand to stop him from interrupting her; this was soul-cleansing time, and she wanted him to hear the whole story. "I started goin' down on'em, but the fucked up thing about it is, I found out lata' on that Zachary wuz standin' right in the doorway watchin' me the whole fuckin' time." Apple reached across the table, tapped Chuck's lap, and yelled, "Can you believe that shit, Chuck? Zachary wuz standin' in the doorway jackin' off, the whole damn time."

Chuck had a confused look on his face again, and he could only whisper, "Get the fuck outta' here."

"Yeah, he waited till I wuz damn near naked, givin' that fat fucka his damn blowjob, before he creep inta the room. An' when he seen enough, he knock Soda Pop in the back of the head wit the butt of his gun." Apple's eyes were red and her cheeks puffed out as she said, "Booooom, that fat bastard fell on the floor jus' like a dead tree…"

Chuck was stunned silent, and he asked Apple if Soda Pop was dead, but she didn't answer him. She just sat there lookin' away from him with her feelings all mixed up. She started laughing and she whispered, "Nah." Apple's lips were poked out, and she shook her head to say no. "But the last time I heard… he wuz still in a coma."

Chuck eyes squinted, "What did ya'll do then?"

Apple said softly, "Well, Zachary cleaned him out. Soda Pop had about two thousand dollas on'em. He had his small bills tucked inside a pack of cigarettes that he kept in his shirt pocket… but the big bills were stuffed in a secret zippa pocket, on the inside of his belt. While I wuz standin' there, lookin' crazy, tryin ta get my head straight, an' puttin' my clothes back on, Zachary wuz rollin' that muthafucka ova an' checkin' his pockets n'shit. When he couldn't find the money, he started kickin' Soda Pop in his ass, an' callin' him all kinda names. He wuz so mad 'cause he couldn't find Soda Pop's stash, that he ripped his belt outta the loops an' he started beatin' him wit the buckle… an' that's how he found the big bills. The damn belt busted open an' all the money fell out, an' Zachary's face lit up like a damn neon light bulb."

"Damn!" Chuck groaned, his hatred for Zachary growing by the minute.

Apple looked at Chuck from the corner of her eye and said,

"We didn't know he wuz hurt that bad till I went back to the club the next night... But fuck it! Zachary had what he wanted, an' he ain't give a fuck... an' neitha did I. I knew we wuz goin' back to New York soon, an' that's all I cared about." Apple suddenly noticed Chuck's expression, and she sneered, "You know... you an' Eyonna have that same look on ya'll face, every time I talk about Zachary."

Chuck quickly pulled himself together, wiping his face with his hands and clearing his throat. "Oh... nah... I wuz jus' listenin' to what'chu wuz tellin' me. I know I'm sittin' here lookin' crazy, but I'm jus' thinkin', that's all." Now that Chuck knew where Zachary was coming from, he would know how to deal with him. "But Apple," he went on, "afta everythin' you jus' told me, why in the hell would you wanna work with Zachary any more?" He waited for her to say something. "Look, I'm jus' gon' tell'em straight out that you and I got sump'n goin' on, an' you done decided to go to school down south where I am!"

Apple sprang up in her chair with her eyes wide open, and in a high-pitched voice she replied, "Oh really?"

"What...you think he won't listen to me, Apple? He don't own you."

Apple had her hands on her hips, being catty. "I don't know Chuck... It might be hard for you to make him stop laughin'."

Chuck was very upset, and he looked like he was about to throw a fit. It wasn't as if Apple was trying to pit him against Zachary, but she obviously felt that Chuck didn't have enough street smarts to handle somebody like that.

"What? He ain't ya damn fatha."

"I know, Chucky," she tried to placate him, "but this ain't yo' problem, baby. You already got problems of yo' own now. You'll jus' be gettin' in way ova ya head."

Chuck was talking low, but he couldn't help pounding his chest with the palm of his hand for emphasis as he replied, "What? Maybe you don't think I'm man enough. You don't think I'm man enough to handle my own business!" Apple began to explain herself, but Chuck was angry, and he wouldn't let her get a word in.

"I'm a man jus' like he's a man, Apple. He bleeds an' breathes the same way I do, an' if you don't wanna be bothered wit him no more, then that's that! Now, we can take care of it the easy way... Or we can get gully an' do it the I-don't-give-a-fuck kinda way!" Chuck's passion was giving Apple goose bumps. She put both of her hands up to his face and kissed him, trying to calm him down. Chuck was still talking, but Apple's lips were muffling his words. "Bump that, Apple - you more important to me."

"I know baby, I know." she softly replied. She still had her hands on Chuck's face, and she continued to kiss him. "Chuck, listen to me... you showed me more affection in these last coupla days then I've had in my whole lifetime. An' I really enjoyed the time we spent togetha down south," Apple exclaimed. Then she looked the other way and blushed. "An' that night in the motel too. But baby, you ain't ready fo' this. It wuz jus' a little while ago you were tellin' me what'cha plans are, right?" Chuck was still upset, but he lethargically nodded his head in agreement. "An' it sounded good," Apple went on. "It sounded real good, but baby, you need to move on. Don't waste yo' time on me. Get'cha degree an' follow ya dreams."

"I don't wanna hear that shit," Chuck replied. He felt in his heart that Apple didn't mean what she was saying. "Apple, you my dream, that's why I'm followin' you." Chuck looked sheepish as he put his hands on her lap and almost pleaded with her, "Apple, you my baby, you got that?"

She didn't reply. She only wished that she was stronger - then it would be easier for her to tell him no. She toyed with her bottom lip, took a deep breath, and looked at the floor.

Chuck whispered in her ear, "Apple, baby, the only reason I don't dream about you is because I stay up all night jus' thinkin' about you."

With a stone face, Apple looked at Chuck from the corner of her eye and sucked her teeth. Then she started to smile and playfully called him silly. "Where you get that cornball line from?"

Chuck tried to look at her with a straight face, but Apple's smile was too contagious. "I jus' made it up," he said.

"Yeah… okay," Apple replied, showing off her pretty teeth. But when she started thinking about what Eyonna had said right before she'd walked out the door that evening, her expression changed. Apple felt sorry for Chuck. She had her hands on his face, and she grinned at his funny-shaped ears, the way they warmed her heart. She grabbed Chuck's hand and placed it over her heart and asked him to promise her one thing, and Chuck agreed. Apple asked him to promise her that he would never hurt her, and it took Chuck a second to realize what she was saying.

His blood raced, and his eyes grew wider. He quickly had to collect himself before replying, so the wine wouldn't make him say something he didn't mean. He licked his lips, grabbed Apple's hand and blurted, "Apple baby, you got my word. You got my word, Big Apple." He then affectionately kissed her on the hand, and if any of the patrons in the restaurant had been watching them, they probably would have thought they were witnessing a marriage proposal. "I jus' want the best for you, Apple. That's all I want."

After they shared a toast of wine with Chuck pledging his ever-lasting loyalty, Apple asked him what he planned on doing next.

"I'm not sure what you're talkin' about," he answered evasively.

"I'm talkin' 'bout you bein' careful 'round Zachary. That's what I'm talkin' about."

"Apple baby, don'chu worry 'bout that. I got things under control."

"See Chuck, that's jus' what I'm talkin' about. You can't have this half-ass attitude when I tell you this stuff about Zachary. You gotta be careful aroun' that sneaky bastard."

"I got it, Apple," he impatiently declared. "I mean, I hear you. I mean, I'm jus' wanna show you so much, that's all."

"I am too, baby… But we gotta handle this situation first. How can we go on wit our lives if he's a danger to you?"

"Apple baby, I'm listenin' to ya… I'm jus' bein' silly… that's all." He pouted and smiled, refusing to be serious.

Apple sucked her teeth in disgust, then folded her arms and turned her back to him. She was stubbornly ignoring him, and he was trying to get her attention by tapping her on the shoulder and calling her name. She quickly turned around and said, "See Chuck, that's the shit I'm talkin about…You playin' aroun' 'n shit. You can't be sleepin' on him."

"I'm not sleepin' on him… but I'm jus' sayin'…"

"What'chu sayin', Chucky?" she calmly asked. Apple didn't listen to his answer; she had already turned her back on him again, and waited until he stopped talking before she spoke. "Chucky, I tell you things that I wouldn't even confess to a priest. I care about you man, an' I jus don't want that bastard tryin' to use you or hurt you…"

"Okay, okay," he said, "I'm sorry. I'm sorry! I know I'm actin' dumb. It's jus' the wine."

"I see," Apple said, as she reached to take his drink away from him. "I think you done had enough to drink for tonight!"

"You right… But hey, Apple… I wuz sittin' here thinkin', when you were jus' tellin' me all that shit Zachary had you doin'… I wuz thinkin' 'bout killin' him anyway."

Apple frowned, then glared at him and said, "Yeah… you right, you did have too much to drink. Because you talkin' crazy right now." She grabbed her bag and got up from the table, leaving Chuck sitting there with his face turned up, asking her what was wrong. "Boy, let's get the hell outta here before you get us locked up."

"What's wrong?" Chuck asked again.

"Nut'n. Ain't nut'n wrong. I'ma use da ladies room before we leave… that's all." She took about two steps away from the table, then quickly sat back down. Apple was talking just above a whisper so as not to draw attention to their table. "Here you are Chucky, a damn college student, one year away from graduatin', an' you talkin' 'bout killin' somebody. Chuck, you betta get yo' shit straight-ened out. Once you a murdera, that's fo' life." Apple felt that she had finally made her point, and she stomped off to the ladies room.

Chapter 14:

When Apple returned, Chuck was standing by the front exit waiting for her. He had already paid for dinner, and his head was still buzzing from the wine. In fact, they were both a little tipsy - but Apple could handle herself a little better than Chuck when she felt that way. Chuck thought they should walk off some of the wine, but Apple's feet started to hurt and she got tired of him staggering against her, so they hailed a cab. The driver tried chatting with the couple as he banged over the city potholes and swerved through the heaving traffic. But they had other things on their minds.

Apple sat embraced in Chuck's arms, and she began to kiss his hands and suck on his fingers. He pulled her closer, and gently turned her face up to his mouth. Soon they were passionately kissing, feeling as if the world were caving in around them. Chuck slowly moved his hand down to cup her breast; he paused to caress her belly, and stopped on the inside of her thigh. His touch was pleasing to her, and Apple's nipples grew firm, protruding through her blouse, while her sex was moist and throbbing under her silk panties. It began to seem as if it was taking forever for the cab to drive uptown, and then suddenly Chuck just stopped. He was still hard, but other than that he showed no further enthusiasm for her tender touch - and she wanted to know why.

By now she was sitting up and looking straight at him, and she firmly asked, "Wassup wit'chu now? What'chu thinkin' 'bout so hard, Chuck?"

He shrugged his shoulders, "Nut'n...How come?"

"Cause you sittin' ova there all quiet n'shit, that's why."

"Nah, I'm just thinkin', that's all."

"About what I told you tonight?"

"Oh, nah." Chuck's offhand manner caused Apple to suck her teeth and leave him alone. They both sat there quietly bouncing uptown, while Apple watched the buildings change from glittering establishments accommodated with doormen and garages, to vacant lots, abandoned buildings and seedy liquor stores. They had a few more miles to drive before they arrived at her doorstep.

Apple finally broke the silence when she sat up and asked, "Chuck, you hear from that boy, since we been back?"

He was staring out the window when he answered, "What boy you talkin' about? I know a lotta boys."

Apple automatically assumed that he was just being sarcastic. She nudged him with her elbow and innocently whispered, "The guy that wuz drivin' you aroun' in that stolen car, rememba?"

It was strange to Chuck that Apple would ask him that, because he'd been thinking about Tone half the night. That had also been the reason why he'd suddenly stopped kissing her. But instead of answering her directly, he shamefully closed his eyes and started massaging his forehead with the tips of his fingers. Tone's murder was still fresh in his mind, and just the thought of Tone's voice the last time he'd heard it made Chuck feel a sharp, throbbing pain above his left eye. Apple curiously waited for an answer, but he only continued to rub his head, finally peeping out at her through his fingertips. He slowly removed his hands from his face, and Apple read from his body language that he must have held true to his word. They looked at each other without saying anything; it was as if they were talking with their eyes.

"You killed that boy, Chucky," she softly stated. There was a long pause, so she put it to him as a question, but still he said nothing. Apple was now looking up at him like a worried child. "Did Zachary do it?"

Chuck maintained his silence, and confirmed her suspicion

by harshly looking into her eyes. Then he just turned his head away and continued to massage his temples while staring out of the window.

Apple sat back and whispered to herself, "That's fucked up, man. That's real fucked up!" Then she nudged Chuck on the shoulder. "I told you he don't give a fuck 'bout nobody, didn't I? An' if you mess aroun' wit'em Chuck... yo' ass is gon' be next, you watch an' see."

"Thanks for the vote of confidence," he sarcastically replied.

"Yeah, okay.... you jus' keep on thinkin' shit is a joke."

"I know it ain't no joke, Apple."

She still had that worried child look on her face, and then she started thinking about Chuck being an accessory to murder. She sucked her teeth, looked out the window, and finally asked, "Were you there when all'a this happened?"

Chuck shamefully covered his face with his hands and just growled. He wasn't directing his frustration at her; he was just trying to release some of the anxiety that had been swelling inside of him. "How you think I know what happened?" he replied.

"Fuck!" Apple whispered. She grabbed his hand and said, "Chuck, I wuz afraid to admit it to myself, but I'm fallin' in love wit you. An' anybody that knows Big Apple knows I don't do that every day. But I'm crazy about you, Chuck, an' I don't want you gettin' locked up, or that bastard hurtin' you. Chuck... let's leave this city, now, tonight. Let's get outta here before it's too late. Fuck that little bitta money that you're supposed to be makin' wit Zachary. It sounds like a lot right now... but in a little while Chuck, you'll look back an' realize how small that shit is."

Chuck was looking straight ahead, and Apple was looking straight at him, waiting for his reply. "An' do what?" he finally said. Bust my ass on some stupid nine-to-five, makin' somebody else rich? Just turn inta some kinda ordinary Joe, right?" He coldly faced her to see if he was saying what she wanted to hear. "Fuck that, you hear me? Fuck that! My fatha ain't bust his ass for nobody, an' neitha am I. I made a promise to myself that I wuz coming back to New York and make my mark!"

"Uh oh," Apple sneered sarcastically. "Somebody's been aroun' Zachary too long."

"I don't sound like Zachary."

"I didn't say you sound like him, but'chu startin' to say the same dumb shit that he likes to say."

"Apple... whose side are you on, anyway?"

Apple didn't like the way the conversation was going, and she realized that her comment had not made things any better. So she put up her hands to stop the back and fourth bickering. "Baby, listen to me. All I'm sayin' is, if the cops come lookin' for Zachary and things get hot, he's gonna try ta find a way to blame it all on you, or at least take you down wit'em." Chuck shook his head but didn't reply, and that seemed to irritate Apple even more. "Zachary murdered your friend, Chuck... do you realize that? Dey throw muthafuckas in jail for that shit, and in case you didn't know, dey throw accomplices in jail too."

Apple was now sitting as far away from Chuck as she could shrink in the backseat of the cab. She was on one side, leaning on the door, and Chuck was on the other, staring out the window at the passing lights. He had his hand up to his head again, fretting about what he should do next. Nevertheless, he managed to convince Apple that everything would be all right.

"Listen," he said, "all the while I been with Zachary, he keep braggin' about how he has you wrapped aroun' his little finger. He call you his 'down-for-what'eva' chick."

"So what? Fuck Zachary," Apple said, shrugging her shoulders.

"Nah, what I'm sayin' is all you gotta do is keep doin' what'chu doin'. Let him believe whateva he wanna believe, okay?" Apple was about to ask Chuck why, but he stopped her short and calmly said, "Jus' listen, okay?" Apple sat back and listened. "I jus' don't want him to panic an' do sump'n stupid." He was looking

Apple in the eyes with his hand on her lap. "Tomorrow I'ma meet'em to get some money, so's I can make anotha run down south. This'll be the last time, I promise. An' when we get down there, we'll have a chance to look aroun' an' check things out. I mean as far as apartments an' all that - an' then you can tell me what'chu think. An' if you like it, then we'll make the move."

"That's cool." Apple replied, finally softening to him.

Chuck slid over, put his arm around her neck and he gave her soft kiss. "I'll even show you where you can buy worms in a vendin' machine," he said, burying his face in her neck.

"Huh…?

"Nut'n…you'll see."

Chapter 15:

Being that Paul was such big guy, it always appeared that he was sitting in the backseat of his car when he was driving. He stood about 6'5" and weighed close to 240 pounds. He was built like a linebacker, with wide shoulders, small hips, and big thighs. He had smooth bronze skin, triple-black curly hair, and two gold teeth screwed into his gums. He wasn't an old-school dresser like Zachary; instead he opted for jeans and boots in the winter, and sneakers and sweatsuits in the summer - and he was a firm believer in gettin' his hands dirty when he had to. He was quiet and polite, the opposite of Zachary - and that's what made him so treacherous.

Paul and Zachary had met a couple of years before, and whenever they bumped into each other at the girls' place they would laugh about their younger years, when Zachary used to bully Paul around. Zachary had also been close with Paul's cousin Sean, and Sean and Zachary had shared a small job running errands for a ruthless numbers banker who lived uptown in the Bronx. The banker never cared for traveling all the way to Harlem for payoffs of less than $1,000, so he would pay Sean and Zachary to make the runs for him.

One afternoon the banker had given Sean a call to drop off a sum of cash that was quite a bit larger than usual, and as always,

Paul wanted to tag along. Zachary and Sean insisted that he stay behind - and that was the last time either man ever saw Sean alive. Somehow during that fateful run, Paul's cousin Sean mysteriously met a grisly end. Zachary was the only person who could have known anything about what had happened, but he was always strangely vague about the details. Zachary always swore that he would avenge his friend's murder, and Paul was too young and innocent at the time to harbor either a lingering suspicion or a deep need for vendetta, so he just let it go. But Paul never forgot his cousin, and at the back of his mind, there had always been an uncomfortable feeling in his regard, as if something remained unsettled or unknown.

Earlier that day Paul and Zachary had talked, and they had agreed to meet near Mr. Ray's Barbershop so Paul could purchase two pistols, get his hair cut, and then go meet Eyonna. Zachary's timing was perfect, because Paul had just finished getting his hair cut when he saw Zachary driving up. He was wiping the loose hair from his neck as he exited the barbershop, and he smiled and said smoothly, "Zach-Zach, wassup, wassup?

"Yo Yo, Big Paul," Zachary replied, returning the smile. "Wassup baby, how you livin'?"

The two men slapped five, patted each other on the back, and chatted briefly together. Then Paul gave Zachary sixteen hundred dollars, and walked off into a building not far from the barbershop, where another young man nonchalantly greeted him. The man gave Paul a sneaker box containing two brand new nine-millimeter pistols. After Paul had checked the guns over, he placed them back into the box, put the box into a shopping bag, and quickly left.

After Paul had stowed the guns in the trunk of his car, he double-checked the lock, then went back across the street to talk to Zachary. All the while they were talking, Mr. Ray and some of his customers were peeping out of the barbershop window, scrutinizing

Zachary's body language and hand gestures.

"He needs ta cut dat shit out...." Mr. Ray grumbled, "an' learn how'ta stand still while he's talkin, like he got some damn sense!" Watching a sixty-six-year-old man mocking Zachary's body movements and hand gestures could make anybody laugh, which was exactly what everyone in the barbershop was doing. "I'll tell you," Mr. Ray continued, "If he wuzn't my nephew, I swear I'd go out there an' shoot'em right in his ass..."

The men in the barbershop snickered at Zachary, who was being his typical self - waving his hands, stomping his feet and grabbing his privacy to stress each point as he talked.

"Yo, bust it," Zachary said to Paul. "I know you know what happen between me an Apple..."

"Nah," Paul answered, only because he knew that no matter what he said, Zachary was going to tell him all about it anyway. Paul always felt that Zachary talked too much, and that's one thing he never cared for. He felt anybody that talked as much as Zachary did had to be lying half the time, and eventually they'd tell on themselves. Zachary went on to tell Paul that it was his job to keep Apple in line, and Paul asked him why.

"'Cause," Zachary said, "The minute she get some new dick, she start actin' stupid... like she don't know what time it is, ya know what I'm sayin'?"

"Nah, why, what happen?" Paul asked with some concern.

"Yo, I had to yoke her up..."

"Word, how come?"

Zachary sucked his teeth, stomped his feet and said, "Yo, I can't prove it right now... but I got a gut feelin' that she tryin' to play me, word up." His accusation made Paul step back with a look that required answering. So Zachary continued, "Yo, I sent her down south wit this dude to get me some joints... an' dey comes back short."

"Word, what dude you talkin' 'bout?"

Zachary began to tell Paul about Chuck, how they'd met,

and why he trusted him. "Don't you know, I gave that kid enough money ta get twelve joints, an' dey only come back wit ten."

"Word? Get the fuck outta here, Zach. So what'chu gon' do? You want me to talk ta E, an' see if she know sump'n?"

"Nah, chill, lemme finish first. I gave that little nigga enough money ta get me twelve joints, right... an' he gon' tell me he lost two of'em!" Zachary stopped talking to see what Paul's reaction would be, but Paul just shook his head. "Can you believe that shit?" Zachary went on. "How can a mothafucka lose two big-ass guns?"

"Did he tell you how he lost'em?"

"Yeah, sure he did," Zachary said sharply. He explained what Chuck had told him, and Paul said he thought it sounded plausible.

"Why can't you giv'em da benefit of da doubt?" Paul asked.

"Nah, fuck that, fuck that," Zachary yelled, "I jus' got this feelin' that connivin' bitch Apple convinced him to do some foul shit."

"Word?"

"Yo, word to my mutha," Zachary growled, hitting his hands together in disgust once more. "Afta all da shit I did for Apple, I can't believe she would do some foul shit like that to me of all people. I mean, I practically saved her fuckin' life. You rememba, don'chu, Paul? You rememba when she wuz livin' in dat rat-infested buildin', wit da fuckin' roaches runnin' across da TV screen? An' now she wanna play me like this!" Zachary was dangerously upset, and Paul knew it. "But yo, bust it," Zachary continued, "anybody that tries ta play me, I'm hurtin'em. Word up I am. I already had to smoke a kid da otha day."

"Nah, Zach, get da fuck outta here! Word?"

"Word ta my mutha, Paul," Zachary insisted, raising his right hand in the air. For a second he looked as if he were being sworn in as the next president. "I had ta smoke dis clown da otha day. Get the papah."

Paul shook his head, "Damn, it wuz in da newspapah?"

"Word to my mutha! But bust it," Zachary said, lowering his voice, "I got Apple an' that kid goin' down south for me again ta get some more joints, an' when dey get back, I'ma kill'em."

"It's like that Zach?"

"Yup, It's like that! I'm tired of dese niggas tryin' ta play me, man. I gotta let'em know what time it is. Plus he might try ta drop a dime on me for smokin' that one dude."

"I hear ya," Paul said without expression.

Zachary put his arm around Paul's shoulders, and they slowly walked towards the corner. It was as if he were about to tell Paul something that he didn't care to share with the rest of the world. Zachary was like a quarterback in a huddle - the game was on the line, and he had to call the decisive play. He whispered, "The reason I'm tellin' you this Paul, is 'cause I know you like makin' money, jus' like I do. An' I know how you gets down." Zachary paused and looked around, and now he was practically whispering in Paul's ear. "If you wanna get down wit dis, den you jus' let me know wassup." Zachary looked Paul in his eyes and patted him two times on the back. But Paul just bit his bottom lip, showing off his gold teeth, and Zachary felt that he had a little more convincing to do. "Well... I'm meetin' this kid tomorrow. He's comin to get some more money for anotha trip."

"How much money?"

"Five G's," Zachary said quickly. "Which belongs ta you... if you take care of this little problem for me..." Then he tapped Paul in his chest, extended his right hand, and waited for him to comply. The men shook hands, and Zachary continued to hold Paul's hand as he told him about the small chain that Chuck wore proudly around his neck at all times. Zachary briefly explained the symbolic value that it held for Chuck, and said that he wanted it as proof that Chuck was dead. "One more thing," Zachary added. "I prefer that you take care of this down in Kentucky, an' that's worth an extra G." Paul gripped Zachary's hand a little harder, confirming their agreement. Now Chuck had a price on his head.

Chapter 16:

The next afternoon, Zachary and Paul met at the same location. Zachary slid into Paul's car, and handed him a small paper bag containing keys to a rental car, directions for Kentucky, and two thousand dollars in cash. Paul would receive the balance on his return to the city.

"Now Paul, listen up," Zachary whispered. "Chuck usually stays in the same motel every time he makes this trip. But if for any reason he don't this time, then jus' forget the whole thing, an' we'll take care of'em when he comes back up here to New York. Now, what I want you to do is beep me as soon as dey gets to da motel - you got that?" Zachary looked Paul in the eyes, resting his left hand heavily on Paul shoulder, and Paul answered Zachary simply by nodding his head. "Then I'll call the room an' tell Apple that I'm in Kentucky, an' I want her to come downstairs. But I'm really gonna be in Philly this week. That way if the police trace the call, it'll be to a public phone numba nowhere near nowhere... You got that?"

Paul had an odd look on his face, "What if Chuck answers the phone?"

Zachary shrugged his shoulders, "So what - I'll jus' tell'em to put Apple on the phone."

"You think she gon' come downstairs fo' you when she got anotha dude in the room?"

Zachary smirked and swaggered, "Uh huh!"

Paul twisted his mouth, "How come? You gotta tell me how

this shit is gonna work, 'cause I gotta know before I get in."

Zachary confidently replied, "How you think I know so much?" He was smiling broadly, not expecting an answer. "Chuck don't tell me shit… I know everythin' 'cause that dumb bitch tells me everythin' she know. Now, if Chuck was to see me in Kentucky, he'd flip on her - an' Apple loves that nigga. So she gon' bring her ass downstairs jus' like I tell her to do."

Paul was now shaking his head and smirking, because the plan was starting to make sense.

"See, Paul," Zachary said, still in a whisper, "the whole purpose for me callin' the room is so you can get indoors an' kill his ass… then grab the guns an' get out."

"That's easy," Paul said with complete confidence.

"So check it," Zachary whispered in the same conspiratorial tone, "I jus' feel that it'd be betta to do'em in Kentucky, because he goes ta school down there, an' his driva's license is from there too. So I'm guessin' that the police investigation won't go beyond the Pennsylvania state line. I know for a fact that Apple is puttin' da rental car in her name, since Chuck is makin' a little money now, an' he's buyin' guns for hisself too. If everythin' goes accordin' to plan, Apple will find Chuck dead, an' since she knows that what she'n him wuz doin' is illegal, she'll panic an' haul her ass back to New York. Once she see'em dead n'stinkin', she'll forget he eva existed. An' afta da smoke blows away, she'll be tellin' me how much she love me again, an' she'll spill where he buys them fuckin' guns from, or who buys'em for him"

Zachary and Paul were still talking through the plan when they saw Chuck arrive across the street. They watched him furtively look around, then walk into the barbershop.

Zachary quickly nudged Paul's shoulder and whispered in a low, hostile voice, "That's him. Yeah, that's that muthafucka that jus' went inta da barba'shop. Did you get a good look at'em?"

"Yeah… I saw'em," Paul replied.

"So now you know what he looks like, but I'ma bring his ass outside and talk to'em for a while, so's you can get a betta look."

Zachary had oozed out of the car, and just before he walked off, he leaned back in the window and reminded Paul one more time not to forget to call him. Then he crossed the street and headed toward the barbershop.

Zachary's royal blue slacks rippled in the wind like a flag on a windy September day, and his grey shades reflected the sunlight like two polished hubcaps. He appeared almost robotic, heartless as cold steel. Every clever thing the streets had taught him was now second nature, and that is what he would pass on to the next generation.

Mr. Ray had just said hello to Chuck when he saw Zachary walking toward the door, and he grumbled, "Here comes that asshole nephew o' mine. I'ma get the hell outta here before he get on my nerves, case I hurt dat boy in dis barba'shop." Mr. Ray called Mr. Allen to the back of the store, and asked him to let him know when Zachary was gone. "I'll be in my office," he said. Then he waved his hand in a fretful gesture at the sight of his nephew's face.

Everyone looked up at the sound of the front door opening and greeted Zachary as he came in - except for Mr. Ray. He was in his office by then, with the door closed.

This was the first time Zachary and Chuck had seen each other since Zachary had roughed up Apple, so neither man knew what to expect. Chuck was uptight, and Zachary pointedly humbled himself so that Chuck wouldn't renege on making the trip. Zachary wanted those guns badly, but even more than that he wanted Chuck in Kentucky where Paul could take care of him discreetly - so he was careful not to give any indication of what he was scheming.

By now Chuck's innocent facial features and boyish smile were gone, and he appeared cold and empty - a change that Zachary did not fail to note. Chuck was beginning to remind him of himself, and that alone was enough to convince Zachary that Chuck was better off dead. The two men shook hands and smiled, the way powerful lawyers do when a large monetary settlement is in question, but reputations matter more. They were just about to walk outside to talk in private, when Mr. Ray called Chuck into his office. The two men stopped in their tracks and looked at each other, and Chuck told Zachary that he'd meet him outside.

Mr. Ray had been surprised and upset to find out that Chuck was hanging with his nephew. He knew that they were on speaking terms, because they would greet one another whenever Zachary came into the shop, but he had no idea about the depth of their recent involvement. Once he had Chuck in his office, Mr. Ray repeatedly warned him that he was headed in the wrong direction, and Chuck repeatedly lied, trying in vain to convince Mr. Ray that he and Zachary had just been talking about the ballgame. Mr. Ray kept Chuck in the office for almost thirty minutes, until he felt that he had made his point clear.

Chuck and Zachary were now strolling toward the corner outside so they could talk. Every so often a passerby would say hello, and Zachary would stop and smile like a campaigning politician, making sure he didn't forget the little man. When the two men walked past Paul's car, Zachary nonchalantly waved to him, and Paul beeped his horn two times, then drove off. Zachary snickered to himself, and Chuck paid it no mind.

Right before Zachary handed Chuck the usual bag of money, he started apologizing to him for what he'd done to Apple.

Chuck had an odd look on his face, and both of his hands were stuffed deep into his pockets. But when Zachary apologized, he pulled his hands out and let them hang by his sides. "Why you apologizin' to me?" he asked.

"'Cause, Chuck...you know?" Zachary cautiously mumbled, making sure not to step on Chuck's toes.

"I know what?" Chuck queried resentfully. He was acting sarcastic and playing stupid at the same time.

"'Cause, Chuck, you know... I thinkin' you an' Apple like each otha, or sump'n like that... Am I right?"

Chuck had that odd look on his face again, because he knew

by Zachary's behavior that something wasn't right. "Why you say that?" he asked, "What makes you think that me an' Apple got sump'n goin' on?"

"'Cause ya'll seem to be gettin' along pretty good n'shit, that's all."

"She a'ight," Chuck replied, ever so casually, "But I think you apologizin' to the wrong person. You should be apologizin' to Apple, not ta me."

'This little sarcastic faggot has a big damn mouth,' Zachary thought to himself, but his face didn't change at all. He gave Chuck a big phony smile, and replied, "Yeah, you right Chuck. Soon as I see huh, that's gon' be the first thing I do, is apologize to huh," adding silently to himself, 'Right after I kill yo' little punk ass.' Zachary then handed Chuck a bag with eight thousand dollars in cash in it, and told him that he wanted six Glock's, six Taurus 415T Brazil models, six Lorcin 380's, and two Uzi's.

"No problem," Chuck replied. "I'll be callin' you or beepin' you on the way down there jus' like always… an' on the way back too. The men slapped five, and Chuck went off to meet Apple. Then they were on their way.

Chapter 17:

Two days had passed since Chuck and Apple had left New York, and Zachary was in Pennsylvania pulling his hair out. He was holed up at a girlfriend's house, wondering why he hadn't heard anything from Paul yet. Countless times he had tried to page him, but no one called back, and he could only hope that Paul was not in police custody. Zachary wasn't too worried about Apple and Chuck. He felt that as long as they made it back from Kentucky, he'd still be able to sell the guns and carry on as if nothing had happened.

At about 3:00 p.m. Zachary got a page from Eyonna, and he immediately returned her call. When Eyonna answered the phone, Zachary could sense the anxiety in her voice. She began to ask him about Apple, but before she could finish her sentence Zachary interrupted her, pretending that he was in New York, and telling her to be ready when it was time to go downtown.

Eyonna said politely, "Fuck you Zachary, an' I ain't thinkin about that fuckin' game, that shit is still gon' be there. I'm worried about Apple. I ain't heard from her. So wassup wit dat?"

Zachary took a deep breath and slowly hissed it out. "Apple, Apple, Apple - that's all da fuck you talk about is Apple. What is it - ya'll eatin' each otha now, or what?"

Eyonna responded by telling Zachary to go to hell. "You're a real insensitive bastard, you know that? An' nut'n betta not had happened to my girl, or I'm sendin' the cops right to yo' damn door."

Zachary frowned and sharply asked Eyonna to repeat herself.

"You heard what I jus' said. An' fo' yo' info'mation, I know what Apple be makin' these trips fo', an' nut'n betta not happen to her... or else!"

"Ain't nut'n happen to ya damn girl, I told you. An' you jus' get yo' ass ready to go downtown lata' on."

"Didn't I jus' tell you to go to hell? I ain't goin' downtown, Zachary." Zachary chuckled, and Eyonna quickly realized that she needed to be the bigger person. She regained her composure and said, "Please Zachary, if you hear from Apple before I do... can you tell her to call me?"

Zachary mocked the concern in her voice, and Eyonna slammed the phone down. He seemed to get a thrill from knowing that he was able to upset her so easily.

Five minutes after he got off the phone with Eyonna, Zachary received another page, and his beeper displayed an out-of-state area code. He really had no idea what to expect, since it could be either Apple or Chuck paging him - but when he called back it was Paul who answered the phone. He was using a pay phone in a convenience store, and being from the city he didn't realize how conspicuous that looked until he noticed the hometown locals eyeing him up and down as if he'd beamed down from another planet.

Paul was wearing a large gold chain, new white sneakers, and a blue and white sweat-suit - in other words, he was dressed like an alien as well. This was a modest, white suburban town where the average income was about a hundred and fifty thousand a year, and Paul thought he looked like a million dollars. He took offense at the constant eye contact with strangers, sometimes snapping at the patrons and rudely asking what were they staring at.

"Yo... somebody beep me?" Zachary asked when Paul

answered the telephone.

"Yeah, Zach, it's me, Paul."

"Yo, wassup Paul?" Zachary was glad to hear from him, but he was also afraid that he was about to hear some bad news.

"Yeah… it's done." Paul secretly replied.

"What'chu talkin' about?"

Paul spoke a little slower this time. "Yo, it's done, an' I got the joints sittin' in the car."

"What'chu mean, it's done?" Zachary hissed. "You wuz supposed ta beep me."

"I ain't have to," Paul casually replied, "It wuzn't necessary…"

Once Zachary realized what Paul was saying, the two of them began to speak in an urban dialect, just in case the phone was tapped.

"I wuz chillin' in the parkin' lot across the street from the spot, waitin' for Home Girl and that dude to show up. She went inta a dolla' store, an' the dude went upstairs. I followed'em to his room an' pushed him in. Afta' I found the joints, I hit'em two times in the back of the head, then I snatched his necklace an' jetted."

"Woooord?" Zachary whispered with relief. The stunned look on his face quickly turned to a smile, and he asked again, "Woooord, Paul, you got da necklace too?"

Paul casually sucked his teeth, "Yeah, word, man! I got the shit right here. Ya friend is dead. He stinkin' right now." Then he paused and added, "An' you ain't neva gotta worry 'bout him no mo'."

Zachary snickered like a fox as he rubbed his hands together, "Yeah, okay, so where you at now?"

Paul peeped out of the store window, and had to put his hand up to his forehead to shade the Kentucky sun. He squinted his eyes and replied, "I'm about three hours away from that place."

"I hope you ain't got that dirty joint on you right now?" Zachary asked, referring to the murder weapon.

"Nah, nah… I got rid that shit, man! But the otha joints is

sittin' in the car..."

"So where's Apple?"

"I don' know. I broke out before she got back. But that's cool, 'cause I ain't want her to see me anyway..."

Zachary cheered, saying "Cool, cool, now that bitch college nigga is out the pitcha, an' we can start makin' some real money. I hope you gon' get down wit me?"

"Who, me?" Paul asked eagerly, "Course I'm down. You know that. You ain't even got to ask me that."

"Yeah, okay... We gon' throw us a little party an' celebrate n'shit, soon as you get back."

"No doubt, no doubt. True... true," Paul said.

"Word, so I'll talk to you when you get back."

"Yeah," Paul replied, and they both hung up.

No sooner had Zachary gotten off the phone with Paul than his pager started beeping nonstop, and he began singing and dancing to the tinny melodies it gave off. Hearing from Paul was good news, and hearing that Chuck was dead was even better. Zachary took his time checking his pager, because he knew that Apple had probably called Eyonna, and now Eyonna was paging him to say that Chuck was dead. After he'd finished dancing around the room, Zachary gathered himself together to give an Oscar performance on the phone. When he finally checked his pager, it was Eyonna who had called, just as he'd suspected. He called her back, and when she picked up the phone, all Zachary could hear was the sound of her crying.

"Zachary...," Eyonna sobbed. "That boy Chuck is dead."

"Dead?" He asked, sounding dramatically shocked. "How can he be dead? I jus' talked to'em a little while ago, an' we had plans." He laid it on a little more. "Dead... what do you mean he dead? I don't believe that shit. Where the fuck is Apple?

"Apple's fine," Eyonna softly wept. "But I knew sump'n wuz wrong... I could jus' feel it in my bones."

Zachary switched to a compassionate tone, and gently asked

Eyonna to tell him what had happened.

"Apple said dat dey got robbed."

"Robbed?" Zachary screeched, as if this were news to him. He sent his voice up a little higher to sound really concerned. "Who the hell robbed them?"

Eyonna started crying loudly again, and Zachary patiently asked her to calm down. Then she collected herself somewhat and said, "I jus' feel bad for my girl. That's why I'm cryin'."

"Damn - umph, umph umph," Zachary grunted. He was waiting for her to spill more of the story.

"She wuz so lovin', that kid," Eyonna whimpered, and then she loudly blew her nose. "Zachary, you should'a heard how she was screamin' an' shit."

"That's a damn shame."

"Yeah, and like I wuz sayin'… Apple told me she went to the store, an' when she got back to the room, the door wuz open, an' Chuck wuz lyin' face down in his own blood."

"Get the fuck outta' here!" Zachary whispered. "Ahhh, shit. Damn, Chucky… My brotha, my brotha." There was a moment of silence, and then he sympathetically called Eyonna's name, dancing on eggshells. "Did Apple stay aroun' an' talk to the police?"

Eyonna sniffed her nose, sobbed twice, and said, "All Apple told me wuz as soon as she saw Chuck's blood n'shit all ova the place, she jetted."

"Damn," Zachary said again, as he moved the phone away from his mouth and silently cheered. Everything was going exactly the way he had planned. He took a deep breath, then called Eyonna's name again. "Where is Apple now?"

"She said she's on the highway drivin' up right now, an' she scared as shit."

"Did she leave any of huh bags in da room?"

Eyonna didn't answer him, but just blew her nose - so Zachary asked her again. "Nah," Eyonna answered, she told me she got everythin' togetha, an' then she jetted."

"So E, you listen to me… Tell Apple to call me as soon as

she get the chance, 'cause we gon' get to the bottom of this. A'ight?" Zachary encouraged her like a child.

"A'right," Eyonna responded.

"We gon' go down ta Kentucky, an' light that fuckin' town up. An' who'eva did this to my boy is gonna pay. Word to my mutha'!"

"A'ight," Eyonna wept quietly into the phone.

Chapter 18:

Fly and his high-school sweetheart had once shared a spacious condo in a quiet, influential neighborhood in Pottstown, Pennsylvania. She was rapidly moving up in the ranks of an advertisement agency, and Fly worked for a security company called 5-Star Kennel. He specialized in training guard dogs for security, and tracker dogs for search and rescue missions. But after they'd both exhausted their excuses for calling in sick and coming in late, they watched their careers go slowly down the drain.

Fly and his girl had come up with this crazy idea that they could subsidize their income by selling crack from the backdoor of their apartment, and when they started experimenting with their own product, that was the beginning of the end. They went from throwing Super Bowl parties to arranging small get-togethers that turned into couple swapping encounters, and that is how Fly had met Zachary.

One night after Fly and his girl had already been evicted from a string of apartments and were strapped for cash to support their drug habit, they stumbled into an after-hour spot called The Pink Tiger in downtown Philadelphia. Fly figured that if he could watch his girlfriend having sex with other men and women for free, then she might as well get paid for it - so she became a regular performer at the club.

Zachary and Apple came into The Pink Tiger one night when nothing much was going on. It was one of those slow nights when Zachary sat at the bar to have a drink while Apple changed into her dancing costume. Fly was howling and whistling at the young girls, excited by the way they contorted their firm bodies, and then he and Zachary started talking. Somehow the subject of dogs came up, and that was when Fly told Zachary that he could train dogs to eat human flesh... and the two men became close associates from that moment on.

Bruce 'Fly' Davis was Fly's whole name, and he'd weighed 175 pounds the day he left Pottstown, Pennsylvania, though only a few years later he'd shrunk to no more than 135. He was 43 years old, with bad posture, a receding hairline, and eyes as wide as Frisbees. Fly was your typical all-bones, no ass, *'the right answer for everything wrong'* crack-head. Everybody in the neighborhood recognized him, and nobody trusted him. Whenever he came around, people knew to keep a close eye on him and on their valuables, or else their valuables would mysteriously walk away. The few people that did trust Fly would send him on errands or have him wash their cars, and if he wasn't doing anything for Zachary, Mr. Ray would pay him to clean up the barbershop. Mr. Ray could do it himself, but since Fly was always begging for a dollar, he felt that he would make him earn it.

Mr. Ray had just finished taking care of a few customers, so the floor was cluttered with hair, and he was looking for Fly to come do his job. Fly had told Mr. Ray that he would be right back, and somehow "right back" had stretched into an hour. Mr. Ray was getting agitated, and he walked towards the window to see if Fly was hanging around outside. He grumbled aloud, "I tell ya, that damn Fly is so unreliable. When I need him here... I can never find him."

"Ya damn sure can't," Mr. Allen agreed.

"Every time he get that damn welfare check, his ass jus' disappears... an' then he'll come aroun' here tomorra, broke an' beggin' for a dolla."

"He'll dolla yo' ass ta death," Mr. Allen sang out loudly.

"How in the hell can a man wit no kids, no cable bill, no light bill, and no water bill, livin' in an abandoned building, get a check on the 1st of the month… an' be broke by the 2nd?"

"I know how," Mr. Allen laughed. "He smoke it up, that's how!"

"That shit don't make no sense," Mr. Ray cried. "He come aroun' here beggin' every damn day of the week. An' when I tell'em to get the broom, he act like he don't wanna sweep. But soon as he see Zachary, he take off like Zachary wuz his damn daddy." Mr. Ray sucked his teeth and went to stand in front of the barbershop in the hope of spotting him. When he did see Fly he called him over, and Fly came hobbling across the street. Mr. Ray scolded him like a boy, and Fly sulked to the back of the barbershop to get the broom and start cleaning up.

Chapter 19:

Zachary had been back in the city for some time now, and Paul had just arrived in Fort Lee, New Jersey. He was calling Zachary to confirm where they would meet. When Paul spoke to Zachary he could hear the excitement in the other man's voice, but he was feeling quite the opposite.

"I'm exhausted," Paul sluggishly drawled, "I got these big-ass bags under my eyes n'shit, man."

"Word?" Zachary asked, "Yo, I know you beat."

"Word," Paul answered, putting his hand up to his mouth and yawning loudly, "I've been on this damn highway for more than twenty hours."

"Yeah…I hear you," Zachary said sympathetically. "That's a long-ass ride."

"It damn sure is," Paul vigorously agreed. "Man, I wuz drinkin' soda all the way up the fuckin' highway."

"Word… why's that?"

"Caffeine, man, that shit helps me stay awake."

Zachary grinned and sucked his teeth, "Damn, you a damn troopa, Paul. Word up, you are. I'm definitely gon' look out fo' you!"

"No doubt. So meet me by ya' uncle's barba'shop in 30 minutes, a'ight?"

"Cool."

"Yo, an' please be on time, 'cause you know it's hot out there."

"I'll be there," Zachary assured him.

One hour later, Paul was already tired of sitting in the car with a bladder full of soda and a trunk full of guns. It didn't help any that the car was a rental, and he was sitting on 8th Avenue. The avenue was known for random police sweeps and roadblocks, targeting rental cars and vehicles with out-of-state plates. Zachary was now thirty minutes late, so Paul decided that he would run into the barbershop to use the restroom, and hopefully Zachary would be outside by the time he got back.

When Paul rushed into the shop, neither Fly nor Mr. Ray saw him come in. They were still in the back, where Mr. Ray had Fly busy with the menial task of tidying his office, taking out the trash and cleaning the sinks and mirrors. Mr. Allen was sitting in his barber's chair with his legs crossed watching television when Paul brush passed him. Paul said hello to Mr. Allen, and just as he reached the restroom door, Mr. Allen told him that it was already occupied.

"Damn," Paul whispered under his breath. He held his urine, anxiously dancing from one foot to the other, but when Mr. Allen started snickering, he realized that he'd only been joking around. Paul sucked his teeth, smiled, and swiftly opened the door. "You a real funny guy, Mr. Allen, ya know that!"

Mr. Allen laughed with that croaky voice of his and said, "When you get to be my age, young man, you might need a pampa'."

"I doubt that," Paul teased back.

Paul had closed the restroom door, but he could still hear Mr. Allen's voice and the television playing.

Mr. Ray came out of his office to see who had gone into the restroom, but Mr. Allen didn't know Paul's name, so he simply referred to him as the chubby, quiet guy with the gold teeth.

"Oh, him," Mr. Ray said simply. Then he briskly walked back into his office to make sure that Fly wasn't stealing anything.

Paul figured that since he was already in the restroom, he

might as well sit down and relieve himself, and as soon as he did, Zachary arrived. Zachary stood outside looking around for Paul, and when he didn't see him, he burst into the barbershop and started running his mouth. "I told that fat muthafucka I'd be here in one hour," he spat resentfully, "an' he ain't out there yet!" He pulled out his pager and checked the time. "Niggas can't do shit right!" he continued.

Mr. Allen didn't feel like being bothered with Zachary or even speaking to him for that matter, but he said hello anyway, out of courtesy and barbershop professionalism. Zachary just looked through him as if he weren't even there, and walked towards the restroom without speaking. His rudeness didn't make any impression on Mr. Allen, who was use to it by now. However, he did feel as if he had just wasted some of his precious breath, and didn't see why he should waste anymore by telling Zachary that the restroom was already occupied.

Paul had heard Zachary's comment though the bathroom door, and he took offense. It wasn't the reference to his weight - he'd heard plenty of jokes about that before - it was the disrespectful way in which Zachary had said it. He quickly and quietly made sure the door was locked when he heard Zachary's footsteps coming closer, because he wanted to eavesdrop and hear what else he had to say.

Fly was still sweeping in the office when he heard Zachary's voice. He dropped the broom and hurried toward the main area of the barbershop. "Yo Zach... yo Zach," Fly anxiously called.

Zachary had just reached for the bathroom doorknob when he heard Fly calling him. He turned around and harshly answered, "Yeah, wassup?"

"I jus' came from checkin' on the dogs," Fly whispered.

"Yeah, wassup? How dey look?"

"Cool," Fly said confidently, "Dey look good, real good... but hungry."

Zachary barely opened his mouth and hissed, "I got some

blood upstairs in the fridge, give that shit to'em."

"Cool. I'll warm it up first…"

"Cool, do that."

Fly was about to skulk off and finish cleaning, when Zachary tapped him on the shoulder and asked if he'd seen Paul.

"Who, Sean's cousin?"

"Yeah!"

Fly twisted his lips and shook his head. "Nope. Last time I saw Paul is when you wuz talkin' to'em the other day."

"A'ight," Zachary said. He was about to grab the restroom door handle again, when Mr. Ray diverted his attention by yelling at Fly.

"I'm the one that's payin' you aroun' here to work, man," Mr. Ray yelled at the cowering figure, "not him. Every time you hear Zachary's voice, you gotta jump an' run, like he da masta an' you da slave n'shit!"

Zachary was angered by Mr. Ray's comment, and a heated argument erupted despite Fly's feeble attempt to mediate, which only seemed to make things worse. The argument escalated to a shoving match, and finally Mr. Allen had to jump in and convince Zachary to leave. All the while, Paul sat on the toilet listening to the ruckus.

"Don't tell'em shit," Mr. Ray said calmly, but he was so upset that a thick vein was swelling across his forehead like a thick earthworm. He turned around and made a beeline towards his office to retrieve his pistol. "I got a trick fo' his yella ass," he yelled. "Let'em stay right there an' keep talkin' shit." He had reached the other end of the shop, and he turned around and pointed one more time in Zachary's direction. "Stay yo' yella ass right there till I get back, an' we gon' see what's gon' happen. I'ma teach you some respect."

"Ah… you ain't gon' do shit," Zachary yelled. "not one fuckin' thing." Mr. Allen had both of his hands on Zachary's chest, firmly holding him back and pushing him toward the door. "Nah, fuck that Mr. Allen! Let'em go get that rusty-ass gun. I'll shoot that shit right outta his fuckin' hands."

Paul had heard every word that passed between Zachary and Fly outside the restroom door, and he was bothered by some of what they'd said. Why had Zachary's mysterious interlocutor mention his cousin Sean, and why did he have dogs that apparently drank human blood? But most of all, Paul was troubled by the conspiratorial tone in which Zachary had spoken to Fly - not as he would have spoken to some crack-head runner, but more in the style of an accomplice in some kind of darker crime. Paul would have liked to linger in the restroom a little longer so he could hear what else Zachary had to say, but he didn't want to get hit by a stray bullet. When Paul emerged, the shop was quiet and Fly and Zachary were gone.

Paul headed out of the barbershop, walking briskly in hope of catching up to the men, so he could match that annoying voice with a face. He thanked Mr. Allen for allowing him to use the toilet, and wanted to say something to Mr. Ray as well, but he was stopped by the look on the old man's face. He had never seen him that upset before, and rather then add fuel to the fire, he just waved a greeting. But just before Paul walked out the door, Mr. Allen called him back. He was still in a playful mood when he said, "Hey there, young man… let me shake yo' hand before you go." The two men shook hands and smiled, and then Mr. Allen continued, "You sho' wuz in there for a long time..."

"Yeah, kinda," Paul replied absent-mindedly, with his attention closely focused on getting out the front door.

"Let me ask you one question, young man."
Paul looked oddly at Mr. Allen, and shrugged his shoulders, "Sure, go ahead."

"All I want to know is… do you feel betta now?"

"Light as a feather." Paul replied with a big smile. The two men laughed as Paul snatched away from Mr. Allen and playfully punched him in the arm. "Man, I said it before Mr. Allen, you a funny guy!"

Mr. Allen continued to laugh as Paul cheerfully raced out of the barbershop, but by the time he got outside, neither Zachary nor the owner of the irritating voice were anywhere to be seen. Paul decided that he would switch cars first, then go to the girls' place and relax with Eyonna until he could get in touch with Zachary.

Chapter 20:

When Paul arrived at the girls' front door, Eyonna looked through the peephole and all she could see was a gold chain with a diamond studded P dangling in the middle of it. She sent her voice deeper as she joyfully called him by his pet name, "Big Daddy." Then she quickly opened the door, flung herself into his arms, and hugged him as if he was a soldier returning from a war. She pulled him inside the apartment and gave him a soft kiss. "Wassup, Big Daddy?" she said teasingly in her low, sexy voice.

Paul was happy to see her. He smiled warmly and said, "I'm tired as a motha, you know what!"

Eyonna gave him a sad puppy-dog look and she softly cried, "Awww, poor baby…" Then she stood on her the tips of her toes and mischievously ruffled up his soft curly hair. "Follow me," she crooned seductively. "Let Eyonna take care of you." She wrapped her arm under his and rubbed his large stomach as they walked toward her bedroom. Paul had his hand firmly on her soft behind, and when they got to her room she told him to make himself comfortable. She started taking off her clothes, ignoring the buttons on her blouse, and Paul tried his best to keep up with her. It almost seemed as if they were racing to undress, and Eyonna was way out in front. Her sex was hot, and the throbbing spread all the way to the center of her belly - and as far as she was concerned, Paul was moving way too slowly. When he finally got his pants off, Eyonna dropped to her knees and slowly worked her way up his legs with her open mouth. Twining like a serpent, she rubbed her face against his balls while gently massaging his erect sex.

"Damn, Eyonna..."he moaned with pleasure. "Shit!" He grabbed a handful of her hair, which caused her to suck on his sex even harder. Paul could feel his legs getting weak, and he started to lose his balance. He fell back onto the bed, and for one brief moment he didn't want to touch her. He didn't even want to smell the sweet womanly odors that most men take for granted. Instead he chose to close his eyes and concentrate on the view of the city skyline, to prevent himself from ejaculating too soon.

Once Eyonna had released his sex, she sat on the edge of the bed with her legs spread apart, and Paul just stared at her. 'Her body is perfect,' he thought, along with the rich perfume exuded from her sex, and the wet stains on the bed sheets. Her brown skin glistened like gold under the city sky. Her breasts were plump with dark nipples, like some delicious forbidden fruit. Paul was in awe; he felt as if this was the first time their naked bodies had touched, and as always, Eyonna had to spread her lips wide to stop herself from crying with joy.

"You are so fuckin' beau-ti-ful." He whispered in her ear. He then asked her to lie back, and she complied, stretching voluptuously under his gaze. Paul placed his hands under her behind, pulling her closer to his face, and gently sucked on her sex. Simultaneously he stroked her anus with his index finger, causing Eyonna to turn her hips and cry his name. She firmly grabbed the back of his head and pulled his face into her crotch, and though he could hardly breathe, he didn't care. Two days in Kentucky seemed like an eternity, and he had so longed for the salty taste of her sex.

"Damn, baby," she softly whispered as Paul's head lingered between her legs. "You eatin' me like you 'bout to face the electric chair... you know that?"

Paul lifted his head from her crotch with the moisture of her sex on his face. He looked her in the eyes and whispered, "Shut-the-fuck-up!"

Eyonna reared back and slapped him across the face. "You shut the fuck up!" she seductively replied. Then she leapt up and stood in the corner of the bedroom with her back to him, as if she was about to be frisked. Her nipples were barely touching the cool white plaster, and the palms of her hands were pressed against the wall. Her back was slightly arched as she poked out her butt, leaving one foot still on the bed. Paul smacked her on the butt three times, leaving his handprint across her soft, brown skin.

"Ssssshit!" Eyonna cried. Unashamed, she called him every dirty name she could think of - and that seemed to arouse his masculinity to its peak. Paul held her by the waist and slowly entered her moist, warm sex with his erect member as she continued to curse him with increasing vigor. The harder he pushed into her, the more she screamed, bending over until she was leaning all the way forward and touching her toes. He pulled her back up with his arm around her neck and his stomach against her back, and her breasts were smashed flat against the wall. Their tongues were tangled as they gyrated together, with no rules or guidelines. Saliva and sweat streaked both of their faces, and they continued to grind into each other while screaming obscenities. Paul grunted like a bull as he squeezed Eyonna's body, and then they collapsed onto the bed to exhale. He was releasing his juices into her, which made his toes snap uncontrollably and the back of his legs sweat.

Eyonna had her eyes tightly shut as she panted through her nose. Her legs were wrapped around his, and his sex was still inside of her. Paul gazed at her curiously, and without opening her eyes, Eyonna just shook her head and mumbled for him not to move. The two of them lay motionless for more then five minutes, Eyonna's legs slightly twitching as if jolts of electricity were traveling through them. She was not finished. Paul knew it, and he didn't want to disturb her. Their faces were lying close together, and finally Eyonna took a deep breath, exhaled and then smiled. Their grip on each other loosened, and she stretched like a cat. She took another deep breath, and then started to fan herself with her hand.

Usually Eyonna would go to the bathroom and bring back a hot towel for him to wipe himself off, but now they were home alone, so she went to run him a bath. Paul was lying on his back with his hands behind his head, thinking about the love they'd just had, and it made him smile. Eyonna returned to the room, and she broke into his reverie when she jumped on the bed and cuddled up underneath him. Then she hit him with a pillow, which led to pillow fight that eventually ended with them kissing again.

Eyonna was about to walk out of the room again when she turned around and waggled her finger at him. "An' you betta not move," she playfully teased.

Paul smirked and asked, "Where'm I goin'? You lovin' me so much that I don't even wanna move."

"Yeah... okay," she said, "you betta not. 'Cause you know, you always pullin' them disappearin' acts on me, tellin' me you gotta do this an' that."

Paul just shook his head and laughed. He was charmed by Eyonna's feistiness. Then he rested back on her soft cool pillows, and the scent of her sex made him hate to remember that he still had to meet Zachary that night. She kissed him once before she left the room, and told him she'd be right back. Eyonna wasn't moving fast, but she moved expeditiously, as if everything she needed was right within reach, and if it wasn't, she didn't have to look hard to find it.

In fact, the girls' apartment was always tidy and well-kept. The furniture was not fancy or flashy, and a lot of the styles clashed due to the girls' differing tastes, but they always found a way to compromise. That was one of the things that Paul found so amazing about both of the girls, and about Eyonna in particular. She was well organized, but on top of that she always seemed to find time to take care of him, especially when he wasn't on his best behavior.

"Tell me," Eyonna asked as she came back from the bathroom to lie down beside him again, "how'd everything go down south?"

"Cool," he answered, "Chuck showed me aroun' an' introduced me to a coupla people, so I can pick up where he leavin' off.
He wuz tellin' me this wuz his last run down there. He even showed
me the apartment where he an' Apple gon' live. It's nice. It's got
wall-to-wall carpet, an' a washer an' dryer. It's cool, E. You might
like sump'n like that too."

"You think Apple gon' like it?"

"Apple in luuuv," Paul teased with a southern accent, "She
pretty much likes everything right now. Dey look like two love
birds down there, building dey little nest."

Eyonna sighed, "I know, that's right! Love make you do
some weird shit."

Paul disagreed, "I ain't sayin' what Apple's doin' is weird…
but love ain't what make people do crazy shit… people do crazy
shit anyway… an' dey jus' try to use love as a excuse."

Eyonna rolled her eyes and waved her hand, "Paul, don't
start with that philosophy shit…"

He smiled, "Nah, all I'm sayin' is love is a choice. It's not
sump'n that you accidentally step in, like shit on the sidewalk - it's
a choice you make. That's all I'm sayin'."

"You just a damn grouch, who don't know shit about love.
That's what'cha' problem is."

"I know plenty about love," Paul boasted. "I know that I
love you, an' if you wuz to eva move down there, I'd even come
check you out."

Eyonna blushed, "Would you, baby?"

"Hell yeah I would. That's 'cause I love you."

"Ahhh… Big Daddy… come give me a kiss. I love you
too." Then she turned over and put her soft hands on Paul's face,
and their lips touched. They kissed, and then she asked him if he'd
met up with Zachary.

Paul sat on the edge of the bed, shook his head, and mumbled, "That Zachary is a real asshole!"

Eyonna sighed, "I thought that you knew that already!" She

looked at Paul with her hands on her hips and a surprised expression on her face. "You shoulda heard how arrogant he sounded when I told him that I hadn't heard from Apple. He thought that shit wuz a joke." Eyonna's voice was slightly louder now, as the thought of Zachary made her blood boil. "Now here's Apple an' that dude Chuck both lookin' out for him, an' he don't even care." Eyonna stopped talking and looked at Paul as he shamefully shook his head. "An' when I called him back lata' on like you told me to, an' I told him Chuck was dead... he started actin' real distant an' cold. He even lied to me, an' told me that he had jus' talked to'em."

"He said that?"

"Word up!" Eyonna barked, and Paul sucked his teeth in anger. "He really thinks it's all about him, don't he. I really hate that muthafucka, word up I do! I'll be glad when all'a this shit is ova wit, so's we can all get on wit our lives. Apple will be down south doin' her thing, an' I'll be up here doin' mine." Then she asked Paul if he had given Zachary his guns.

"Nah," he replied. "I'ma give'em his shit lata' on tonight."

"But I thought you wuz gon' give it to'em today. What happened?"

"Yeah, I thought I wuz too, but some bullshit jumped off."

"What'chu mean?"

Paul then told her about the fight in the barbershop, how he'd overheard Zachary talking about him while he was in the restroom, and how cheerful Zachary seemed when he'd told him about Chuck.

"Do you have Chuck's necklace on you?" Eyonna asked.

"Yeah... I got it right here," Paul replied. Then he picked his pants up from the floor and reached into his pocket to show it to her.

"What did Chuck say when you told him that Zachary put a price on his head?"

"Chuck ain't stupid. He knew Zachary wuz schemin' on him a long time ago. He's jus' happy that we wuz on his side."

"Did he say what he gon' do now?"

"Well, he said he jus' gon' lay low for awhile, but he also

said he ain't gon' run. Not when he still got friends an' family up here in New York that he gotta come visit."

Eyonna shook her head. Then she threw Paul a towel and they walked into the bathroom together, where the hot water had fogged up the mirrors, and beads of sweat immediately formed on the tips of their noses. Eyonna closed the lid of the toilet and she sat there, watching Paul take his time stepping into the hot water.

"So Paul, Zachary paid you half'a the money already, right?" Paul nodded his head yes. "An' you s'posed to get the other half from him lata' on tonight, right?"

"Uh huh!" He assured her. He was now settled in the tub, letting his body adjust to the heat, and Eyonna sat there with a concerned look on her face.

"So what'chu gon' do if Zachary jus' happen to see Chuck walkin' aroun' alive, when he s'posed to be dead?" Paul shrugged his shoulders and continued to wash his body. "So what?"

Eyonna sighed, then she walked over to the tub and Paul handed her his bath towel. She kneeled down next to him and submerged the towel in the water. Then she rubbed it on a bar of soap and she started washing Paul's back and shoulders. "Lay back," she urged. Eyonna washed his stomach and in between his legs while he closed his eyes and relaxed. "Then that means that he's gon' try an' kill you… right?"

"Eyonna baby… you let me worry about that. A'ight?

"Okay," she answered sadly. She let the towel drop into the water, then stood up and kissed him on the forehead. She was about to leave the bathroom when he called her back.

"I wanna tell you sump'n, come here." Paul knew by her body language and the way she was moping that something was troubling her. Eyonna came back and kneeled down by his side again. He placed his wet hands on her face, and told her how much he loved her.

"I know, Paul. I'm jus' worried, that's all."

"Jus hear me out, okay?"

Eyonna nodded her head.

"You know how I'm always lookin' out for you an' Apple. An' you know I don't give two shits about Zachary... but if I can make money an' look out for y'all at the same time... then that's even betta."

"But Paul, I don't want Zachary tryin' to step to you."

Paul stopped her from talking by putting his index finger up to her lips. "Shhhhh..." he whispered, as he confidently looked her in the eyes. "Let me worry about it... Okay?

"Okay," she softly replied.

Paul then switched the subject and asked her whether Zachary owned any dogs.

Eyonna twisted her mouth while she thought for a minute. "Not that I know of.... But Apple said sump'n about Zachary an' some dogs before. Ask her - she know everythin' about that bastard. Why you askin'?"

"'Cause, when I wuz in the bathroom at the barba'shop, Zachary wuz talkin' ta some dude that sounded like a damn crack-head, an' dey wuz talkin' about a fridge full'a blood n'shit... an' feedin' it to some dogs."

"So what? Zachary knows a lotta weird people, crack-heads included."

"Nah... but this dude's voice sounded familiar."

"Maybe it wuz Fly."

"Fly, who's that?"

"One of Zachary's crack-head runners."

Paul's face reflected his frustration, and he hit his hands together saying, "I gotta find out who that dude was."

"Well... Apple should be here before you leave, an' you can ask her."

"Okay... cool."

After Paul had finished taking his bath, he got dressed, and Eyonna told him to take a seat at the table. She followed the recipes her grandmother had taught her mother, which pleased Paul no end.

Her cooking always tasted better the second day, and whenever she wanted to persuade him to stop by, she would make his favorites. Her herb-n-garlic, light-n-fluffy mashed potatoes never added an inch to her perfect size two; instead it all went to Paul's stomach. The potatoes were fresh and piping hot, with a pool of rich gravy from the pot roast that had been simmering for hours with succulent vegetables and a splash of red wine. The smell alone could lift Paul off his feet and pull him by his nose all the way into the kitchen. The meat could be cut into slices with a spoon, and the cabbage always brought back memories of his grandmothers cooking.

After Paul ate two hefty servings and washed it down with a cold beer, he wanted to lie back down and enjoy digesting his supper, but he wanted to get the rest of his money from Zachary even more. Apple hadn't arrived yet, and Paul had gotten tired of waiting. He kissed Eyonna a couple of times, promised her that he would see her later, and then he left. As soon as he got downstairs and out the front entrance, Paul saw Apple coming up the block with her bags in her hand.

"Big Paul Big Paul, Wassup-wassup-wassup?" Apple playfully smiled while doing a silly dance to the music she made with her mouth. "Wassup Paul, how long you been back?"

"I got back this mornin', but look at you - you all happy n'shit. Why you come back so soon? You ain't like it down there?"

Apple was slightly out of breath from all that dancing when she replied, "Nah, I wuz lovin' it down there, Paul. I ain't wanna come back, but I had to bring that car back up here."

"Oh yeah, that's right. I forgot about that rental car." Then he asked her about Chuck.

"Chuck is Chuck," Apple happily said, "He's doin' his thing. We gettin' ready for school, an' he still gettin' things togetha for that magazine o' his. You should see him Paul, that's all he talks about." Then she balled up her fist and started bouncing around like a boxer. She playfully punched Paul in the shoulder and said, "He done showed me so many boxin' tapes from his fight collection, man I'm ready for somebody to try an' step to me now. I'll knock dey ass out!"

Being that Paul was such a large man, Apple appeared even smaller when she stood next to him, almost like a little girl playing with her father. He smiled as he looked down at her, and she continued to bounce around him.

"Word up Paul. I wuz lovin' it down there. Plus I know my way up an' down the highway by myself now." Apple started doing her silly dance again. "I'ma have me some fun this year, Paul. Word up I am."

"How long did it take you to drive up?"

"I'm not really sure, 'cause I drove about eight hours, then I stopped in V A to see some family. You know I got people from here to Miami. But that ride is too long for me to drive non-stop like you an' Chuck be doin'. I don't see how ya'll be doin' that."

"Well, once you put'cha mind to it, then the rest is easy."

"Oh shoot, I forgot you wuz a big ol' philosopher," she teased, "You an' Chuck be soundin' jus' alike, I swear."

Paul laughed, and mentioned how happy she'd been acting for the last couple of days. "You been lookin' real good Apple, you know that."

"Thanks, Paul." She was really pleased at the compliment.

"I'm glad to see you happy, Apple. That dude is crazy about you. I can see how he looks at you when you're not even payin' attention."

Apple started blushing, "Yeah?"

"He smiles at the silly things you do, an' he laughs at those corny-ass jokes you be tellin' all the time. Stick with'em, Apple, an' ya'll gon' go places."

"Yeah, I believe that too, Paul. Word up I do."

Paul then changed the subject and asked her it she knew anybody by the name of Fly. Apple looked strangely at Paul; she'd thought he would know who Fly was, since he knew so many people, and Fly was a gofer for everybody in the neighborhood.

"You don't know who Fly is?" she asked, incredulous. "Hum... that's weird."

Paul shrugged his shoulders, "Nah... I don't know him."

Apple tapped Paul on the shoulder, "That's the crack-head dude that's always hangin' aroun' Zachary, like he's Zachary shadow or sump'n."

Paul thought about it for a moment, but he still didn't know who she was talking about.

Apple snapped her fingers, remembering something else. "Hey, Fly's the one that found your cousin Sean dead. Rememba?"

Paul recollected most of the details about his cousin's murder, but that one had escaped his notice.. "Nah, I don't rememba that," Paul mused, suddenly thinking back. "Do you know if this Fly dude got dogs, or sump'n?"

"He use'ta have two big-ass dogs that looked like wolves, but I don't know what happened to them. Now he jus' got those two big black ones. I don't know what kinda dogs dey are, but dey look like devil dogs to me."

"Rottweilers?"

"Yeah, that's it," she said with a surprised look of recognition on her face. "That's the name of those big-ass dogs... Rottweilers."

"Do you know where he keep'em?"

"Downtown, ova there in those stinkin'-ass buildings on 109th Street."

Paul had heard enough. He thanked Apple for the information, because he knew exactly the place she was talking about. That was his old neighborhood, and that's where he was headed right now. Before he walked away he spoke to Apple as a big brother would, warning her to be careful. "An' leave that jerk-off Zachary alone," he added.

"Don't worry, Paul..." she replied, "I am."

Chapter 21:

After Paul had talked to Apple that night, his intuition told him to go around to the old neighborhood and check things out. If memory served him right, the block she'd mentioned was very dangerous, and he wasn't about to go around their alone - so he went to pick up a friend first. The meeting with Zachary was now put on the back burner, because for the moment he was intent on finding out who this Fly person was.

Paul hadn't been around his old neighborhood for quite some time, and he knew it would bring back memories, good and bad. Before he even got there, he started having flashbacks of the cars that used to cruise through the block for one reason only - to cop a hit.

Paul parked his car on the avenue, and he and his partner reached under their seats for their pistols. They casually tucked them into their waists as they walked toward the building Apple had mentioned. The block itself was dark and desolate with no signs of life, and the avenues were kept alive by the merengue music that pulsed through the air. On one corner there were a couple of older men wearing short-sleeved guayaberas and fedoras straw hats. Some were sitting on milk crates playing dominos beneath the bodega's flashing lights, while others were drinking beer out of plastic cups or bottles wrapped in paper bags. At the other corner there was a group of young guys standing around their custom-made low rider. They had the stereo blasting, and they were calling every girl that passed them by them a *Mah-me* . As Paul and his partner walked down the block, the abandoned buildings exuded a stale damp odor that caused their muscles to tighten reflexively, and though they didn't understand the lyrics to the music, it seemed to help them relax.

They looked up at the building before they walked in, and saw that there were no lights on in the hallway, and most of the windows were broken out except for those on the top floor. The two men were somewhat skeptical about entering the abandoned building, but their pistols were already cocked and ready. Paul was dubious about the whole venture, but a sneaking suspicion had been forming in his mind as he slowly traced the connections between Zachary and Fly, and between Fly and his cousin Sean's murder. And somewhere in the middle of it all there were two big black dogs with an unusual thirst for human blood.. When the men cautiously entered the building the rotten stench assailed them, while the moon, beaming through broken windows, served as the only source of light.

Paul whispered to his partner to stay downstairs, while he cautiously tiptoed upstairs to reconnoiter. The building was much darker on the inside than the men had expected, so they had to creep along at first, waiting for their eyes to adjust. When Paul got to the top floor, he put his ear to the apartment door, but he couldn't hear anything inside. Then he got down on his knees to peer under the door, but could see nothing either. He groped the large bolted locks, nudging them a few times to see if there was any give, but to no avail. Then he walked up one more flight to investigate the roof, and when he opened the door he caught a glimpse of the city skyline, sparkling and seductive, but there was nobody up there either. He was now talking aloud to his partner as he carefully edged back down the stairs, but he received no answer. Paul guessed that he had gone back outside, and thought nothing of it.

The only thing that was keeping Paul from panicking that night was his awareness that there wasn't anything he could do, other than keep a firm grip on his pistol and make sure he didn't fall. When he finally got to the last landing, which opened onto a long hallway, he heard somebody entering the building. He could see a man's silhouette, but he couldn't make out who it was. He also noticed that the man was making his way through the dark building effortlessly, as if he had been here before. Paul called out his partner's name, and was astonished to find that he had been hiding in the shadows right beside him. Paul nearly jumped out of his skin with fear as his partner vainly urged him to keep quiet - but it was too late.

The dark mysterious figure was accompanied by two large dogs, and soon as Paul raised his voice, the command was given for the dogs to attack. The ferocious beasts came charging at the two men with their fangs bared. Paul and his partner stood there in the dark, sweating bullets and shooting wildly, with nothing to aim at but a hideous growling. The sparks from their guns flared out in the dark building like a strobe light in a nightclub, and the two men seemed to be hitting everything except the dogs.

They could hear the vicious beasts charging towards them, and then they leaped on Paul's partner, knocking him to the floor and the pistol from his hand. He was dragged across the dirty tiles, screaming for help, and Paul tried to come to his aid - but he couldn't see a thing in the pitch-black hallway.

All Paul could do was put out his hands and run around in circles until he found where his partner lay. The beasts growled in a fuming rage, latching onto the man's foot, and nearly ripping off one of his fingers. Paul didn't want to aim his gun at random and risk hitting his partner, but he didn't seem to have many options. The only other alternative was to feel around with his foot and start kicking wildly.

The first kick hit the dog in the ribs, causing it to yelp and back away, but in a moment it came charging at him again. Paul had to risk stretching out his hands toward the growls, in the hope of finding the beast's neck. He felt the dogs under his hands almost at once, their hairy, muscular bodies twisting and squirming as they tried to get a better bite on his partner. Paul now felt that he had the beasts where he wanted them, so he quickly emptied his gun into one of the dog's head, killing him instantly. Hearing his partner's screams of agony in the silence that followed, Paul could only draw satisfaction from the knowledge that he was not yet dead.

Paul barely had time to recoil before the second dog lunged at him. He screamed for help, and his partner tried to struggle to his feet, without success. The dog had bitten him quite badly, and his leg crumpled beneath him. When the second dog latched onto Paul's forearm, he fell back onto a piece of metal that bit into his back even more deeply than the animal's fangs.

Then in a moment of relief, Paul realized that the metal object was in fact his partner's pistol, which had fallen to the floor when the dogs first attacked. He quickly fired two shots into the beast's stomach, and the dog died on his chest, leaving trails of saliva and blood all over Paul's body. He pushed the animal off of him, then jumped to his feet and went after the mysterious intruder, who at that moment was running out of the building. Paul was not far behind as he chased the man up the block with his arm throbbing from a deep bite - but he would worry about that later. There was only one thing clear in Paul's mind now - when the man had given the dogs the attack command, Paul had recognized that voice. It was the voice from the barbershop, and it was the same voice that Eyonna had said belonged to Zachary's crack-head runner Fly - and that made Paul run even faster.

Fly dashed into the bodega, leaving Paul behind - but then Paul slowed down and stopped. He wasn't about to run into the bodega breathing heavily with his gun exposed, alarming the men who were sitting around a table, calmly playing dominos. The last thing he wanted was to be mistaken for a robber, and risk getting into a shootout with the store clerk. After he had straightened out his clothes as best he could, Paul pulled himself together, and gingerly walked into the store like an ordinary shopper. He knew that most bodegas have surveillance mirrors placed up in the corners and in the aisles, and he would use these to his advantage. When Paul looked into the mirror behind him, he could see that Fly was on one side of the store near the beer and soda aisle.

Fly was over forty years of age, but he was still fast on his feet. He thought that he had left Paul behind in the chase, so he was hoping that it was safe to leave the bodega, and he briskly walked past the store clerk. The store clerk just stood there eyeing him suspiciously as Paul came out of the cereal aisle not too far behind him. Paul smiled at the clerk as he was leaving, trying to defuse his suspicion so he wouldn't call the cops.

Paul had his gun in his front pocket with his finger on the trigger, patiently waiting until Fly crossed the street, and that's when he skipped up behind him. Fly was startled, and he looked like a turtle trying to duck his head back into his shell when Paul tapped him on his shoulder. He quickly turned around with his eyes and mouth wide open as if he were trying to scream, but no sound came out. Paul snatched him by his collar, practically lifting him off of his feet as he slammed him into a nearby telephone booth. Fly's back hit the phone, knocking it off of the hook as he slid to the ground, pleading for his life. Paul got down on one knee and feverishly beat Fly in the face with his pistol until his hands were sore. Paul's lips were tightly tucked into his mouth, his eyes were dark red, and it seem as if the more Fly screamed, the more he wanted to hit him.

Paul wasn't a detective, and he wasn't trying to be one. The pieces of the puzzle had simply fallen together in his mind; Zachary's association with Fly, Fly's apparent penchant for using attack dogs as murder weapons, and his connection to the old neighborhood, where Paul's cousin Sean had been murdered... In Paul's mind Fly had already been tried, convicted and sentenced - and street justice would be served.

After Paul had beaten Fly unconscious, he put his pistol into Fly's open mouth and let the barrel rest on his bottom teeth. He slowly squeezed the trigger, firing two shots into Fly's head. The young men of the neighborhood who were out on the streets flirting with the girls that night had their music playing so loud that they never noticed anything out of the ordinary.

Paul tucked his pistol away as he jogged back to his car, then jumped in and drove down the block to pick up his partner. The wounded man staggered into the vehicle with his T-shirt wrapped around his bleeding hand, and his facial expression plainly showed that he was in excruciating pain.

"Did you get that muthafucka?" He asked Paul.

Paul was trying to keep his eyes on the road. "Yo, you a'ight?"

"Yeah, I'm cool," the man said through clenched teeth, "I'm fine. Did you catch that dude?"

"Yeah, I got his ass."

"Cool, that's all I wanted to know."

Paul looked over at him again. "Yo, you sure you a'ight?"

"Yeah, jus' drop me off uptown. I'ma change my clothes at my girl's house and get her to take me to the hospital so dey can sew this shit back togetha. Jus' beep me later on, a'ight?"

"Cool. You sure you a'ight?"

His partner forced a smile, "Yeah… man, I'm good."

Chapter 22:

I t was 11:30 in the evening when Apple came charging through the front door, and Eyonna could see that she was in high spirits. Apple had been on the highway for a while now, and she was happy to be home. She also knew that Paul had just left the apartment, so she started teasing Eyonna as soon as she'd dropped her bags. Apple frowned, sniffed the air and playfully asked, "Why it smell so funny in this place?" She waited for Eyonna's response, but all she got was a "hello" as Eyonna walked right past her. Apple thought her friend hadn't heard her, so she continued to tease. "Umph, umph umph, smell like somebody wuz gettin' it on up in here!"

Eyonna just grinned as she headed towards the kitchen to clean up and put away the food. "Girl, you so silly," she said, waving Apple away.

Apple was still standing near the front door, and she could tell that Eyonna wasn't falling for her mischievous behavior. Nevertheless, she put her hands on her hips and continued to taunt her. "Look who tryin' to get stank, jus' 'cause dey got some." Then she rolled her eyes and stormed into her room in mock frustration.

The girls went about their separate routines, cleaning up and bathing at opposite ends of the apartment, each feeling comfortable and secure knowing that the other was nearby.

Apple still hadn't managed to engage Eyonna in their usual

bouts of teasing fun, and she wanted to know what was troubling her friend. She went and stood in the doorway of Eyonna's bedroom for a brief moment without saying anything. Eyonna was lying on her stomach with her head down at the foot of the bed, so she did-n't even know that Apple was standing there till she walked into the room and she sat down on the edge of the bed.

Apple was still playing games, and she looked around the room like a child in awe. "Wow," she burst out, "You done change the sheets on ya bed n'shit. I knew sump'n looked different aroun' here." Then she hit one of the pillows and said, "Yeah girl, you an' Paul musta been gettin' it on up in here!" Apple laughed aloud at her own joke, but Eyonna's face remained blank. Apple's big smile slowly disappeared, because Eyonna was still not saying anything. Now Apple was concerned. "Eyonna, what's bothering you. Why you so quiet?"

Eyonna started to mumble, and Apple couldn't understand what she was saying, so she leaned over and put her ear closer to her friend's mouth. Eyonna then sat up and asked Apple point-blank whether she knew why Paul was in Kentucky. Apple thought for a moment, then replied that she had never stopped to give it any thought. "Why?"

"Chuck didn't tell you why?" Eyonna prompted.

"No," Apple replied with a curious look on her face.

"'Cause yo' ex-lover, yo' ex-boyfriend Zachary, paid Paul five G's ta kill yo' man, Chuck. Did you know that?"

Apple sucked her teeth, looking stunned. "What?" She said flatly.

"You heard what I jus' said. Zachary paid Paul five G's ta go to Kentucky and kill Chuck." There was a long pause as Eyonna glared at Apple. "Chuck ain't tell you that?"

Apple was speechless. "No."

"You need to get'cha shit straight Apple... How do you think Paul found his way down to Kentucky...?" Apple started try-ing to think, but Eyonna blurted out "Zachary told'em how to get down there, 'cause yo' dumb ass told Zachary."

Apple continued to sit there looking lost.

"Apple, you talk too damn much. You tell Zachary every damn thing like he's ya fuckin' fatha. Girl, sometimes you gotta think first. You hafta use yo' head, and know when ta shut the fuck up."

"But E, I ain't know."

"How come you ain't know, Apple? You know everything else."

"Zachary is capable of anything, but I ain't know he paid Paul to kill Chuck, I swear it." Then Apple put up her hands to prevent Eyonna from cutting in. "Wait," she said, dropping all affectation from her voice. "E... listen to me. I'm not gon' stand here and say that I'm in love with Chuck. I'm not gon' even lie to myself. But there are some things about him that I do love. I think Chuck is a wonderful person, an' I wouldn't be movin' down south if I didn't. I'm talkin' 'bout goin' back to school an' all'a that shit, jus' fo' this kid."

"That's yo' problem Apple, you always doin' shit for these kids out here that don't give a fuck about you. You need to do shit jus' for Apple, that's what'chu need to do. Not for Zachary. Not for Chuck but for Apple."

"So what'chu sayin' E, I shouldn't go down south?"

"No, what I'm sayin' is... goin' down south is cool... if you goin' down south 'cause that's what you wanna do. That's what I'm sayin'." Eyonna was standing up on the other side of the bedroom, looking out the window with her back towards Apple. "But let's not forget the main point fo' right now," she fumed. "Do you realize that Chuck is supposed to be dead at this minute?" Apple didn't answer her. She just started fidgeting around as if the question made her uncomfortable, so Eyonna turned around and addressed her again. "An' now Paul is caught up in this mess too, 'cause Chuck ain't dead."

"So what'chu 'spec me to do?"

"You say that you love Chuck... but'chu still fuckin' wit

Zachary. An' I warned you that all'a this beef wuz gonna happen when you made up ya mind to do him dirty."

"I ain't fuckin' wit Zachary." Apple yelled. "I told you that, Eyonna. An' that other mess wit the guns wuz jus' a mistake."

"Yeah... okay. A mistake that's done started a whole lotta' shit."

"Look E, I know what kinda person Zachary is," Apple finally sighed. "an' I know what he's capable of doing. That's one of the main reasons why I decided to move down south wit Chuck. I know that shit ain't gon' be easy... but I'm ready to give it a try." Then she walked over to stand right in front of Eyonna and said earnestly, "E... you lookin' at the new Apple."

Eyonna listened, and in the back of her mind it all sounded like a bunch of gibberish, only because she knew Apple and her selfish tendencies. She glared out of the corners of her eyes and asked, "Yeah... is that so, Miss Apple?"

"Yeah," Apple assured her, "an' I wuz hopin' that once I got settled, then you would come down there an' visit me sometimes." She smiled and tapped Eyonna's shoulder, "A'ight?"

"But what'chu gon' do about the situation we in right now, Apple" Eyonna could scarcely contain her frustration.

"What'chu tryin' to say... You want Chuck to run from Zachary an' jus stay down south for the rest of his life?"

Eyonna didn't respond, only because that's exactly what she'd been thinking.

"I dunno, E..." Apple went on, "That's some crazy shit you talkin'. I can't see Chuck runnin'. He's got a mother livin' up here that he's gotta come an' see."

"Well then, you betta' tell'em to watch his back, when he do come up this way."

"But what about Paul... You ain't worried about him?"

Eyonna was about to reply, but the phone interrupted her. She went to answer it, and Paul was on the other end. He told Eyonna that he was coming by, and she asked if he was all right -

but he had already hung up. Eyonna looked worried when she got off the phone, and Apple asked her what was wrong. Eyonna stood there looking dazed, until Apple tapped her on the shoulder.

"Who wuz that?" Apple asked. She was staring into Eyonna's face as if she were trying to read her thoughts.

Eyonna was holding the phone with both hands, and her mouth was slightly open. She told Apple that it was Paul. "An' he sounded kinda strange," she said.

"Strange, how?" Apple fearfully asked. Eyonna's behavior troubled her, and she was afraid that her friend might have just received some bad news.

"Like he wuz anxious about sump'n," Eyonna softly said, "He wuz talkin' fast an' breathin' real hard... like he wuz nervous."

"Did he say where he wuz at?"

"Nah... he jus' said that he wuz stoppin' by, then he hung up."

Eyonna was thinking to herself that whatever Paul's problem was, she wanted to help. She quickly started getting dressed and taking the pins out of her hair, so she would be ready when Paul arrived.

Chapter 23:

Paul was coasting uptown with his pistol sitting on his lap, touching it every now and then to make sure it hadn't evaporated into thin air. He was still edgy from all the excitement, so he turned on the radio to help him think as he drove to the girls' place. He carefully kept the car at a moderate speed, even slowing down for the yellow lights, and he arrived at their building in a few minutes. This time he had to ring the downstairs intercom, and Eyonna buzzed him in without checking to see who it was. She had recognized the way he didn't ease up on the buzzer.

Once inside, he briskly loped up the three flights, to find Eyonna standing in the doorway with one foot over the threshold. His brand new sweat-suit was soiled and ripped from the knees to the elbows, and she started to cry as soon as she saw the expression on his face. She gently lifted his forearm, and gasped at the ugly bruise. "Damn, baby," she whimpered anxiously, "what happened? You need to go to the hospital?"

"Nah," he answered through clenched teeth, "let me catch my breath first." He was winded, and stress had cut his breath even shorter.

Eyonna walked him over to the couch, asking if she could get him anything. He answered that he wanted some water, so she rushed to the kitchen and came back with a tall glass. Apple had stood watching all of this in silence, with her mouth hanging open. Paul took his pistol from his hip and laid it on the coffee table, and

Apple could see that it had been used. It was dirty, with visible fingerprints and a dull gleam to it. She watched Paul's Adam's apple move convulsively as he gulped down the water, then asked him what had happened. He wiped his face with his shirt, and briefly told them all he thought they needed to know. The way he saw it, if they remembered anything about the old neighborhood, it wouldn't be difficult for them to fill in whatever details he left out.

Eyonna blamed Apple indirectly for all of this trouble, and she couldn't help glaring at her friend as she rushed to get some bandages for Paul's wound. He was unaware of the tension that had been developing between the girls, though he could sense it in the air. It wasn't until Apple loudly snapped at Eyonna that his intuition was confirmed.

"Would you please stop lookin' at me like that," Apple yelled.

"You know wassup, Apple," Eyonna shot back, "An' you know ezzackly why I'm lookin' at you like that. But then you'll jus' sit ova there lookin' all innocent n'shit, like you don't know what's goin' on."

Paul sat up and looked at the girls. "What's goin' on here?" he asked, with his eyes trained on Apple.

Eyonna ran to the bathroom again and returned with a bottle of peroxide and a towel in her hand. She continued to glare at Apple out the corner of her eye while she gently wiped Paul's arm.

"What's happened?" Paul asked the girls again, as he twitched and gritted his teeth every time Eyonna wiped his bruises.

"Ain't nothin' happened," Apple replied, though she immediately regretted opening her mouth, because she felt that Eyonna and Paul would team up against her.

"It's that fuckin' Zachary…" Eyonna blurted out, "an' she act like she can't leave his ass alone."

Paul continued to twitch as he shook his head. "Wassup wit that, Apple, why Eyonna say that?" Eyonna maintained her stony expression, and Apple didn't answer, so Paul just shook his head again and said, "I dunno what's goin' on in here." Then he struggled to get to his feet, and slowly walked down the hallway. "But somebody gon' get hurt real bad, an' it ain't gon' be me. I know that much."

Eyonna jumped up along with him, and asked him where he was going.

"Bathroom," he grunted, "I'ma take dese clothes off, an' I'ma burn'em soon's I get outta' here."

Eyonna followed him into the bathroom and closed the door behind them. She was helping him undress when she heard the phone ring, and when she asked Apple to answer it, she got no response. The phone's ringing finally became annoying, so Eyonna rushed to the living room to answer it herself - but rather then picking it up right away, she screened the call. When she heard Chuck's voice through the answering machine, she picked up the receiver. They talked briefly, and then she asked him to hold on.

"I'll go get Apple for you," she said. Eyonna searched the apartment, calling Apple's name - but to no avail. This puzzled her because she hadn't heard Apple leave, and when she went back to the phone to tell Chuck that Apple wasn't there, he became suspicious too.

They were about to hang up, but when Paul realized whom she was talking to, he quickly picked up the receiver in Eyonna's room. He now had on a different outfit, and his old sweat-suit was stuffed into a paper bag. Paul said "Wassup?" to Chuck, and then without taking a breath, he asked Eyonna where Apple had gone.

"I dunno, Paul," she yelled, "I wanna know where she is too, jus' like you do."

"What the hell is goin' on aroun' here?" Paul asked, losing his patience.

On the other end of the line, Chuck was completely confused, and as he listened to Paul and Eyonna shouting back and forth, he tried in vain to put the pieces together. Eventually he had to hang up the phone and call back just to get the others' attention, and Eyonna coldly advised him to talk to Paul, banging down her receiver.

"Shit is crazy right now," she yelled, "an' ya'll about to make me pull my fuckin' hair out."

"What's goin' on?" Chuck anxiously asked, "What happened to Apple?"

Paul was still deeply aggravated, but he kept his composure and told Chuck that Apple had stepped out.

"What?" Chuck retorted, "It's one thirty in the morning. Where the hell is she goin' this late? An' why does everybody sound so crazy up there?"

"It ain't nut'n, Chuck," Paul replied calmly, "E's jus' a little jittery right now, that's all."

Eyonna loudly yelled from the back of the apartment, "Jittery my ass! I ain't jittery… shit … An' why you tryin' to protect her, Paul?" Eyonna was deliberately yelling so she could be overheard by Chuck on the other end of the phone. "Apple prob'ly ran her ass off to go be wit dat damn snake… but that's okay," She calmed herself and went on. "'Cause I got a trick for her ass soon as I see her!"

Eyonna was completely dressed now, and as she stormed towards the front door, Paul had to drop the phone to go stop her. They tussled briefly, and Chuck could faintly hear the commotion, but he couldn't make out what they were saying - which frustrated him even more. Paul came back to the phone after he'd convinced Eyonna to sit tight, and Chuck asked him if there was something wrong.

"What'd I tell you I wuz gon' do to that kid?" Paul calmly asked, referring to Zachary and his associates. "I hope you rememba what we talked about right before you left, Chuck, 'cause shit is startin' to get real."

Chuck took a deep breath and whistled, "Damn!" He put two and two together, and automatically assumed the worst. There were a few seconds of silence between them before Chuck asked Paul if he was all right.

"Yeah man, like I said before. Shit is just a little crazy right now, but I'ma handle it."

Eyonna was anxiously calling Paul's name from the living room, and he wanted to go to her. He told Chuck to call him when he made it to New York, and then they both hung up. Paul met Eyonna halfway down the hall, rushing in to find him. Her eyes were wide with fear, and her voice was hoarse from yelling. "Paul, didn't you put yo' gun on that coffee table?" she asked, almost in a whisper.

He calmly told her yes, "An' I hope you know betta then to touch it. As a matta of fact, I'ma get rid of it when I dump these clothes. That shit is dirty baby, it's got a body on it."

"But I thought you moved it already."

"What?" he asked, with a bad feeling forming in his gut. He limped past her to search the coffee table. When he didn't find the gun, he knew that things were about to get worse than he'd ever imagined. He and Eyonna practically turned the apartment upside down looking for it, and she could see the frustration in his eyes as he stood in the middle of the living room, beginning to panic.

Eyonna was walking around the apartment with her socks on and her jeans rolled up like a farmer. She had her hands on her hips when she looked at Paul and said, "Well, baby, we looked everywhere in this damn apartment an' a gun can't just get up an' walk away." Then she put words to what Paul had feared. "You know, Apple ain't here, an' yo' gun ain't eitha."

Paul dropped his face into his hands as if he was hiding tears. "But why would she take that shit outta' here, knowin' that it's dirty? I jus told her that I smoked somebody wit it."

"Maybe she ain't know."

"What the hell do you mean, she ain't know?" He yelled, scaring Eyonna and causing her to jump. Then he stormed towards the front door, and just before grabbing the doorknob he barked, "Eyonna, don't get stupid on me now! I wuz jus' right here tellin' ya'll what happened. I don't even know how you could stand there an' say some dumb shit like that." Paul was about to leave, and Eyonna ran to stop him. "Do you realize that I'm a condemned man right now?" He cried with fury. "If Zachary finds out what happened before I get a chance to cover myself, I'm fucked! An' knowin' him an' his little fuckin' crew of old men... ain't no tellin' what's gon' happen."

"Please take me wit you, Paul," Eyonna begged him. "I know where Zachary hangs out at, an' I betcha that's where Apple went."

"Where's that?"

"Ova there on the East Side. 110th street an' Lexington Ave."

"You sure about that?"

"I'm positive. That's where Zachary's at every Saturday night afta we finish hustlin'."

"A'ight, so cool, I'ma go get rid of these clothes real quick, then make some phone calls, an' I'll be back in a few minutes."

"Baby, you promise?"

Paul walked back over to her and he gave her a kiss on the forehead, "I promise," he answered. Eyonna smiled, and then he told her to lock the door.

She sadly watched him hurry off, and then she rushed to the window to peep from behind the curtains. Paul limped and jogged down the block to his car, and she waited until he was out of view. Then she quickly walked to her room, put on her sneakers, grabbed her keys and left the apartment.

Chapter 24:

There was a crowd standing around the Starlight Social Club on 124th Street and Broadway. It was one of those makeshift storefronts that appear lifeless during the day, but alive and kicking at night. Some of the patrons were standing around talking and drinking, while others were just enjoying the music. Zachary was standing off to one side, counting a wad of money and laughing with some friends, his gold pinky ring glistening under the city lights. At first he appeared surprised when a woman jumped out of a cab and ran screaming towards him, but once he'd realized that it was only Apple, he sneered and glanced away. He crammed his money into his pocket, and the men who were standing around him snickered and slowly backed off. They assumed that Apple was just a jealous girlfriend, and they didn't want to get mixed up in that kind of scene. In any case, they could get a better view of her body from a distance. She was properly dressed for the southern heat, but the city breeze gave her goose bumps and made her small body shiver in her baby-blue T-shirt. Her vulnerable appearance, contrasted with her healthy brick-red suntan, made the men drool.

Zachary was aware that they were gawking at Apple, and he wanted to put on a good show. With open arms and a fake smile, he appeared overjoyed to see her as he solicitously asked about her trip.

"Don't ask me shit,'" Apple replied as she stormed towards

him, "'cause you ain't shit. You know that, right?" She had her index finger in his face, and he immediately recognized that she wasn't broken up over Chuck's death, as he'd expected, but simply furious - and that puzzled him. In an effort to put up a good front, Zachary added some bass to his voice when he told her that he didn't know what she was talking about, which only upset her more.

"Don't be playin' dumb, Zachary, you know ezzackly what I'm talkin' about!" Then she punched him on his arm as hard as she could. It didn't hurt him, and he giggled along with the other men who stood back watching them. Nevertheless, he did put up his guard in case she tried to swing again.

"Why you playin' dumb, man?" Apple fumed.

Zachary's smile disappeared and now he looked suspicious, "You need'ta 'splain to me what'chu sayin'."

Apple yelled back at him, "Why you playin', Zachary, you made those dogs attack Paul." Then she hit him again as she continued to vent her rage. "Now Eyonna's breakin' on me n'shit!"

All of a sudden Zachary stared into Apple's eyes and his hands dropped to his sides. He asked her to repeat herself, but she stood there with her arms folded and her lips shut tight. He nudged her arm, and they stepped a little further away from the crowd of gawking men as he whispered, "I dunno what'chu talkin' 'bout, Apple. My dogs is upstairs, at the spot, mindin' dey own business."

Apple kept her arms folded across her chest as she rolled her eyes and said, "Well then, somebody's lyin'… 'cause Paul jus' came back to the crib wit blood n'shit all ova his clothes, talkin' 'bout your dogs attacked him."

Zachary stretched his arms wide and protested his ignorance of the whole thing. "What'chu talkin' about, Apple!" Then he stopped as if struck by a sudden thought. "Wait a minute," Zachary said suspiciously, "how does Paul even know I got dogs?"

"I dunno," Apple shouted, "I jus' know what he said."

"Paul neva even seen my dogs before…" Zachary countered, while Apple just stood there with her arms folded and her mouth twisted to the side.

"Well, he told me he went downtown, an' yo' dogs tried to kill'em."

"What the fuck he go down there for?" Zachary mumbled. He had a feeling that Paul had been up to something, but he didn't want to talk about it in front of Apple. He started thinking aloud as she stood there rolling her eyes at him. "Apple, did Eyonna know that you wuz comin' aroun' here to see me?" he asked, beginning to construct a picture in his mind,

"No, why?"

Zachary didn't answer her. He was fuming and kicking the ground, and out of pure frustration he cursed violently, as if he were about to burst open. He walked off, leaving Apple standing alone and lost, and the group of men who had been checking her out got suddenly quiet. Zachary glanced over at the men and slightly nodded his head, so they walked over to him and they began to whisper together.

Once the men had arranged their business, they strolled off, and Apple walked over to Zachary and tried to calm him down, but he snatched away from her. He had enough rage pumping through his body to jump-start a diesel engine, '*This nigga Paul is tryin' ta beat me outta' my money,*' he thought to himself, and that made him very upset. When he finally looked around for Apple, she was already walking up the street.

Apple was hurt and aggravated, and when Zachary called her back, she just started walking faster. He caught up with her and tapped her shoulder, and she whirled around to face him.

"What, Zachary? What the hell you want?" she harshly asked. "I wuz tryin' to talk to you back there… an' you runnin' away from me like I'm the bad guy." Zachary started to apologize, but she continued to castigate him. "I'm tired of kissin' yo' ass, Zachary. I put up wit'cho' shit long enough, an' I'm jus' plain sick of it. Word up I am!"

After Apple had finally spoken her whole mind, Zachary looked almost as if he were about to get on his knees and apologize

- but she knew he would never go that far. "I'm sorry, Apple baby. I jus' wanna talk to you for a minute... that's all... Okay?" He stood as close to her as he could without their bodies actually touching, and he smiled as gently as he could. "Okay?"

Apple knew the grin Zachary had on his face could only mean one thing, and that made her very uncomfortable. She raised her hands in front of her and told him to step back.

"What happened to us, Apple?" Zachary asked, soft and smooth as butter. "How come we don't get along like we use'ta? We wuz a team, Apple, you rememba that, don'cha? A tax-free, cash money-makin' team."

Apple sucked her teeth and looked the other way. "What the hell you talkin' about, Zachary?"

"I'm just tryin' to be a betta man fo' you, Apple, that's all. I wanna laugh wit'chu like we use'ta. I wanna go out an' eat like we use'ta. I wanna share my dreams an' my ideas wit'chu, baby. You rememba all that... don'chu?"

"Man, you wuz gon' have Chuck killed, to prove how much of a betta man you tryin' to be."

Zachary stopped grinning. He appeared hurt and offended, as if he were being wrongly accused. "I wuzn't gon' have nobody killed," he sulked.

Apple sneered, "Yeah okay, there you go lyin' again, jus' like always."

Zachary put both of his hands on his chest like a repentant sinner, and earnestly told Apple that he'd never meant to do Chuck any harm. "That wuz jus' a big misunderstandin' 'tween me an' him. 'Besides, I ain't know you had feelin's fo' him like that, Apple."

"Like what?"

"Like you wuz thinkin' 'bout movin' down south, n'every-thang."

"Listen, Zachary," Apple said kindly, "Chuck is my man, an' I'm stickin' by his side no matta what. An' I ain't thinkin' 'bout movin' down south wit him... I am movin' down south."

Zachary was putting on his best performance when he

dropped his head and sadly replied, "It's like that, is it, Apple?"

"Sorry Zachary… but yeah, that's the way it is."

Apple's words seemed to slow down the city, and for once in his life, Zachary appeared beaten. He heaved a deep sigh, and in a low compassionate voice he said, "Well Apple, if that's the way you want things, then that's the way it's gon' be - an' I can't do nut'n but accept it, right?" Then he looked her in the eyes with a somber expression on his face, and asked her again, "Right?"

Apple just nodded her head.

Zachary took a deep breath and exhaled. He shrugged his shoulders, and with a grim look he said, "Well." Then he smiled and reached to take Apple's hand, "I'ma miss you, Apple. You know that, right?"

"I'ma miss you too, Zach," she murmured sadly.

"You know Apple, we had a lot of fun togetha, 'specially downtown, right?"

Apple looked as if she were about to cry. They were still holding hands and looking into each other's eyes when she replied, "We sure did, Zachary. We sure did." They smiled and hugged, and Apple wiped her eyes with her hands. After she'd regained her composure, she asked Zachary to do her a favor.

"What kinda favor?" he asked her, handing her a piece of tissue.

Apple wiped her face again, and then she asked him not to say anything to Paul and Eyonna. "Please Zachary," she pleaded. "I can get'cha money back if that's what'chu worried about."

Zachary was frowning, and Apple could see how upset he was. "That nigga tried ta play me, Apple… an' you know how I am." He was about to say something else, but she quickly interrupted.

"I'll get'cha money for you," she confidently said, "an' then you can go on wit'cha life… an' E an' Paul can go on wit theirs. Okay? Please?"

Zachary didn't answer. He was just being stubborn, and

Apple knew it. She stepped closer to him, and gently grabbed his sex. He jumped back, then grinned at her and said, "Apple, you my girl, you know that, right?"

"I hope so," she said seductively.

"It ain't gon' be easy fo' me," he crooned, "but if that's gon' make you happy… then I'll see what I can do." Apple smiled, and Zachary told her that he would do anything for her. "I owe it to you, Apple. We been through so much shit togetha, man, I'd be crazy to turn my back on you, right?" Apple nodded her head, and then he whispered her name. He bashfully stuttered, "Apple, I want you to know, the only reason why I acted that way is 'cause I wuz jealous." She blushed as he continued, "An' I want'cha to know that I still…"

"You still what?" she asked. She couldn't believe the look on his face, and for a moment she thought that she was hearing things.

"I still love you, Apple," he said softly.

Those were three words that Zachary seldom if ever spoke, and it was difficult for her to remember the last time she'd heard them from him. His mouth was soft and round, and Apple remembered the taste of his succulent lips, and the way he smelled when they kissed. It was almost as if his words exerted a magnetic pull on her heart, and she toyed with the idea of kissing him one last time - but Chuck's voice played like a tape loop in the back of her mind. Apple dropped her head and softly said, "Zachary… don't do this to me." They were standing face to face, and he leaned forward to kiss her, but she turned her head away.

Chapter 25:

Eyonna had held a gun before, and she would have no problem using one if she had to. After she exited the lobby of her building, she dashed across the street to hail a cab, and from the corner of her eye she saw two strange men heading in the opposite direction. She had never seen these men in the neighborhood before, and she immediately noticed that they both were overdressed for the warm weather. One of them had on a dark blue baseball jacket with a matching hat, and the other man was wearing a denim jeans-suit, with his hands tucked into his pockets as if he felt cold.

As the two men approached her building, they kept looking up at her window - and that was enough to make her duck behind the parked cars and watch them furtively from a distance. When they were unable to get into her building, she saw them stroll off. She thought to hang back and confront them, but she wanted to hurry up and catch Apple. She got into a cab, and told the driver to take her to 124th street and Broadway, all the while thinking only of Paul. She prayed that he wouldn't return for her as he'd said he would, because those strange men were clearly lying in wait. Something about them made her feel scared and vulnerable, and soon as the cab had dropped her off, she immediately paged Paul. She impatiently waited by the phone for him to return her page, but when she spotted Apple about to get into Zachary's car, she rushed to stop her.

"Yo Apple, wassup?" she yelled, as if expecting an explanation.

As soon as Apple heard Eyonna's voice, she turned around with a surprised look on her face - and Zachary grumbled.

"Fuck," he barked. He balled up his fist and hit the roof of his car, making a small dent in it. He sucked his teeth at the sight of Eyonna's face, and her voice made his skin crawl. Zachary had been confident that Apple would leave with him, but when he heard Eyonna's voice, he knew that it would never happen. '*What the fuck does she want?*' he thought to himself, rolling his eyes in disgust.

"Zachary, don't you say shit to me," Eyonna spat as soon as he opened his mouth to protest. She felt that he was up to no good, and she pointed her finger in his face saying, "I'm comin' to get Apple, an' you ain't got nut'n to do wit this."

The small crowd of people backed away, then curiously looked on as Apple tried to explain herself. Zachary smiled with his hands spread wide apart as he sarcastically protested, "Oh, I get what's goin' on now, you must be Apple's motha, right?"

Eyonna turned around with a glare that was worth serving life in prison without the possibility of parole. She held Apple's hand the way girlfriends do and said, "Zachary, You a no good nigga wit a capitol N, you know that? An' yo' days are numbered, you watch an' see. But in the mean time, jus' stay away from us… okay?" Then she walked away.

Zachary smirked, "An' if I don't, what'chu gon' do about it… Call that faggot-ass boyfriend of yours?" He smirked, and then just above a whispered he added, "You betta hope he ain't dead yet…" Eyonna barely heard his comment, so she paid it no mind and just continued walking, pulling Apple along beside her.

"You know what, Eyonna," Zachary continued, "I showed you how to make a little bit of money, an' now you all conceited. Talkin' like a white girl, an' usin' pretty words n'shit. You think you betta than me, don'cha?" He smiled and continued, "Yeah, that's what it is. You think you betta den a muthafucka. That's a nigga fo' ya. The minute ya'll get a little education, then ya'll too good for a muthafucka, an' can't nobody tell you nut'n." Arrogantly he rubbed his hands together, then put them in his pockets. He looked Eyonna up and down as if she were a beggar. "But let me tell you sump'n, Eyonna. You a zero. A nut'n - you got that? You - are - a - nothin'," he enunciated, making sure she could see his tongue scrape against his teeth, as if she were a child learning her first words.

"An' what are you, Zachary?" Eyonna stopped to ask, as the crowd quietly looked on in astonishment. Zachary outweighed her by eighty pounds or more. He was much taller and stronger then Eyonna, and she was firmly standing her ground before one of the most respected and feared men in the neighborhood. If anything, the crowd expected that Zachary would the last word, and Eyonna would walk away with her tail between her legs. But instead she continued, "Keepin' it real, Zachary, you ain't nut'n ya damn self. You just a high yella punk wit a lotta mouth! Keep talkin' shit an' I got a trick for yo' ass, ya no good son of a bitch!"

He walked over to Eyonna as if he were approaching another man. His eyebrows were high on his forehead, and his bottom lip was tucked under his teeth. He pointed his index finger at her and said, "Let me tell you one thing, you cum-sippin' slut. You know me, Eyonna, an' you know what I'm about. So don't you get beside yourself. You threaten me one more time an' I'll smack ya inta the middle of next week, an' I won't think twice about it!"

"Get'cha damn hands out my face," Eyonna demanded, shoving him away.

Zachary frowned and he covered Eyonna's entire face with the palm of his hand, like a basketball player palming the ball. He pushed her backwards, causing her to lose her balance and fall into the crowd of onlookers. Apple rushed to Eyonna's aid, but Zachary snatched her away. He was enraged, as was evident in the way his nostrils flared open and his mouth was tucked in tight. He kicked Eyonna repeatedly as she lay stretched out on the ground, screaming and crying in agony. The crowd of club-goers looked on in confusion as Apple tried to pull him off of her friend. Then Zachary turned around, grabbed Apple by the neck, and slammed her backwards into the parked cars.

A young lady in the crowd bravely came to Apple's defense yelling, "Why don't you be a real man an' leave them alone?"

"Why don't you be a real woman an' mind ya fuckin' business?" A female friend of Zachary's vigorously retorted.

"Word up," Zachary growled, "before I come an' kick the shit outta you next!"

The two ladies exchanged derogatory remarks, and in a matter of seconds there were three or four fights going on simultaneously, while Zachary stood there bare-chested in the middle of it all. Apple had ripped his shirt when she tried to pull him off of Eyonna, and now he looked like an animal out of control. He wanted to teach Eyonna a lesson. He picked her up by the neck, threw her against the wall, and punched her as hard as he could. Just as he went to hit her again, Apple jumped on his back, wrapping her arms around his neck and pulling him to the ground. Eyonna remained slumped over on her knees, leaning against the wall, gasping for air and vomiting convulsively. She tried shaking her head to collect her senses, but the world wouldn't stop spinning - everything was a blur of bright colors with no sound.

Then Zachary jumped to his feet, leaned over Apple, and hit her with an open hand. She was on her back, kicking wildly in an effort to protect herself, while he kicked back as if she were a stray dog with fleas. He then dashed back over to Eyonna with his fist balled up, ready to hit her again, but he was stopped short by rapid gunfire that cut through the crowd. *'Pop, Pop, Pop,'* Zachary ducked and took off in the opposite direction, screaming with his eyes wide open as he punched and kicked his way through the milling onlookers, and when he got to the other side of the street, he jumped into his car and sped off with screeching tires. He was now fearfully frisking his own body to make sure he wasn't wounded, as he wove through the Broadway traffic, cursing under his breath and vowing to get revenge.

The crowd of club-goers was still screaming with fear, as they panicked and trampled one another, storming off in all directions, leaving trails of shoes, pocketbooks and other personal belongings in their wake. The local hooligans took advantage of the mayhem, and started snatching jewelry or anything else they thought valuable, while most of the other club-goers ran off and didn't even bother to look back. The scene was horribly chaotic, and when everyone had stopped running and the street was mostly clear, there were several bodies lying on the ground in urgent need of medical attention. Some people tried calming the moans of the wounded until the ambulances arrived, while others went back to find lost love ones or possessions. The neighborhood residents watched the pandemonium from their windows, or came out to stand on their stoops for a better view. A few minutes later you could hear police cars and ambulances racing up the avenue.

Apple woke up lying in a pool of blood, whimpering Eyonna's name. She grabbed onto a car door handle, pulled herself to her feet, and looked around - but she didn't see her friend. She slowly staggered through the chaos until a young man rushed to help her, telling her that she was bleeding. He repeatedly asked her if she was okay, but she didn't respond. She just stood there in a daze with her mouth slightly opened, and her clothes drenched with blood. She was overwhelmed by the pandemonium, and didn't realize that she had been shot twice until she touched herself and felt a wave of pain. She started to black out, and the young man cradled her limp body until the ambulance arrived.

Chapter 26:

On the other side of town, Paul was sitting shotgun in his car along with two other men, waiting for Zachary to arrive. They were parked one block away from the address Eyonna had mentioned, beginning to doubt that he would ever show up. After waiting for more than thirty minutes, they decided to call off the hit until the next day, and headed uptown to drop Paul off. He was going to stay with Eyonna that night, and the men were on their way to Brooklyn to hide his car for him. They didn't bother to say much to one another until Paul was about to get out the car. He was worried about Eyonna, and couldn't understand why she wasn't answering his calls.

"Yo, Paul, you think you gon' be okay out here?" asked the man sitting in the backseat. "If you want some extra protection, I can chill."

"Nah, I'll be a'ight," Paul said confidently, "I'm cool."

"I could hang wit'chu at least until daybreak. That's only a few hours - it's not a problem."

Paul opened the car door and gave the offer a quick thought, then answered, "I'ma be a'ight, jus' beep me first thing in the mornin', a'ight?"

The man who'd been sitting in the backseat now stood by the car with a stony look on his face as he examined the neighborhood with a discerning eye. "It looks like dey sell a lotta work out here," he said, noting the drug dealers and the heavy traffic on the opposite side of the street.

"Yeah, those kids'ova there do," Paul replied. "Dey makin' good money on that corner."

"Yeah?"

"Yeah, man," Paul assured him. "Those young muthafuckas is clockin' G's."

"Yo, jus' be safe out here - shit look crazy."

"Nah, I'll be a'ight, this hood," Paul tapped his pockets two times to show the imprint of his pistol, "plus I got my thin' right here waitin' for a muthafucka to get stupid."

"Yeah cool," the man said, "but we gon' chill right here till you get in the buildin', a'ight?"

As Paul was walking across the street towards the girls' apartment, he noticed that all of their lights were out, and wondered why. He rang the intercom, but there was no answer. He then backed away from the door and looked up at the window again, hoping that he had checked out the wrong apartment. When he turned around to tell the guys that there was nobody home, they were talking to a lady who had walked up to the car like a ghost from out of nowhere, causing them to jump and reach for their pistols. She was well-groomed with pretty teeth, a dark brown complexion, and a short Afro-centric hair cut.

When she opened her mouth to speak, she smiled first and then spoke rather low and humbly, as if she was embarrassed to be outside in the wee hours of the morning. "Excuse me fellas," she softly said, "ya'll busy?"

The man who was standing outside the car asked her to repeat herself, and once he realized what she wanted, he gave her the cold shoulder. The lady then walked around to the driver's side of the car and asked the same question, speaking a little louder this time. By now Paul was walking back towards the car with his face frowned up, wondering what was going on. He assumed that the lady was soliciting sex for money, and he told her that they weren't interested.

"Yo, you buggin'," the man in the driver's seat playfully said. "I ain't had my dick sucked in a while. Let me throw that freak in the backseat an' hit her off real quick."

Paul rolled his eyes and yelled, "Stop playin' wit these nasty bitches out here, man. Shit is serious right now, word up!"

The lady put her hands on her hips and snapped, "I ain't no nasty bitch!" But Paul wasn't paying her any mind. He was still looking around wondering where Eyonna could be, and he simply told the woman to leave.

"Yo, I ain't got time to be playin' right now, lady, word up I don't."

The men could see that she was really getting on Paul's nerves, so they asked her to leave also, but she insisted on standing her ground.

Paul stormed around the car and yelled in the lady's face, "Yo, break out, bitch, befo' I smack the shit outta you."

The lady jumped and quickly complied. She turned around and walked off, animatedly switching her hips with a smirk on her face. Once she got a few feet away from the men, she stuck up her middle finger and erratically started shouting at them, "Ya'll betta not be here when I get back, you faggots. 'Cause I'ma get my man to kick your ass."

"Go to hell, stank-ass base-head," The man in the driver's seat yelled back at her.

Paul sternly looked at him and asked, "Why you playin' wit huh, man. We out here to take care of business, an' you playin' aroun'."

The lady went about her way, and the men were now getting into the car to leave, still trying to figure out where she'd come from.

Chapter 27:

All manner of thoughts were going through Eyonna's head as she jumped into a gypsy-cab to escape the mayhem. She slammed the door behind her, slid to the middle of the car, and covered her face with her hands. The leather seats in the cab were badly worn and smelled horribly of mustard and onions, but she didn't even care. Normally she would have jumped right out of the cab and caught another, but tonight it didn't matter. She just wanted to get as far away as possible from everyone she knew, because she was intent on killing herself. She still had the pistol in her hand, and after thinking about what she'd done to Apple, suicide seemed like a good idea. 'It was an accident...' she kept saying to herself, as the cab driver asked her repeatedly where she would like to go. He was a foreign man who spoke broken English, and that night, so did she. She was hysterical, and every word that came from her mouth was mispronounced.

The communication breach between the two escalated into a heated argument, until the driver didn't care what Eyonna's problem was. He just wanted her to get out of his cab, or else pay him first before he would drive her anywhere. Eyonna quickly calmed down and complied with his request.

Twenty minutes later the cab was a few blocks away from

the apartment, and Eyonna sat staring at the pistol in her lap. She picked it up and pointed it towards the back of the cabdrivers head. She pressed it against the fiberglass partition and held it there for a few seconds without him noticing. Then she turned it around and put the barrel into her mouth. She had her finger on the trigger, ready to end her life - and even if she had only been pretending, it wouldn't really have mattered. The cab was only one pothole jounce away from a disaster, and then that gun would have had another body on it. That's when Apple and Paul's faces began to flash through Eyonna's mind, along with everybody else who she loved or who loved her. That's when she slowly removed the pistol from her mouth, wiped it off with her shirt, and stuffed it into the torn seat. She got out of the cab and started running towards her building, when Paul spotted her from across the street. He jumped out of the car calling her name, and they met each other on the corner. He was about to ask her where she'd been, but when he saw how rough she looked, he just hugged her close. Eyonna buried her face in his chest, moaning Apple's name, and he automatically assumed that they had been fighting. Paul consoled her, and asked her what happened.

Eyonna stood there in a daze with tears streaming down her cheeks. She was slowly and shamefully shaking her head as she whimpered, "I shot her."

Paul's face frowned up. "Damn," he whispered, in shock and despair. His arm was still around her when he dropped his face into his hand. After a moment of quiet, he asked about the gun. Eyonna told him what she had done with it, and he assured her that everything would be okay. He wanted to find out more about what had happened, but he knew it wasn't safe to stand on that corner. He still had his arms around her as they walked towards her building, and he asked her if was Apple dead.

"I dunno Paul," she cried, "It wuz so many people out there tonight, I dunno what happened." She then slowed down and loudly cried out, "I wuzn't tryin' to hit her, Paul. You know that, right? That's my girl, man."

"I know," Paul whispered.

They were just about to enter the doorway of her building when Paul asked her to wait while he told the men it was okay for them to leave. He and his men were slapping five and making plans for the next day when the same lady they had argued with before returned, but this time she was not alone. She was accompanied by a small frail man, and the two of them stood a few feet away from them, cursing and pointing their fingers. Paul and his men were convinced that they had been drinking, or were simply crazy. He brushed off their remarks as he headed back towards the building, warning his men not to pay the couple any mind. However, curiosity and male bravado combined to make his men stand their ground.

Then like gray clouds gathering in the sky, the suspicious figures that Eyonna had seen snooping around earlier also returned. Eyonna screamed Paul's name as she madly ran towards him. Paul suddenly realized that something was going wrong, and his heart started pounding while his eyes grew wider. He quickly turned around and glanced at Eyonna, then looked back at the lady. He tried to reach for his pistol, but he didn't stand a chance, and neither did his men. The suspicious strangers had been lurking in the shadows, waiting for the right moment to strike. They ran up to Paul yelling obscenities, then stood just at arm's length from him and the car, firing shots with total abandon, leaving all of the men riddled with bullets, as shell casings and shards of glass flew everywhere.

The man in the driver's seat died with his seatbelt around his chest and his foot still on the accelerator, revving the engine. Thick black smoke mixed with the fumes from burning motor oil rushed from the exhaust pipes, making the hit-men's eyes water like clouds of teargas. They had come with a mission, and they weren't going to leave until it was accomplished. Paul's man in the front passenger seat only had time to put up his hands in a vain gesture of self-protection. The man sitting in the backseat was shot so many times that he dropped to his knees and died in that position, like a pious man in prayer. Paul had used his body as well as his affection as a shield to protect Eyonna, and she lay under his heavy corpse too afraid to scream or cry. The hit-men were gone, Paul's two men were dead, and so was he, with his hand still on his pistol.

Chapter 28:

n all five boroughs, black leaders were holding demonstrations calling for an end to the senseless killings. And when a meeting was held in front of the Harlem State Office Building, as if to make a mockery of the city's misfortunes, Zachary jumped into the crowd and started handing out flyers.

"This is what the white man wants us to do," he crowed, standing in the midst of the marchers. "Brothas an' Sistas, we don't have cocaine factories or gun factories in Harlem... now do we? My black people, we must come togetha as one, an' call for an end to this madness." That summer afternoon Zachary played his role so well that he even got a couple of signatures on the clipboard that he was waving around.

The authorities saw Paul's murder as just another sideshow. Another drug-related death. Another black-on-black crime and to demonstrate to the community how eager they were to find the killers, they would stage random police sweeps, promoting police brutality rather than law and order.

Eyonna sat in a small room at the police station early that morning, being questioned by an over-zealous detective who took pleasure in upsetting her as much as possible. He was a heavyset man with coffee on his breath and an army-style crew cut. His herringbone suit was tight over his shoulders, his tie pattern didn't match his suit, and he walked as if he had his shoes on the wrong feet.

"Someone really had a vendetta against your baby, Baby," he said sarcastically. He had even changed the tone of his voice to get under Eyonna's skin. "There was no money taken... so this wasn't a robbery," he continued. "Or else your boyfriend just had generous friends, because whoever smoked your homeboy, did it quick, so at least he didn't suffer."

The detective went on to tell Eyonna how the gunshot residue found at the crime scene showed that the perpetrators had taken this killing personally. "He must have really loved you," the officer sneered, "'cause it looks like he used his big body as a shield."

Eyonna sat there in a daze with tears streaming down her cheeks, working her way through a box of tissues. Most of the time she answered their questioning by shrugging her shoulders, and eventually her honest appearance and distressed behavior removed her from the possible suspects list. The only time she appeared agitated was when they asked her about her bruises, and she told them she had fallen. The case had no merit as far as the authorities were concerned, and since Apple's name never came up, Eyonna never volunteered it. The police detectives gave her their card, told her they'd stay in touch, and then let her go.

When Eyonna finally got home, she made herself a cup of raspberry tea, lay down across the couch, and cried on and off for about ten hours. Her whole world was in utter chaos. She felt that it was only a matter of time before the police would be knocking on her door to tell her that Apple was dead, and she would be charged with murder. There were so many messages on the answering machine that she thought about simply erasing them all. Most of the calls were from friends expressing their sympathy about Paul's murder. Some asked her if she needed anything, while others suggested that she get out of the city and take it easy - but no one had called about Apple, not even Chuck.

As always, there were various accounts of what actually happened the night Apple was shot. There were some on-lookers who claimed to have seen the whole thing. Some said it had been stick-up kids from Brooklyn, while others said it was just a jealous girlfriend. No one actually knew what had happened that night except Eyonna and Zachary, because Apple's mind had gone completely blank. There was a small bump on the top of her forehead, and since she couldn't remember much at all, the doctors diagnosed amnesia. They were counting on her regaining her memory eventually, but they couldn't say when. After all of the neurology test and x-rays had revealed no broken bones or life-threatening conditions, they assumed that she would make a full recovery. She was left with a couple of scratches on her face and a scar on the left side of her cheek, caused by the gunshots. There were also some bullet fragments that remained in her left shoulder, which made it difficult for her to move her fingers, but other than that, it seemed she would live.

It was around 5:00 a.m. when Eyonna was awakened by the phone, and as always she screened the call before answering. Ever since her fight with Zachary, listening to the answering machine had become a routine she would have to stick to until she left the city. This time it was Apple's voice that she heard over the speaker, as she lay motionless across the couch. In an odd way, she was afraid that if she moved she would be awakened from a dream, and it would all become suddenly true. But once she realized that this was Apple's voice in real time, she snatched up the receiver, crying tears of joy and sorrow at the same time. "Hello?" She pronounced the word like a question, her heart pounding and her hands trembling. Eyonna was so jumpy that she had to hold the phone with both hands so she wouldn't drop it. "Apple, is that you?"

"Hey… wassup," Apple sluggishly replied. Her voice was rough, as if she had just awakened from a deep sleep. She cleared her throat and asked once more, "Wassup, E?"

Eyonna didn't know what to say next. She was expecting to hear the worst, and all she could do was to tell Apple how happy she was to hear her voice, and how bad she felt about what had happened.

"Bad about what?" Apple cried, "I'm the one still laid up in this damn hospital. But what's worse than that Eyonna, is that I don't even rememba gettin' shot, or how in the hell I got here."

"So you gon' be a'ight, right?"

"Yeah, the doctors said I'ma be fine. I jus don't rememba shit."

"What'chu sayin', Apple, I don't unda'stand what'chu mean."

"I can't rememba nut'n," Apple repeated, and Eyonna could sense the muscles in her throat tightening with anxiety, causing her voice to crack. "I can rememba talkin' to you, Eyonna, an' I can rememba talkin' ta some dude. I'm not sure if it wuz a dream… but I think the dude's name wuz Peter, or sump'n like that." Apple was now sitting on the edge of the bed, rubbing her head and looking at the floor. She was trying as hard as she could to think back, and at the same time, hoping that Eyonna could give her some answers.

However, Eyonna was just as confused as Apple was, and on top of that, she didn't fully understand what Apple was saying. She had heard of people having amnesia before, but she'd never known anyone personally who'd had it - so she just kept asking Apple to repeat herself.

Apple stuttered and slowly intoned, "All I can rememba is talkin' to you, an' to some dude named Peter. The cops went through my bag an' found the house numba, an' once dey read it back to me, my memory started to come back a little, so I asked them to call you."

Eyonna sniffed, wiped her eyes and cleared her throat. "Apple, you don't rememba gettin' shot?"

"Nah."

"Do you rememba goin' down south?"

"Huh?"

Eyonna repeated her question. But Apple was confused, and instead of verbally responding, she shook her head to say no as if Eyonna could see her reaction through the telephone.

Loudly Eyonna asked once more, "Do you rememba that, Apple?"

Apple continued to shake her head, and softly said no.

"Neva mind," Eyonna comforted her. Then she loudly cleared her throat to make sure that she had Apple's undivided attention. "Apple, the guy you talkin' about, his name is Paul, not Peter... an' that wuz my boyfriend."

"Oh."

"You use'ta joke aroun wit'em, an' call'em Big Paul, rememba?"

Apple tried her hardest to think back. "Yeah," she slowly replied. She wasn't really sure of herself, but she agreed anyway so that Eyonna would continue, and hopefully something she said would help jar her memory. "He wuz ya boyfriend?" she continued, "What'chu mean wuz, what happened?"

Eyonna started crying again, and it took her a few seconds to reply. "He got killed last night. You don't rememba that eitha?

"Nah."

"That's why I'm so upset," Eyonna said, and by this time Apple was so confused that she didn't know what to say or do to console her. "It jus' seem like shit is goin' so crazy right now," she moaned.

"Damn," Apple whispered, "How'd he get killed?"

Eyonna collected herself, thought for a second, and said, "It wuz me, you, Paul an' ya boyfriend Zachary..."

"Zachary?" Apple asked loudly.

"Yeah, ya boyfriend Zachary," she repeated, "You don't rememba him?"

"No, not really."

"Damn," Eyonna whispered, "Yo' memory is that bad?"

Apple sucked her teeth in sheer frustration, "E, you jus' dunno how lost I feel right now. I been layin' here starin' at stuff, jus' hopin' I can rememba sump'n, so's I won't be walkin' aroun' here lookin' crazy like a damn base-head."

"Man, Apple, people wuz callin' here askin' for you, an' I ain't know what to tell'em, 'cause I ain't know what dey wuz talkin' 'bout."

"Yeah? Well all I know is I got this bangin' headache" Apple whimpered sadly.

"Apple, listen to me," Eyonna tried to focus her friend's attention, "It wuz the four of us, an' we had jus' came back from down south..."

"Down south...? What we go down there for...?"

"To hustle wit'cha boyfriend Zachary. All he eva talk about is makin' money, an' we wuz tryin' a new game."

"So we went all the way down south, jus'ta hustle. Damn, what kinda hustlin' did we do?"

"We went down there for some otha stuff too, but I don't wanna talk about it ova the phone..."

"Did we get paid?"

"Yeah, we did our thing."

"How long we stayed?"

"Like, two days."

"What state we go to?"

"Kentucky."

"Kentucky?" Apple moaned, "Man, E, I'm scared as hell right now! I don't rememba none'a that shit. But tell me some more about what happened, maybe it'll come back to me."

"We got paid," Eyonna boasted. She was now speaking with confidence, and every bit of grief she'd been holding in her body was momentarily released. "We wuz clockin' G's, Apple, an' those country-ass people ain't know what time it wuz."

"An' we only stayed two days? We should'a stayed longa if we wuz makin' money," Apple replied. She now had the phone wedged between her mouth and shoulder as she searched the room for her clothes. She found them on the chair, balled up and stuffed into a clear plastic bag with the hospital logo going across it. With her left shoulder bandaged, she did her best to slowly remove her belongings, and saw that they were soiled, stretched out of shape and ripped. Her shirt was stiff with a large patch of blood that had hardened and caused it to stick together. At any other time the sight of her own blood would have made Apple heave, but her stomach was still empty, so instead she only gasped. She let her shirt drop to the floor, and kicked it under the bed. Then she walked over to the sink to spit. "Damn," she whined, gently touching her face. She was looking into the mirror when she called Eyonna's name. "Damn, how'd I get all these scratches n'shit on my face?"

Eyonna continued to fabricate her story. "We got into it wit these bitches that wuz tryin' to play you."

"An' what happened, we wuz fightin'em?"

"Yeah, that's what I wuz gettin' ready to tell you. The four of us wuz jus' chillin' when these girls come to the club, right? An' dey started flirtin' wit'cho' man n'shit while you wuz standin' right there talkin' to'em."

"I wuz standin' right there?" Apple asked bitterly, "an' dey wuz tryin' to play us like that? Damn, bitches be gettin' bold dese days."

"Yeah, so listen. Me an' you stepped to them bitches, an' we fucked'em up!"

"Get out'?"

"Yeah, then dey left, but dey came back wit dese rowdy kids from Brooklyn, an' dey started shootin' n'shit…

"Is that how I got shot?"

"Yeah, that's when it happened." Then Eyonna cautiously asked Apple what had happened with the police.

"Them bastards don't give a damn about me. Dey jus' wanted to know if I saw the people doin' the shootin', cause dey don't want no guns on the streets. Dey jus' scared somebody might turn aroun' an' shoot dey ass."

"So what'chu tell'em."

"Man, E, I wuz so high offa all that damn medicine, I don't even rememba."

"Dey ain't mention Paul's name to you?"

"Nah, not to me dey didn't."

"So listen Apple, I'm on my way ova to the hospital to see you. Which one you at?"

"I'm in Harlem."

"Dey gon' let you leave, right?"

"If dey do or if dey don't, I dunno," Apple said defiantly, "I jus' know I'm gettin' outta' here, so you hurry up. Oh, an' bring me sump'n to wear outta this place, 'cause all my shit is messed up."

Eyonna arrived at the hospital in a matter of minutes, and when the doctor walked into the room and saw the girls gathering Apple's things, he insisted that Apple really should stay another day. But once he saw that she was determined to leave, he had no choice but to let her go. Just before the girls left the room, the doctor pulled Eyonna to the side and informed her of Apple's condition, and then they left. The girls briskly walked through the hospital corridors, stopped downstairs to pick up Apple's prescription, and then they hailed a cab. All the while, Apple appeared lost and nervous like a child in a big city. She was tightly holding on to Eyonna's arm, taking short steps and staring at everything with a confused look on her face. Apple didn't know it, but Eyonna was walking fast because she was afraid of being ambushed by Zachary. For all she knew, he had been hiding out at the hospital all the while, lying in wait for them.

Chapter 29:

The warm August weather had the neighborhood children swarming around an ice-cream wagon when Apple and Eyonna finally arrived home. The children's parents were sitting on the stoop keeping a watchful eye over them and talking, while other neighbors were huddled around a makeshift card table playing Spades. When Eyonna and Apple got out of the cab and headed towards the building, Eyonna quickly noticed the shady looks on her neighbors' faces. It irritated her to see the way they whispered without moving their lips. It was as if they wanted to ask her about the shooting, but they were too afraid. Apple didn't recognize anyone, and Eyonna was not in the talking mood, so they just breezed past everyone without speaking. Moreover, she felt that the only reason they smiled at her was to strike up an informational conversation, and in her opinion, that only proved how nosy they were.

As soon as the girls entered their apartment, Eyonna double-checked the locks on the door, then started pulling down the window shades. She was trying to create the perception that no one was home, but when she went to pull down the shades in the living room, the outside view grabbed her attention. With a heavy heart and teary eyes she sighed and thought, 'That's where those bastards murdered my baby,' and in the back of her mind she vowed revenge.

That dreadful night, numerous emergency units had been

called to the crime scene, but the homicide unit was the last to leave, and although Paul and the other victims had their faces covered, they stayed laid out on 8th Avenue for close to seven hours. In fact, the detectives were so adamant about nothing being touched that the man who died on his knees in a praying position remained that way throughout the entire night. Eventually the bodies were taken to the city morgue, and once they were gone, someone washed down the blood that had stained the sidewalks like the floor of a slaughterhouse. The only sign that remained of the carnage was a small stretch of the curb that was slightly cleaner than the rest, and that's what Eyonna was staring at. She softly whispered Paul's name, then wiped her tears away and pulled down the shade. She was on her way down the hallway when she noticed Apple still standing by the front door. "Apple, girl, what's wrong wit'chu - you waitin' to be invited in?"

Apple started fidgeting with her bag, and helplessly murmured, "I dunno."

"You don't recognize nothin'," Eyonna sighed.

Apple touched the bandages on her face, then shook her head and said, "No."

Eyonna slowly walked back down the hall, trying to comfort her friend by putting her arms around her and patting her on the back. Then she took her by the hand and showed her around as she had when she'd first moved in. The apartment was not that large, so it didn't take her long. Apple walked around touching the linen in the closet, the lamps on the tables, and even the mop that they kept in the bathroom.

"We like to hang the mop outside the window to let it dry," Eyonna explained, "'cause it stinks sometimes, plus it attracts roaches."

Apple listened to everything she was told, and then she went into her bedroom and continued exploring all the things that should have been so familiar, while Eyonna went to her own room to make some phone calls. Apple took a shower, and then she went and sat on Eyonna's bed to talk. Every now and then the phone would interrupt the girls' conversation, and Eyonna told her why she was letting the answering machine screen the calls. Whenever there was a call for Apple, Eyonna explained to her who was calling and how they had met, but Apple still didn't want to talk to anyone.

"What are you afraid of, Apple?" Eyonna asked.

"I jus' don't feel right," Apple explained. "How you think it feel talkin' to people an' you don't even rememba dey name n'shit."

"Well, you gotta start somewhere. You can't jus' turn your back on the world an' live in a box."

"I dunno, E. It's a crazy feelin'."

"You worried about those scratches on your face?"

"Nah," Apple replied as she lightly touched her scars, "Don't worry, I'll talk to everybody when I feel ready."

"Yeah, okay, wheneva you say - but what if Zachary calls. You don't wanna talk to him neitha?"

"I dunno, maybe."

And no sooner had she said that than the phone rang four times, as it was programmed to do before the answering machine came on. Chuck's voice crackled out of the speaker, and just as he was about to tell Apple how much he missed her, Eyonna snatched up the receiver. She rapidly untangled the cords and headed towards the doorway with the phone in her hand.

"Who's that?" Apple asked oddly as Eyonna skipped over her feet.

"Nobody," she quickly answered, "I'll be right back." Eyonna vigorously sped down the hall, telling Chuck to hold on until she was in the living room. Once she got there, she walked over to the living room window and peeped out of the curtains, then started telling Chuck her story.

"Damn," he cried with a sound like something breaking. At first it seemed as if he had hung up the phone, and Eyonna kept calling his name. When he finally answered her, he was in a furious rage. "That muthafucka," he harshly yelled, "When I see his ass, he's dead. He's dead, Eyonna. That muthafucka is dead! I'm in the city right now wit my motha, an' she keep tellin' me she been havin' bad dreams," he cried. "So I ain't got nothin' to live for anyhow, and when I see Zachary, it's ova. I'ma shoot'em right in his fuckin' face."

Eyonna tried to calm him down, but he continued to swear into the phone.

Just then Apple came to the living room and stood in the doorway, "Who you talkin' to, Eyonna?"

"Nobody," she replied flashing Apple a phony smile with her hand over the receiver.

"Everythin' a'ight?"

"Yeah, everythin' is cool, you can go back to my room and wait, I'll be right there."

Apple slowly headed down the hallway, and Eyonna continued talking into the phone.

"Where's Apple right now?" Chuck asked.

"She's in my room, waitin' for me to come back."

"Can I talk to her before I get outta here?"

"She's not gon' know who you are, Chuck, that's what I wuz tryin' to tell you."

"So Eyonna, tell me this. What am I s'posed ta do? I love Apple, you know that. That's my girl, man, an' I'll do anything for her."

"I believe you Chuck, but there's only one thing I can think of."

"Whateva it is, I'll do it," Chuck passionately cried, letting Eyonna know that there was nothing he wouldn't do to prove his love for Apple. He was still breathing heavily, and his chest heaved up and down. "Jus' tell me what it is," he begged once more. "I'll do whateva you say."

"Are you sure about that?" as she continued plotting.

Chuck sucked his teeth, "Eyonna, man I'd shut down this city for Apple if I had to. I been lovin' that girl wit no brakes, from the very first time our lips touched."

Eyonna went to sit on the couch and lowered her voice even

further, "Chuck, I don't think you know it, but Apple still act like she got a thing for

"E, are you tellin' me that even afta he shot her and killed Paul, she still in love wit dat bastard?"

"Yeah maybe, but you can't go out there actin' all buck-wild an' killin' him or nut'n like that, then you'd wind up wit yo' ass right in jail, an' Apple would hate you. An' I know you don't want that."

"I dunno what I want right now, Eyonna. What'chu tellin' me has my head spinnin' aroun' an'…"

"Chuck, listen to me," Eyonna calmly continued. "I wanna talk to you, in private. Tomorrow, a'ight? Then we'll have more time, 'cause right now it's not really cool. A'ight?"

"A'ight. Meet me at the dina' on 145th street."

"An' 7th?"

"Yeah, eight o'clock is good wit me. How 'bout you?"

"That's cool," Eyonna said. Then she flicked off the phone and went back to her room.

Apple was still sitting on the bed, and she innocently asked, "Who wuz that, E?"

"Um, it wuz Zachary. We were talkin' about what happened. He asked about you, and I told'em that you were fine. You want me to call'em back for you?"

"Nah."

"Cause I will if you want me to."

"That's a'ight."

"Okay," Eyonna said, then after a brief moment of silence she added, "Oh, an' he told me to tell you that he loves you, an' he can't wait to see you."

"See me when?"

"Tomorrow," Eyonna said as she smiled, "But only if that's cool wit you?"

"I dunno. Lemme think about it."

Chapter 30:

Chuck was sitting at the back of the diner drinking a glass of water, anxiously waiting for Eyonna to show up. The forecast had called for a bright clear day, with temperatures expected to reach the high 80's, but when she finally arrived, it was still cool and windy. "Damn," Chuck grunted under his breath when he first saw her bruises. He didn't say it loud enough for her to hear him, but his eyes said enough.

That morning Eyonna had on a yellow T-shirt and a pair of faded blue jeans that firmly covered her small athletic shape like a second skin. She wore a brown pair of sandals, and her baseball hat was pulled down tightly on her head, with her hair slightly covering her scar. Even though she wasn't dressed for the weather, she still looked neat and girlish.

"I look that bad?" she smiled as she reached to shake Chuck's hand, noting the grimace on his face.

"Zachary did that?" he asked with the anger returning to his eyes.

Eyonna continued to smile, "You ain't answer me, so I must look real bad."

"Nah, it's jus' the idea that he put his hands on you," Chuck placated her, then gently touched her face as if they were the best of friends, even though they had rarely talked before. "Who the fuck does he think he is?" Chuck asked, with a fire growing in his heart that only revenge could satisfy.

Eyonna shrugged her shoulders and pointed at her face, "Don't sweat this Chuck, this shit'll heal in no time, an' Zachary will get his."

Chuck was still agitated and jumpy, and Eyonna had to ask him to sit still and relax. They ordered some orange juice, and Chuck asked her about Apple.

"She's fine, Chuck. When I left the house she wuz still layin' down, which is crazy," Eyonna chuckled, "'cause you know Apple don't like to sleep."

"Like she gon' miss sump'n," they simultaneously said with a smile.

"Does she eva talk about me?" Chuck asked wistfully, leaning forward over the table.

"She doin' okay, Chuck. The doctor said she jus' needs time…"

"I loved that girl," he sharply interjected, and Eyonna jumped slightly. "Sorry," Chuck went on, "I ain't mean ta scare you like that - I jus neva expected all this bullshit ta happen."

"It's alright, Chuck. I know how you feel."

After Eyonna had gulped down her entire glass of orange juice she immediately ordered another, while Chuck was still waiting for an answer to his question. She took a napkin and wiped the corner of her mouth and said, "I'ma be straight wit you, Chuck, 'cause I like you. Plus I think you're the best thing for Apple. To answer yo' question - no she didn't ask about you." She looked him in his eyes and put her hand on his hand, "I wuz at the hospital when she first came around, an' the first thing she asked me wuz, where am I, an' the second thing wuz, where's you-know-who."

Chuck sat back in his chair and sucked his teeth, "Zachary?"

Eyonna slowly nodded her head to confirm his suspicion.

"But that's not to say that she don't care about you too, Chuck. An' jus' cause she asked about Zachary don't mean that she don't still love you."

Out of frustration Chuck bent down over the table and lightly hit his head on it three times. Then he looked up and said simply, "I wanna see her."

"I ain't got a problem wit that Chuck, but rememba what I told you. She ain't gon' know who you are. Her memory is shot all ta hell."

"She won't know me at all?"

"Nah, I'm sorry. So what I wuz thinkin' is, you should call her first, before you go aroun' there."

"I ain't got no problem wit that."

§

An hour after Eyonna had finished talking to Chuck, she walked into the apartment and greeted Apple, then sat down on the couch next to her. Eyonna tapped Apple's leg and asked, "How come you lookin' at the television an' it's not even turned on?"

Apple shrugged her shoulders, "I dunno."

"You jus' sittin' here lookin' at a blank TV screen?"

"Nah, I wuz gon' turn it on in a few minutes. I wuz listenin' to some of the messages on the answerin' machine, tryin' ta see if I can recognize anybody's voice."

"Well?"

"Oh, some of'em sound a little familia..."

"Cool," Eyonna said cheerfully. Then the phone started ringing, and her face frowned up. "I wonda' who that could be?"

The girls waited for the answer machine to switch on, and then they heard a man's voice leaving a message.

"What's up Apple?" the voice said, fumbling over the words. "It's me, Zachary, an', um, I wuz jus' callin' to say 'wassup' to the most beautiful girl in the world. I wanna tell her that I missed her so much." Then he cleared his throat and continued, "Apple, sweetheart, if you're listenin' to this message, I wish you'd pick up the phone an' talk to me." But Apple didn't. Instead she continued to sit there looking baffled, while Eyonna encouraged her to answer it by nudging her arm. After a brief moment of silence, he continued, "Baby, I wrote you a poem. It's a short one, 'cause I don't want the answerin' machine ta cut me off, okay? Anyway the poem goes like this… The Mayor of New York, should rename this city afta you Apple, an' call it, beautiful. Apple I guess the only reason that I never dream about you…is because I stay up all night just thinkin' about you." Then there was a moment of silence, and the faint sound of paper being folded. "That wuz the poem," he said bashfully. "I hope you liked it. Oh, baby, if you listenin', um… I wanna talk wit you. I wanna hear you voice. I wanna smell you, Apple baby. I wanna help nurse you back to health. So… if you get this message, please call me. I love you…Zachary…" and then he hung up.

The girls sat there quietly looking at the phone, and then Eyonna nudged Apple's arm again. "How come you didn't answer it?"

"I dunno."

"I'ma call'em back for you. Okay?"

"You think you so slick," Apple cautiously smiled, "That's where you went this mornin', huh? To meet'em. Didn't you."

"Nah, I went to the store."

"Yes you did, Eyonna. You went to see Zachary."

Eyonna finally confessed, saying, "'Cause Apple, that's all he talks about is you, so I promised him that I'd get you to talk to'em. Please… will you?"

"What if he starts talkin' an' askin' me stuff I don't rememba? I'ma feel stupid."

"Nah, that's the whole point of you talkin' to'em, so he can help you rememba stuff."

"I'm not sure, Eyonna."

"Apple, listen, there's been a lot of things goin' on in these last couple of days that needs to be straightened out. Plus ya'll got a nice big apartment waitin' fo' you down south, an' he's probably wonderin' wassup. When ya'll gon' have a chance to chill wit each otha?"

Apple sat silently for a moment. "Yeah, what kinda drama?"

"He can explain it all to you if you give'em the chance."

Apple sat on the couch giving Eyonna's words some thought. "Did you see the apartment?"

"How you think I know what it looks like. I told you, all four of us had jus' came back from down there."

"Oh."

"We wuz makin' plans for a big move real soon."

"Yeah... all of us?"

"Well, it wuz gonna be all four of us, until Paul got killed," Eyonna said with a somber look on her face.

"Fo' what, ta hustle?"

"Nah, we planned on movin' down there for good. To live, an' go ta school n'shit."

"Oh."

"So listen, I'ma freshen' up ya memory a little bit more an' tell you everythin' that you use'ta tell me, that way you won't feel so lost. Okay?"

"A'ight," Apple nodded.

Chapter 31:

New York City's murder rate was at an all-time high, with rashes of petty crime and unexplained fires that burned down tenement buildings. It was now late June, the weeds were in full bloom in the vacant lots, and Zachary had switched professions again. He had opened up a game room on 151st Street where he sold the morning paper along with buttered rolls and coffee. Then after hours, Zachary's Playhouse turned into a typical gambling hole. He charged thirty dollars at the door, and held a raffle drawing that stopped the music at 1 o'clock in the morning, followed by chicken and rib dinners. Every first and third Friday of the month he employed female dancers to entertain the regulars. It seemed as if every move he made was building him a stronger presence and influence in the neighborhood.

Apple and Eyonna had been in Kentucky for about a year. About a week after Paul was killed and Apple was shot, they'd decided to pick up and leave the city with nothing but the clothes on their backs and whatever they could cram into a rental car. Once they'd finally adjusted to the slower lifestyle down south and had made new friends, Eyonna had started dating again, and she was now seeing an enlisted man who she called simply by his last name - Rice.

It was a clear afternoon, and Eyonna was comfortably reclining in the passenger seat of Rice's car with her hands folded behind her head, as they toured the military base. Suddenly Eyonna called his name, and casually broached a new subject.

"Baby, I know it gets to be a hassle drivin' all those miles to my place, and then you jus' gotta turn aroun' an' drive right back."

"What… let me see…" Rice said, counting quickly in his head, "We've been seeing each other for about four months now…"

"Six months," Eyonna interjected, slightly annoyed.

"Oh yeah, sorry. We been seeing each other for six months now, and hell, Eyonna, I don't mind the ride. I'm used to it."

"Yeah I know, but wheneva I come down here ta see you, all we do is drive aroun' wastin' gas. An' I can't even chill wit'chu for the night, cause you livin' in the barracks."

"So what do you suggest?"

"Well, you know I don't like stayin' in no damn hotel. I don't trust those sheets!" Then she seductively rubbed his leg, "An' the way it is now, I can't relax like I want to." Rice's eyebrows rose up high on his forehead as she continued. "Baby, feel so good when we be makin' love, an' I jus' wanna let go an' get loud - but I can't, 'cause I don't be wantin' Apple to hear us."

"Well?" He prompted her again.

"Well, you should get'cha own place," she suggested, and before he could give her an answer she continued, "An' jus' think, when you come see me, an' your superior officers be pagin' you, then you don't have to get up an' drive back so late at night."

"I'd like to get a place, but I told you earlier Eyonna, there's a good chance I might get deployed soon."

"To where?"

"Germany. I'm really just waiting for my orders, plus you know how Uncle Sam pays us."

"No I don't know how he pays you," Eyonna snapped. She was acting snobbish because she knew Rice was fascinated by her New York feistiness, so she stood firm and remained cold.

"We only get paid on the 1st an' the 15th of each month," he modestly explained. Then he tried to change the subject by pointing out the various types of military tanks and helicopters they were passing, and the soldiers who were marching by in cadence - but Eyonna remained silent.

She had her arms folded across her chest, and she was reclining in her seat enjoying the scenery, though she gave no outward sign of her pleasure. She had never seen a place that looked so spotless before. There wasn't even a scrap of stray paper on the well-trimmed lawns, or a single weed touching the curb. There were no cracks in the sidewalks, or people hanging out on the corners. Everybody was busy doing something useful, such as trimming the trees, cleaning weapons or painting the barracks. There was no loud music blaring from the passing traffic, and the vehicles actually stopped at the stop signs, and never exceeded the 15-mph speed limit. She even saw black men who looked just like the men in her neighborhood respectfully saluting each other, and although she was really dying to know the purpose behind all their formal procedures, she continued to pout and pretend indifference.

Twenty minutes later she and Rice were cruising down the parkway, when suddenly he slowed down near some motels and turned into a trailer park.

Eyonna looked over at him and asked, "Where we goin'?"

"You said I needed a place, right?"

Eyonna sucked her teeth and sighed, "What, you gon' rent out a motel room?"

"Nah. You said I needed my own place, and this is all I can afford, Eyonna."

Her eyes grew wider as she turned on her brilliant smile. "These are nice," she said excitedly, sitting up in her seat to look out of the window, "And what are those?"

"Mobile homes," he answered.

"Whaaat? Dey don't look like it."

"They are, though. They still have the wheels on'em, but the people that own'em hooked'em up like houses, so you can't see the wheels."

"Yeah, I get it," she said with an astonished look on her face.

Rice parked his car, and the two of them stood beside it as he explained to her the options she could choose from. "Those over on that side are the ones they rent out to the soldiers."

Eyonna hinted, "I bet'chu gotta sign a long-ass lease, right?"

"Nah, you can sign a lease for jus' four months."

"Yeah, that's all? Why's that?"

"'Cause the soldiers are always getting sent to other posts on short notice."

"Ooooh, that makes sense."

The two of them walked into the management office, and forty-five minutes later Rice came out with a set of keys to the trailer at 808 Lutz Lane.

"These are for you," he said as he handed Eyonna the keys, and then he took her by the hand and they walked over to inspect the trailer.

Eyonna cut on the lights and smiled. "It's bigger inside these things than I first thought." She walked towards the back, running her hands along the thin plywood walls. Then she jumped up and touched the low ceiling.

Rice opened the refrigerator door, and the hideous odor made him jump back with a pained look on his face that made Eyonna laugh out loud. "Whoever was here before us sure was nasty," he cried, "It stinks like a dead dog in that damn thing!"

"It sure do," Eyonna laughed as she pinched her nose. "But look here, Rice. It's even got a back door," she said eagerly, opening it and looking out.

"Yeah I see," he said with less enthusiasm, glancing at the thick brush and high grass that made it nearly impossible to see the surrounding trailers. "I jus' don't like all those trees n'shit back there. I see enough of that shit when I get sent overseas."

The two of them went out the back of the trailer, carefully stepping down the rickety stairs, and began to tour the backyard.

Eyonna was being mischievous when she grabbed a couple of grapes and tossed a few at Rice. "These things don't look that sweet," she said, "but they will be soon, when the weather gets hotter." Then she took a few and put them in her pocket. "I'ma take some home wit me and put'em in a paper bag. That'll make'em ripen up quicker."

"Yeah I know," he said. "And look at the pear trees right here. Shit, if we ever get hungry, we don't even have to go grocery shopping," he playfully added.

"They don't look ripe, though."

Eyonna was a few feet ahead of him, bravely exploring beyond their new property through the thick brush, until she stumbled upon some railroad tracks. The bright sun made her squint her eyes and cover her face as she continued walking. "Rice, check this out," she called to him.

"Its railroad tracks," he calmly answered, "so what's the big deal? You thinkin' about tying me up an' letting the train run over me?"

"I jus' might," she smiled, "They still use these tracks?"

"Yeah, they use the trains to ship coal n'shit around to different parts of the state."

Together they crossed over the tracks and pushed on through some more bushes, discovering another community of small homes on the other side. After they had seen enough, they started heading back towards the trailer, and Rice was picking the twigs and leaves from her hair when he asked her what she thought of the trailer.

"It's cool," she said, "I felt like we jus' did some exploring into a new land all our own. I especially liked those houses. Dey wuz nice, huh?"

Rice smiled, "I thought you told me you were from Harlem?"

"I am," Eyonna blushed.

"Yeah? Are you sure? 'Cause you sure got a lotta country in you."

"Nah, that wuz cool," she replied with her eyes wide with excitement, "It felt like we wuz on a expedition. All you have to do is cut the grass an' watch out for the snakes. There'll be a lot of shade to chill out under on those steamy hot days." Then she hugged him and added, "An' maybe on those quiet nights we can go back there an' get it on in the high grass."

"Sssshit," Rice smiled, "not me. I don't want no ants trying to crawl up my butt."

Eyonna laughed and kissed him again, then they locked up the trailer and headed back toward the realty office to sign the lease.

Eyonna did most of the talking, about how nice the trailer was, and how it only lacked a women's touch, while Rice just held onto her hand and listened. He was happy to do her a favor and see her smile.

§

Chuck had graduated with a bachelor's degree in graphic arts, and now he was getting ready for the first print run of his new magazine. He had never realized how difficult it would be to get distributors to carry the magazines, so he went by the bookstores and the newsstands with his portfolio under his arm, and set up deals on consignment. That weekend he and the girls drove to New York and he dropped them off at their old apartment and then he went by his mother's place to pick up the magazines. After Chuck had stacked up a few magazines he set out to drop them off, and just as he was about to walk out of the door, Eyonna called.

"How's your motha doin'?" she asked.

"Mom's cool," he answered, "Thanks for askin'." Then he asked Eyonna if she had heard anything about Zachary.

"Nah, but me an' Apple goin' downtown in a little while to see some old friends, an' I know dey gon' have sump'n ta say."

"Eyonna, please be careful out there," he urged, realizing

that this was the girls' first time back in New York. He was worried about her being seen by Zachary or any of his associates. "Ya know how shit is," he added.

"Don't worry about us, Chuck. We gon' be a'ight."

"Okay," he cautiously acquiesced, and then he asked Eyonna about Apple.

"She gettin' dressed - ya wanna talk ta her?"

"Nah, that's a'ight. If she asks about me, jus' tell her I'll see her lata' on, a'ight?"

"A'ight Chuck. Oh yeah, I heard from Rice, an' like I told you before, everythin' is still good."

"Cool."

"He's still in Germany. I got a letta from'em the otha' day, sayin' everything is fine. Okay?"

"How long he gon' be ova there?"

Eyonna grinned noting the anxiousness in Chuck's voice, "At least six more months, man, so relax."

"Okay, cool." Then he called Eyonna's name with the voice of a concerned father, asking, "Apple's head ain't botherin' her, is it?"

"Nah, she's straight."

"E, please make sure she takes her medicine," he pleaded, "An' make sure she gets the word out."

"No doubt."

He then looked at his watch to make sure that he wasn't running late, and once he'd seen that he had ample time to talk, he sat the bag on the floor and took a seat. "Eyonna," he began, "of course you've known Zachary a lot longa than I have…"

"Uh huh."

"So how long you think it'll be before he tries to come down there?"

"Shit. As mad as he wuz at me for standin' up to him in front of everybody… I wouldn't be surprised if he showed up in Kentucky tomorra night."

Chuck sucked his teeth. "I don't even know how that should

make me feel right now."

Eyonna snickered, "Trust me, the minute Apple start runnin' her mouth aroun' them bitches, dey gon' run right back to Zachary's ass and tell'em everything.

"I hope you right."

"Listen to me," Eyonna said confidently, "Down south, you know that little motel right across da street from 808?"

"Yeah?"

"Well that's where Zachary's gonna have to check in at. He ain't got no choice." Eyonna stated emphatically. "Listen to me, man, I can give you five reasons."

"Yeah…what are they?"

"Okay, one: he won't be able to sleep in a car wit a bunch of sweaty-ass men unda that Kentucky sun. Two: Zachary is a neat freak. You seen how he dresses n'shit. He always worried 'bout how he looks. Three: he's gotta watch the trailer to see when we're goin' an' comin'. Four: he don't know his way aroun' Kentucky, so he's gonna feel more comfortable in that motel. An' five: he can't drive aroun' wit a bunch of guns in his car. He'll be too afraid of gettin' pulled ova."

"Yeah, that's true. You got a point."

Eyonna relaxed and added, "Zachary ain't the brightest man in the world. He's jus' muscles, and not much brain. So trust me, man. I know what I'm talkin' about."

"I am trustin' you, Eyonna, but'chu know what - you slipped up da otha day an' called me Chuck in front of Apple."

"Yeah, I know man, I'm sorry about that. I do be forgettin' shit sometimes, but…"

Chuck sternly cut her off, "That's what I'm sayin', Eyonna, we gotta be real careful."

"But Apple ain't even pick up on it."

"But still, we can't be takin' no chances. So E, please drill it into that girl's head before you get around your friends - Zachary, Zachary, Zachary. A'ight? Don't forget."

Eyonna smirked, "Listen, I hate that Zachary muthafucka twice as much as you do, an' if I had it my way, I'd tie his ass up to the back of a car and drag'em all the way down to the highway by his ankles."

Chuck was evidently worried, but he finally smiled. "E, you my girl, man. I dunno what I'd do wit'out you."

"No problem man."

"So we'll meet up around eight o'clock tonight so we can get back to Kentucky. Cool?"

"Cool man, talk to ya lata."

§

When Apple and Eyonna surprised their girlfriends by unexpectedly showing up around their old neighborhood, they were smothered with hugs and kisses. They had been greatly missed, and everybody was smiling and crying all at the same time.

Eyonna cheerfully cried, "Wassup Asia? Wassup Tamika? Wassup Nee Nee?"

"Apple an' E, wassup ya'll," Toni said with high spirits, "Look who jus' pops up outta the blue n'shit? Girl's, ya'll know ya'll ain't right!"

Once everybody finally settled down, they asked Eyonna and Apple why they'd suddenly moved away without telling anybody.

"'Cause girl, the city wuz makin' my nerves bad," Apple cried.

"Get out!" Toni smiled, fiddling with the large gold chain that she stylishly wore around her neck. "Girl, how come you gon' jus' up an' leave in the middle o' the night like that?" Then she stepped back with her hands on her hips and looked Eyonna and Apple up and down. "Ya'll know ya'll ain't right," she teased again.

Eyonna grinned, "I wanted ta go somewhere where it's nice

an' quiet."

"Yeah, I hear you," Asia smirked, "I got those pictures you sent."

"Oh yeah?" Eyonna asked, "How dey look ta you?"

"It's pretty down there," Asia said, "Ya'll got a nice big yard n'stuff. I know ya'll doin' good down there."

"Girl, that's a damn traila park," Eyonna said, "but it's all good."

"A traila park?" Nee Nee came from the back and loudly interjected, "Get outta here. That look like a big-ass house."

Eyonna proudly replied, "Yeah girl, dey be hookin' dem things up like houses n'shit. Dey have'em all furnished wit carpet, a dishwasha an' all that otha stuff."

"Yeah?"

"Yeah dey sure do," Eyonna assured her.

"Stop playin'," Asia said. Then she turned towards Apple. "How come you wuzn't in any of the pictures Eyonna sent?"

"What pictures?" Apple was barely following the conversation, but stood on the edge of the circle looking vague and a bit overwhelmed.

"Oh nut'n," Eyonna quickly said, "She jus' talkin' about some ol' pictures I took."

"Oh," Apple whispered.

"I been meanin' to write ya'll," Asia continued, "but I jus' ain't get aroun' to it yet."

Eyonna playfully rolled her eyes, "Yeah, okay."

"Nah, I'ma write," Asia said, "You watch an' see. Ya'll at that address on the envelope, right?"

"Yeah, that's it," Eyonna assured her, "808 Lutz Lane."

"What's that address again?" Toni asked.

"808 Lutz Lane," Eyonna answered, while Apple stood there with an odd look on her face. She was about to tell Eyonna that she had never heard that address before, but her intuition told her to hold fast and let her friend lead.

"808," Toni loudly repeated, "I'ma play that numba tomorrow, an' if I hit, I'm comin' down there to live wit y'all." All the girls laughed aloud while Apple still stood looking confused and feeling left out.

"That's the address," Eyonna assured her, "but we don't have the phone turned on right now, or else I'd give you the numba too."

The minute Eyonna said that, Apple knew she was lying - and although she didn't know why, she was glad that she'd kept her mouth shut.

Asia sucked her teeth. "How in the hell you been livin' in the woods for damn near a year wit no phone. You ain't scared down there?"

"Nah," Eyonna bravely answered, "An' those people down there is real strict. Dey do credit checks an' all that stuff, jus' to get a phone. Can you believe that shit? An' my credit is real fucked up, so you know dey wuzn't hearin' what I had to say."

"What?" Toni frowned, "Get outta here. Jus' for a phone?"

"Yeah, that's what I wuz sayin' when I first found out, but fuck it. I don't need a phone right now anyway. Nobody down there knows us an' we don't know them, an' that's how I wanna keep it."

Asia then turned around and smiled at Apple. "An' look at you, Apple. You still got that small waist wit a big ol' butt. I... am... mad... at... you!"

Apple laughed and did a silly dance to show off her shape. Then in a feisty way she smacked her butt and said, "Yeah girl, all I do down there is eat."

"Ssshit, my skinny ass can't gain no weight for shit. Hell, I need'ta be down south," Nee Nee smiled.

"So where you workin' at now?" Asia asked Apple, "I know ya'll ain't hustlin' down there in the country."

"Hell no!" Eyonna quickly interjected. "You know we saved a little money, so I'm in school right now, plus I'm seein' this dude that's in the army."

"Get outta here," Asia laughed, "As long as he salutes you

in the mornin' wit a good military stick, then it's all good." All the girls started laughing again.

"An' what about you, Miss Apple. What'chu been up to?"

Apple shook her head. "Like I said before, jus eatin'. I can't work right now anyway." Then she pulled down the collar of her shirt to show the scar on her shoulder and the one behind her ear.

"Oh yeah," Asia squirmed, "I forgot you got shot." Then she examined Apple's face and neck and said, "But'cha healed up real good though." Then she asked Apple if they had heard anything from the police lately.

"Nope," Eyonna answered.

"Girl, I don't even wanna think about it," Apple cried. "I get sharp pains in my head when I do."

"Get out!" Asia yelled with her eyes wide open.

"Yeah, right in the top of my head," Apple reiterated.

While all the girls' attention was focused on Apple, Eyonna pretended to spot another friend who she wanted to go speak to, and stepped away, leaving Apple to stand alone with the group of gossiping girls.

"If it wuzn't for Zachary helpin' me," Apple said, "I don't know what I'd do."

"Zachary who?" Asia quickly asked, and although there was a hint of animosity in her voice, she continued to smile. "The same Zachary that wuz out there when you got shot?"

"What otha Zachary you know?" Apple asked, "Cause I only know one."

Asia was bitterly jealous, but she kept her composure, "What that nigga doin' down south?"

All the girls were now looking at each other with puzzled faces, while Apple stood there wondering what she'd said that was so strange. Asia was still smiling, but all the girls could see that it was not genuine. She started fidgeting with her pager as if it were vibrating, but all she really wanted was an excuse to leave, and go find out what Apple was talking about.

Just then Eyonna returned to the small group of gossiping girls, and all of them appeared uneasy. "Why everybody lookin' so crazy?" she asked.

"Shit, I dunno," Apple said, "We wuz jus' talkin', an' I must'-ta said sump'n Asia ain't like."

"So what happened?" Eyonna asked, "Why she break out like that?"

"Don't know," Apple said, thoroughly confused. "She said she was gonna make a phone call."

"There's a phone booth right there. Why she ain't use that one?"

"Apple shrugged her shoulders, "I dunno."

The girls continued to stand with stunned faces until Eyonna broke the silence by smiling and starting to share old stories. Apple just watched silently, looking puzzled. Suddenly Eyonna glanced at her watch and told the girls that it was time for her and Apple to get on the road. They all hugged, cried and promise to stay in touch, and then Apple and Eyonna left.

Chapter 32:

Zachary had just gotten off the phone and had started sweeping the game room floor when his partner, Sam rushed in.

"Yeah Zach, wassup?" he greeted him anxiously.

Zachary never lifted his head to acknowledge him, but just continued sweeping, making sure that he touched every corner of the game room floor. "Hand me the dustpan," he calmly ordered. Once he'd finished sweeping underneath the pool table and behind the arcade games, he stood the broom in the corner and went to wash his hands. He dried them off, then pulled a stool away from the bar and placed it next to Sam. He took a seat, flicked a piece of lint off of his pants and snickered, "Guess what?"

Sam's face was vacant. It was as if nothing in the world mattered to him except what Zachary had to say. He slowly folded his arms across his chest, indirectly letting Zachary know that he had his full attention.

"We breakin' out tomorrow," Zachary continued, and Sam responded by cracking his knuckles. Zachary brushed his pants off again, "Check this out. Home-girl jus' left outta here a minute ago."

Sam frowned, "Who?"

Asia. An' she wuz buggin' out too. Breakin' glasses at the bar n'shit. She asked me why wuz I creepin' down south... an' at first I thought she wuz talkin' 'bout Philly. But nah, it turns out she wuz talkin' about *down south* down south."

Sam nodded his head, "Okay…?"

"An' guess who told her that?"

Sam shrugged his shoulders. "No idea."

Zachary sneered, "Apple." Sam stood there looking puzzled but intrigued. "You look like you thinkin' the same thing I'm thinkin'," Zachary added then.

There was a brief moment of silence while Sam collected his thoughts, and then his face lit up as he hissed, "Fuck she doin' back?"

Zachary smirked, "That's jus' what I wuz thinkin'. What the fuck is she up here for? But if you ask me, I think she came up here wit dat faggot man of hers. That school nigga that cheated me outta' my cheese."

"Huh?"

"Yeah, but bust it. Apple wuz tellin' Asia an' them that I live down south wit her."

"What? Why she say that?"

"Belligerent!" Zachary growled, "She's a no-good belliger-ent bitch." Then he placed the stool back under the bar. He slowly walked back over to his partner, and it was evident that he was upset when he smacked his hands together loudly. "Eyonna's the girl that tried to kill me. Rememba… out there at the club?"

"Yeah, I rememba… That's the night Apple got shot in the arm, right?"

"Yeah no doubt. You know Eyonna did that."

"No kiddin'. For real?"

"Yeah, that's the same night I sent my man to kill Paul."

"Word."

"But it's on now. You know, at one time Apple an' Asia wuz cool wit one another, right? But on the low, me an' her had this thing goin' on. An' I use'ta hit Asia off wit a little paypa, an' Apple wuzn't feelin' that. Now, I bet'chu she tryin' ta keep shit stirred up. Her an' Eyonna came back ta laugh in my face. They wanna let

everybody know they chillin' down south afta Apple convinced
Chuck ta take my money, an' Eyonna tried to kill me."

"Well, wassup?"

"I got dey address from Asia, and we gon' go to Kentucky
an' light his ass up. An' that dyke Eyonna too." Zachary's comment
caused Sam to snicker. "You know I'm tellin' the truth," he continued, "she act jus' like a butch."

"Well, whateva you wanna do, you know I'm down."

"Cool. So what we'll do is go ta Kentucky, get a map of the
area, an' learn our way around the hood. We'll case the crib, an' once
we get comfortable, we'll kill'em."

"Or we can follow'em aroun' an' wait to catch'em off guard."

"Nah," Zachary said, shaking his head. "At night. I wanna
catch'em at night. Everybody's got to sleep sometime."

"But all of'em might not be livin' togetha."

Zachary thought for a second. "Fuck that… we jus' gotta
take our chances."

§

After baiting the trap in New York, Chuck and the girls
headed back to Kentucky, and Eyonna devised a way to make herself a decoy for Zachary. She would drive her car to the trailer-park,
enter the trailer through the front door, and exit out the back. Then
she would cut through the bushes, cross the railroad tracks, and
come out in the other neighborhood. There Chuck would be waiting for her with his car running, and they'd leave for a while and
come back a few hours later.

The next afternoon, the sweet smell of Honeysuckle lingered in the air when Eyonna came through the bushes while Chuck
sat in his car other side of the railroad tracks waiting for her. He was
now driving off with both hands on the steering wheel and Eyonna

safely settled in the seat beside him, he asked her why it had taken her so long to get back from the trailer.

She cut her eyes at him. "I was gettin' you some grapes. Didn't you ask me to bring you some?"

"Yeah…" he said as he tossed a few in his mouth, "but I ain't want all of these. No wonda' it took you so long."

Eyonna frowned and called him nasty. "You ain't gon' wash'em off first?"

"Nah."

"Bugs n'shit be all ova' them things man. You gross, word up. I can tell yo' ass been in the country for a long time."

"So?" Chuck said peevishly, and then he asked her if it looked like anybody had been tampering with the locks on the doors or stepped in the flour.

"No," she mumbled. She was just as uptight as he was, and when he asked her again, he still couldn't understand what she was saying.

Chuck sucked his teeth, and asked if she had remembered to sprinkle flour behind the doorstep. In answer she simply lifted up her feet, showing that the soles were covered with white powder. Then Chuck hit the steering wheel with the palm of his hand, and said in sheer frustration, "I dunno wassup. We been back for a day an' a half now, an' no signs of that muthafucka. You sure that girl told'em?"

"Who, Asia?" Eyonna asked. She sucked her teeth and sneered, "Hell yeah she told'em. That triflin' bitch. You shoulda seen how she looked when Apple started runnin' her mouth."

"Well the way that you wuz talkin', I thought they'd've been here by now!"

She ignored him, and started fumbling with the cassette tapes. After she'd found the one that she was looking for, she popped it into the tape deck. Then she lay back and put her arm across her face. "Jus give'em some time. They'll show up."

Chuck took a deep breath and loudly exhaled, which sounded more like a roaring lion rather than a yawn. He was very nervous and frustrated, and he wanted to let Eyonna know that he was disappointed and losing confidence in her.

Suddenly Eyonna sat back up and noticed that most of the other cars were passing them. "Why you drivin' so slow?" She asked, annoyed and suspicious.

"I'm doin' the speed limit," he answered, glancing at the speedometer. "If I get a ticket, I gotta pay for it, not you."

Eyonna rolled her eyes, silently mocking him, "Well, we ain't got all day," she said sulkily.

"Eyonna, if these rednecks run this car through the system, we'll be fucked, and then we won't be able to take care of business."

Eyonna sucked her teeth and waved off his comment. "Whateva, man."

"We not in New York. If I get stopped it's gonna fuck up our timin', an' we won't be able to get aroun' without the car - that's whateva. So I'ma do the speed limit. A'ight?"

"Why you talkin' to me like that?" she screamed at him.

"'Cause, man, you actin' stupid."

"You know what Chuck, ever since me an' Apple came down to Kentucky, you been actin' real shady, you know that. If things ain't workin' out between you an' her, don't be takin' it out on me."

"Yo, jus' sit back an' relax, a'ight?"

"You know what, Chuck? I use'ta think you wuz a cool dude, but I've gotten to know you a little betta since me an' Apple been down here, an' I've noticed how fuckin' desperate you are.

"What?" Chuck was taken completely by surprise by the sudden attack.

"It's fuckin' pitiful. If you wuzn't listenin' to Apple in the first place, we wouldn't be goin' through all this bullshit, an' you know it."

"That shit happened a year ago. Why you bringin' it up now?"

"If you wuz a real man, you woulda killed Zachary a long

time ago, an' we wouldn't be doin' all this Secret Squirrel shit.
Pushin' through the bushes, n'shit."

"What the fuck are you talkin' about?"

"Puttin' flour on the floor, and talkin' in codes n'shit when
we 'round Apple. That shit is wack, word up it is. That's what I'm
talkin' about."

"That shit wuz your idea, Eyonna," Chuck yelled. "It wuz
your idea ta get Rice ta rent that traila, put flour on the floor ta show
who been in there, an' then get Zachary ta come down here afta us.
Not mine. So I don't know what the fuck you talkin' about... But I
know what'chu gettin' at. I know what'chu up to. You tryin' ta find
a way to blame me for Paul, that's what it is. You been mad at me
ever since he got killed. Don't think I ain't noticed."

Chuck had struck a nerve, and Eyonna yelled, "Paul is
dead!" Then she whispered, "God bless his soul. An' he ain't here ta
speak for hisself, so jus' keep his name out cho' mouth."

"But that's what it's about, isn't it - you wanna blame me for
Zachary killin' your man. But'chu know that Paul had a vendetta
against Zachary, for some shit that happened years ago. An' since
he knew I wuz gon' stop fuckin' wit Zachary, he asked me wuz it
okay if he picked up where I left off."

"Wait a minute," Eyonna yelled with her hand up in Chuck's
face. "Wait a damn minute." Chuck was trying to get a word in, but
she kept cutting him off. "Paul ain't have to ask you shit. Paul wuz
a man's man. Are you stupid or sump'n? Or maybe you think I am."

"He jus' got sloppy an' slipped up. An' now you wanna
blame me for what happened to him."

"You know what Chuck - you a asshole. That's what you
are. You could've stayed in New York an' took on Zachary like a
man, but you didn't. You chose to run down here an' hide. An' now
you got me an' Apple down here playin' cat an' mouse games n'shit
wit'chu."

"Eyonna, what the hell are you talkin' about?"

"If you wuz a real man, you would've took care of Zachary
before you even left New York, back when you first found out that

he wuz up to sump'n. An' besides that, how can you live your life wit a girl who's callin' you by anotha man's name. But what's even crazier, it's the name of the man that smacked your girl up an' tried ta set you up."

"It's called unconditional love, Eyonna. Sump'n you have no concept of."

"No, it's called stupidity, that's what it's called. As a matter of fact, let me outta this fuckin' car, and I'll take care of the shit myself. I know some real army niggas that'll help me take care of my own business. Pull this bitch ova right now."

Chuck immediately stopped the car and let her out as she'd asked. Then he went to talk to Apple.

§

The sun was beginning to set on the Bluegrass State, and Zachary and Sam had checked into the hotel just as Eyonna had said they would. They were traveling a few days behind Chuck, and soon as they got to Kentucky, they went to case the trailer. After they had seen enough they went back to the motel, and Zachary sat down on the edge of the bed to wipe off his pistol and count his bullets.

"So, what'chu think?" he asked Sam "You got any advice before we make this move?"

"It looks risky," Sam calmly answered as he peeped out of the motel window. Then he closed the curtains and turned around to face Zachary. "But then again… life is a risk. It's all about taking chances."

"True, but if I ain't think we could get away wit it, I wouldn't be makin' this trip." Then he shook his head in sheer frustration, and Sam asked him if everything was all right. "Yeah, everythin's cool," he sighed, "I'm jus' sittin' here thinkin' about the bullshit I gotta go through, that's all."

"Yeah?"

"I jus' don't like the fact that Chuck thought he wuz gon' play me like that," Zachary growled as he covered his face and rubbed his forehead. "Can you believe that shit? For a chick? For a chick? Man, listen, I don't care if it wuz a thousand dollas or ten thousand dollas. It's the principle. You seen how much money I done spent jus'ta get down here."

"You want'em bad, huh?"

"Man, I spent more money than a little bit just'ta get down here," Zachary said, rolling his eyes. "Bad is a weak word, man. I want'em more than bad. I showed that kid how ta make money. I showed'em where ta shop an' cop his gear when it's time ta get fresh." Zachary then stood up and smacked his hands together. "I took that fagot downtown an' introduced him to some real live niggas. I took'em clubbin'. Showed'em how Apple an' Eyonna be workin' wit me an' trickin' those cornballs downtown. I showed'em how I use'ta wait outside of the unemployment office an' get a white dude ta work wit the team..."

"Huh?"

Zachary explained, "I use'ta get white dudes and let'em win money at the Three Card Monte table. An' once all the spectators seen'em winnin', then they wanna try dey luck." Zachary then gave a brief description of how Eyonna and Apple would hustle the tourists. "Dey would be trickin' the vics an' makin'em bet all of dey paypa," he smiled.

"Word?"

"Word. I'd leave 42nd street wit a stupid knot. Then I'd hit the white dude off wit some money. Then me an' the girls would go clubbin' for the night."

"Word?"

"Word to my mutha," Zachary exclaimed, hitting his hands together again. "Apple masqueraded as a college student wit her schoolbooks under her arm. Her job wuz ta help charm an' divert the vic's attention while the white dude sidetracked any hecklers. She'd be in the mix, patting the vics on dey back, confusin'em, an' deviously suggestin' the wrong card."

"Word?"

"Yeah, an' Eyonna would be dressed like the corporate lawyer. She be sportin' her navy blue power suit wit her black pumps an' some little pearl earrings. Those long-ass fingernails of hers wuz her only giveaway. But she was good at convincin' those tourists ta bet as much money as possible," Zachary smiled. "When them chicks gave the impression of bein' average Joes, that convinced others ta join in an' try dey luck."

Sam was practically in Zachary's face, smiling as he listened to the adventurous story.

"I would shuffle the three cards around, briefly flashin' the red card an' tellin' the vic ta keep his eye on it, cause that wuz the money card. Right? Afta a brief shuffle, I'd place all three cards face down on the table. Then I'd give the vic time ta choose the card that he thought wuz the money card... which is the red card. Right?"

"Uh huh," Sam answered, nodding his head.

"'This game is simple,' the vic is thinkin' to himself, cause I'm movin' the cards real slow. So he's thinkin' he gon' go home wit some easy money! So he chooses a card, an' he points to it. So I ask the vic, 'Are you positive that's the money card?' Mos' times dey convinced, cause dey had dey eye set on the card all the time. Right? So then I'll say sump'n like... 'How much money do you have sir... because I need to know how to pay you.' Zachary was now speaking in a soft gentle tone, demonstrating to Sam how he'd play the timid role in an effort to convince the gambler to bet as much money as possible. "I gots verbal skills," he laughed. "So then I'd tell the vic, 'If you got a hundred dollas, then I'll match it.' Then I'd put my money on the table, an' some poor chump would go in dey wallet an' put dey money were dey mouth is."

"What Eyonna be doin'?"

"She'd be behind the vic yellin' out loud an' tellin' em how much money she got."

"Oh, okay."

"She'd be doin' that to help persuade the vic ta bet, cause she dressed all respectable n'shit, an' the vic is greedy. He don't want her to win the money before he do."

"Yeah?" Sam laughed.

"Word up. Then if the vic is still too scared ta bet, then the white dude would come from the back of the crowd an' pick up the money card, pretendin' ta be the lucky winna. I'd pay'em, an' the girls'd start clappin' an' pattin' the white dude on his back n'shit."

"You a funny dude, Zachary."

"Word, but check it. You know how most black people be thinkin'."

"Wat'chu mean?"

"You know, dey be thinkin' white people validate every-thing. The minute dey see a white dude wit a suit an' tie on, an' he winnin' sump'n... den dey wanna give it a try too. The think every-thang is on the up an' up." Zachary snickered, "So some sambo would take the bait an' step up to the table, every time."

"Word?"

"Man, da minute dey step up to the table... dey at my mercy then. An' me an' my team neva lost, an' I mean neva!"

"I wouldn't fall for that shit," Sam smiled. "You wouldn't beat me wit that bullshit."

"That's 'cause we from the hood," Zachary laughed, "We know betta!" He then extended his hand and the two men slapped five. "But tourists don't."

"How you be spottin'em?

"Who, the tourists?"

"Yeah."

"That's easy. We use'ta jus' stand on the corners an' watch whoever jaywalking."

"Huh?"

"Most native New Yorkers jaywalk, but tourist don't. So

we'd jus' chill on the corna, an' once they stopped for the light, then the team would start makin' noise, drawin' attention to the table."

"That shit is slick," Sam laughed.

"So check it. The spectators would be aroun' the table screamin' like it's a game show n'shit. Cars be honkin' dey horns, the cabs be racin' up an' down the street, an' the subway is rumblin' unda dey feet. And everybody think dey know the right card. But keep in mind, this game always seem easia from the spectator's viewpoint."

"Damn, that shit is crazy. I wuz wonderin' how ya'll use'ta do that shit."

"No doubt. Once the Vic is standin' front an' center, then the game takes on a whole new meaning. But if the Vic still seems skeptical, then I'll go through my routine again. I'll reshuffle the cards an' say sump'n like, 'This time I'ma do it nice and slow, so slow that Stevie Wonda' gonna be able ta guess it... but Ray Charles is gon' know.' Then I'll briefly flash the two black cards an' say, 'These two are the bread.' Then I'll flash the red card, an' say, 'This the honey... if you pick the red card... then you take home all'a the money.' I'd shuffle the cards in a gauntlet, then lay'em face down on the table. The vic puts his money on the table ta confirm his bet, an' then he confidently points to the card that he thinks is the money card. I'll tell'em ta turn it ova, an' when he does, he gets the shock of his life. 'Cause he thought he was gon' get that money."

"Word?"

"But it's the black card, and the victim has jus' been sprung. The white dude would be in the crowd ready ta yell, 'Heads up!' Then I would snatch up the money, and disappear in the crowd. Eyonna would kick ova the cardboard table an' jet - an' we'd jus' disappear... a hundred dollas richer... while the vic is left standin' there lookin' stupid. Now, you figure we'd do that about twenty or thirty times a day, that's like two G's, right?"

"Yeah, true."

"Me an' the team would break out and go our separate ways,

jus' in case we wuz bein' followed, an' then we'd meet up at that photo place on 42nd Street."

"You mean the one on 8th Ave.?"

"Yeah, where dey make those ID cards at. We'd regroup, an' before goin' back out we'd drop our money in a nearby mailbox, jus' in case we get snatched up."

"Yeah? How'd that work?"

"We'd write one of our addresses on the envelope."

"Ohhh."

Zachary smiled, "I moved those cards back and forth so smooth... I'd make you think you saw something you didn't. I wuz like a snake charmer, drawin' some sittin' duck right into the game... jus'ta be conned outta his cash. Red card you win, black card you lose... It all depends on the cards you choose!"

"Why you leave that shit alone?"

"Nah, runnin' guns make more money, an' the risk is less. Plus my gameroom is makin' money too."

"Yeah, true."

"But gettin' back to what we wuz talkin' about earlier... I had a feelin' Chuck wuz gon' do sump'n stupid, 'cause he wuz payin' too much attention to Apple. Plus he wuz busy listenin' to my uncle's preachin' ass."

Sam sighed, "Speakin' of your uncle. What he gon' do since his shop got burned down?"

"I dunno," Zachary cried, "Fuck'em. He needed ta retire anyway an' stop fuckin' up everybody's hair."

Sam chuckled.

"You know he pulled a gun on me not so long ago?" Zachary loudly protested.

"Word, for what?"

"I don't even know, man. I wuz jus' jokin' wit'em, an' he got serious all of a sudden. So fuck'em. I wish his ass wuz in the shop when I burnt that shit down."

"Damn, that's shit is crazy. Word up it is."

"But getting' back to what you wuz askin' me jus' a minute

ago... Do I want Chuck bad... Naaaaah. But I get a bad taste in my mouth when I mention his name, an' the only way to get rid of it is ta get rid of his ass. An' that stank-ass Eyonna too."

"True dat, true dat," Sam agreed. "But bust it. You seen how sloppy that traila wuz?"

"Yeah, I did. That's not like Eyonna an' Apple. Especially Eyonna - she's always been a neat freak."

"Yeah, but I'm sayin' that 'cause I'm thinkin' about sump'n."

Zachary glanced curiously at Sam. "What?"

Sam picked up one of his sneakers and held it up to show Zachary that the sole was covered with flour.

"Yeah, so, what'chu sayin'?"

"I think somebody tryin' ta set us up."

"What?"

"I think that's why all that flour wuz on the floor."

"Zachary frowned, "Huh?"

"They prob'ly knew we wuz comin' down here, so they put the flour down so we'd leave footprints, that way they'd know somebody wuz in the traila."

Zachary had suddenly stood up, and was thinking rapidly about what Sam had just said. He was biting his thumbnail and slowly pacing back and forth around the room. "That sneaky bastard," he grumbled, "That sneaky muthafucka!" Zachary sat back on the bed with his pistol still in his hand. "So what'chu think?"

Sam grabbed the map and they quickly went over their escape route again. Then he looked at Zachary and said, "What we should do is get some flour an' go back to the traila an' cover our tracks. That way they'll neva know what's goin' on."

"They might be layin' for us."

Sam looked at his watch. "It's still early. Plus, if dey ova there right now, then fuck it. We'll jus snatch'em up, throw'em in the car an' take'em somewhere else ta kill'em."

Zachary thought for a second, while a cold glare settled over his face. "Fuck it, let's go."

Chapter 33:

Apple was comfortably lying across the couch watching television when Eyonna came storming through the apartment. She went straight to her room, and when Apple spoke to her, she didn't reply. The only answer Apple received was the thump of a slamming door - and this puzzled her, since Eyonna usually didn't act that way. Apple automatically assumed the worst, and slowly sat up, allowing her toes to crawl into her slippers. She peeped down the dark hallway calling Eyonna's name, but there was still no answer.

The apartment was now quiet again except for the chatter of the television, which made it sound as if she had invited strangers over for dinner. As she headed down the hallway, her slippers scrunched over the floor like sandpaper, and just as she reached Eyonna's door, her friend came charging out.

Apple froze in her tracks, and Eyonna stopped like a speeding truck about to hit a deer. She glared at Apple, and then breezed right past her. "Chuck is a faggot man," she harshly yelled, while frantically smacking her hands together. "He's a punk man, word up he is."

Apple stood there with her face twisted up in a knot, and then she followed behind her friend. She turned on the living room lights and stood rubbing her eyes to help them adjust to the brightness, which made her feel as if she was looking at a solar eclipse. "Who's Chuck?" she asked, hopelessly lost. "Somebody you messin' wit?" Apple wanted to smile because she figured Eyonna was just having man trouble, but when Eyonna gave her a glare that could bend steel, she got serious.

Eyonna continued to frown. She rolled her eyes, and in the back of her mind she thought, 'Apple, you are such an airhead.' Then she sucked her teeth and said, "Chuck, Apple... The man's name is Chuck, not Zachary. You got me? The man you screwin's name is Chuck. Okay?"

Apple was still rubbing her eyes, but now she was using the bottom of her T-shirt. "What'chu talkin' about, Eyonna?" She was utterly bewildered by what her friend was saying.

Eyonna put both hands on her hips and looked Apple up and down. "How come you ain't gettin' dressed?"

"Gettin' dressed for what?"

"Chuck ain't call you? I know he did, so you can stop actin' all confused n'shit."

"What are you talkin' about, Eyonna? And who the hell is Chuck?"

Eyonna looked Apple in the eyes and yelled, "The man that you spend your nights wit. The man that you call Zachary ain't Zachary. His name is Chuck. Okay?"

"Huh?" This was beginning to be too much for her, and she had the frightened look of a lost little girl.

Eyonna pointed at the ground with her other hand still on her hip and said, "Apple, this whole last year that you an' me been living down here has been a lie." Then she slowly walked over to Apple, put her hand on her shoulder and softly whispered, "Zachary is not Zachary, Apple, his name is Chuck, and he had us both fooled." Apple's bottom lip was trembling, and the more Eyonna talked the more her head hurt. "The only reason I lied around Asia an' them is because they always braggin' about what they got, an' I ain't wanna feel left out. So I lied an' told them that traila was ours."

"I don't get what'chu sayin'..."

"Apple, sit right here," Eyonna said as she reached for Apple's hand. "I got sump'n to tell ya."

§

Zachary and Sam had gone to the trailer as they'd planned, and erased their footprints by sprinkling more flour on the floor. Now they were peeping through the curtains of the motel window, watching Chuck leave the trailer and get into his car.

Zachary whispered, "That muthafucka think he sooo slick. You seen what he did, right?"

"It looked like he was checkin' the ground for footprints," Sam answered.

"Word," Zachary agreed, "Who the fuck dey thought dey wuz foolin' wit that bullshit?" Then he laughed out loud, knowing that Chuck could not hear what he was saying. "We already been in the traila, Chucky baby. Your cover is blown."

"Word up," Sam snickered, and then the two men slapped five.

"But'chu know me," Zachary said like a villain from the pages of a comic strip. "I... don't... give... a... fuck. Let's go kill his ass right now!" He tapped Sam's shoulder and tucked his pistol in his waist as he rushed towards the door.

Sam quickly jumped up to stop him, whispering, "Man, don't be stupid, we ain't in New York. We can't just disappear in a crowed afta we shoot'em. You see all those nosey-ass people sittin' out there?" Zachary thought a minute, then looked out the window again and saw the park residents relaxing in their folding chairs and calmly barbecuing, while their children played freeze-tag and wrestled in the high grass. He turned around and looked at Sam, and Sam smiled. "When you ever seen white people drinkin' Kool Aid?"

"So what, fuck that!"

"Zach, don't be stupid. Man, this place ain't seen no excitement in eons... They'd love for some shit to jump off so dey could see dey self on the news tonight."

Zachary's face was flushed with anger. He glared at his partner, and asked if he was having second thoughts. "I hope you ain't bitchin' out on me now?" he challenged him.

"You stupid? No I ain't frontin' on you, man. You know how I gets down… But we gotta be smart in this hick town. You'll fuck aroun' an' get us both hung." Zachary looked oddly at Sam, who continued with a sly tone, "Now, I don't mind dyin', but I don't want it to be at the hands of no redneck."

Zachary took heed of Sam's words, and suddenly relaxed and listened. "So, what's up?"

"Since we erased our footprints, Chuck is gon' go back an' tell Eyonna that we ain't showed up yet."

"True, I get what'chu sayin'. So we'll jus' chill for a few minutes."

"Right. 'Cause she gotta come back ta get her car."

"You right, you right, man." Zachary then took out his pistol and toyed with it for a few seconds. "Bet it won't be long before the sun's gone down and we gon' go across that highway an' get his ass."

"No doubt."

§

Chuck's heart was throbbing as he got into his car and sped up the highway. He arrived at the girls' place in a matter of minutes, and urgently knocked on the door. When no one answered, he ran back outside to look up at their window, and putting his hands up to his mouth to help his voice travel, he started calling out their names. He waited a few seconds for a response, and when there was none, he ran back inside and put his ear to the door. He was hoping he would hear the television playing, or anything that would indicate that the girls were home. He started knocking again, and a few seconds later he was relieved to hear footsteps coming towards the door.

"Yeah, who is it?" a soft voice firmly demanded.

"Apple, it's me Zachary," he anxiously panted, "Baby, open the door."

Chuck's voice was like a knife piercing through Apple's heart. She kicked the door hard and told him to go away.

"But Apple baby, I got sump'n to tell you, and it's real important!"

"Go… a… way," she sobbed, and Chuck could hear the pain in her voice.

"Apple, come on, baby" he exclaimed, "You gotta let me in."

Chuck continued to beg until she eventually began to unlock the door, but instead of inviting him in, she cracked it just enough for him to see her eyes. He tried to walk in as he normally would, but she stopped him. "Yeah, what. What'chu want?"

Chuck noticed that her eyes were red and puffy as if she had been crying. He frowned, with a thin line of sweat trickling down the side of his cheek. "Apple, wassup?" he panted, "It's me baby. Ain't you gon' let me in?"

"Why?" she sobbed, "Why should I let you in?"

Chuck snatched off his baseball hat to wipe the sweat from his forehead. He took a deep breath and swallowed, "Apple, I love you, an' I need ta talk to you."

Apple looked him up and down, and then she tried to shut the door - but he used his foot to stop her. "Eyonna ain't here, so move yo' damn foot before I break it."

"Baby, what's the matta wit'chu?"

"Baby my ass," she yelled, "You been lying to me man, so move yo' damn foot so I can close this door."

"Apple, I don't know what Eyonna told you, but I can explain everything if you jus' let me in."

"No, no, no!" she yelled, "An" I told you to move ya feet two times already." She then slammed the door on his foot, and he screamed aloud in pain, falling against the wall and then onto the hallway carpet. He removed his shoe to massage his toes, and after he'd recovered slightly, he limped right back to the door. He stood as close as he could to it, and continued to beg Apple to talk to him. "Apple... I need'ta know where Eyonna is. It's real important. I got sump'n ta tell her."

"She left, so you get away from the door before I call the cops."

"She ain't tell you where she wuz goin'?"

"Go away."

"Listen, I know Eyonna prob'ly told you some crazy shit, but I can explain it all if you'd jus' gimme a chance. But I also need ta know where she went. It's very important."

"She jus' left!"

"Wit who?"

"I... don't... know!"

"Apple, I know I lied to you in the beginning, but it wuz the best thing for us, believe me..." he pleaded. When he called her baby again in a wheedling tone, she stopped him short.

"Don'chu call me baby. I ain't cha damn baby."

"Apple, it wuz the best thing for us. That's why Eyonna moved down here too. Did she tell you that? She didn't, right? I ain't think so."

Apple didn't answer him.

"Apple listen, I wuz so caught up in impressin' you that I did some dumb things, and it almost cost us our lives. And I'm payin' for it, Apple. I'm payin' for it, an' it's hurtin' me too."

"Would you please leave? The neighbors gon' think you crazy."

"I don't give a shit. I am crazy about you Apple... The light of day don't mean a thing to me, if I can't share it with you. Nothing matters to me. I'll live my life in total darkness if I can't share the sun with you!" He stopped talking to catch his breath, and the hallway grew quiet. Apple then softly said something that he didn't hear, and he asked her to repeat herself.

"You heard me," she boldly shouted this time as she swung

the door open. "You ain't think I wuz gon' find out, huh? You ain't think I wuz gon' find out that you wuz tryin' to get wit Eyonna?"

Chuck was about to answer her, but the sound of a police radio in the street outside diverted his attention. He shoved Apple into the apartment and told her to keep quiet.

She was still standing by the door with her hands on her hips, staring at him. "Somebody called the police on your ass, 'cause you in the hallway actin' like you done lost your damn mind," she said accusingly.

Chuck put his index finger up to his lips, signaling for her to keep quiet. He tiptoed over to the television and turned up the volume, and then they walked together into her room.

"What'chu talkin' about?" he frowned, "Where you get that shit from?"

"Wassup wit'chu rentin' a traila for Eyonna?"

Chuck's mouth hit the floor. "Apple, what the hell you talkin' about. "I ain't rent no traila for nobody."

"Yeah? Well your punk ass is busted!"

"Apple I know you don't believe that shit... Eyonna is crazy, man."

"Why'd she say what she said then?"

"I don't know!" Chuck yelled as a deep silence fell between them.

§

Eyonna was so upset with Chuck that night that she showed no concern for the plan they had previously laid. She was sitting in the passenger's seat of a friend's car, not saying much of anything, until she suddenly asked the girl to pull over.

"I thought you were going to 808?" the girl asked.

"I am," she whispered, and then she told the girl to turn off the headlights.

"But this mail box sez 708," the girl said anxiously.

"Yeah, I know. I'ma walk from here."

"Girl, are you crazy? It's dark as hell out here, plus this is hillbilly territory. Let me drive you up there."

"Nah, that's a'ight. I'ma jus' get my hoopty, and then you can follow me back up the highway."

"Okay, try to hurry up."

"I'ma be right back," Eyonna assured her. She was looking over her shoulder with a wary eye as she approached her car, even though there were no footprints around it - she was still not taking any chances. As a precaution she kept her pistol by her side. Then just as she went to unlock the car door, she felt a sharp crack on her wrist. She wanted to scream, but Zachary had already wrapped his skinny fingers around her mouth. He had used a nightstick to hit her so hard that it tingled from her fingernails to the ball of her shoulder. She tried fighting back, but to no avail. Sam had picked up her pistol, grabbed her by her feet and locked her ankles under his armpit. In a matter of seconds they had Eyonna sitting on the trailer floor, franticly crying, with her hands tied behind her back and a torn T-shirt tightly wrapped around her mouth.

Zachary was a scoundrel - an evil spirit that came alive in her nightmares - and all she could do now was hope that her prayers would be answered.

"Yonna Yonna Yonna…we finally meet again," Zachary sneered. "I know you ain't think you wuz getting away wit dat stunt you pulled. I'm in your fuckin' neck of the woods now, and ain't shit you can do." Eyonna tried to kick him, but he just laughed. "Eyonna, you need ta be nice and tell me who brought you here… Was it Chuck?"

Eyonna ignored his question, letting her eyes drop to the floor, so he lifted her head back up with the cold tip of his pistol. He let the gun rest under her chin for a moment, with an evil smirk on his face. "I see you like playin' games," he snarled. He glanced at Sam shaking his head in mock shame, and Sam just shrugged his shoulders.

"Don't be too hard on her," Sam said, "She's jus' a girl."

"What, you some kinda humanitarian now?"

"Nah, but I'm sayin' we came down here to take care of business an' then step. I'm not into torturin' no women."

Zachary snickered, "Pope, just chill. A'ight? Don't start gettin' too fuckin' holy on me, n'shit."

§

Eyonna's friend was still sitting in her car waiting for her to return, and when she glanced at her watch she realized that Eyonna had been gone for more than ten minutes. She turned on the car's headlights for a better view of the dark street, but all she could see was a bunch of trees and a couple of trailers. She was confused, and she felt terribly vulnerable. After sitting still for a few seconds more, she decided to cruise towards the trailer. She stared at it for a moment, and saw that it appeared abandoned. There were no lights on inside, and the paint was badly worn due to the rough winter. The grass around the concrete foundation was high, and the trees were in dire need of pruning. When the girl flashed her high beams towards the trailer, all she could see was the glowing eyes of a stray cat that stood still for a moment and then dashed into the darkness. She honked her horn a few times, but there was no answer, so she anxiously sped off.

Once the car was gone, Zachary squatted next to Eyonna as if he were talking to a small child. He toyed with his tongue, whisking it along his lips, and then he sat his pistol on the ground, not too far from where she was sitting. He knew she would want to reach for it, and he also knew that she could not. He put his index finger in her face and said, "Now, I'm gon' ask you one more time, an' if you don't answer me… you gon' have some problems." Eyonna was panting heavily, and the T-shirt that was wrapped around her mouth was soaked with her saliva. "Who brought you here, was it Apple, or that ho-mo Chuck?"

Eyonna responded by kicking and squirming as if that

would help to ease her predicament, but it only made matters worse - and this gave Zachary a feeling of power over her.

"I'll remove this shirt from your mouth, if you promise ta calm down, Eyonna. I mean, I don't wanna hurt'chu. I just wanna know where Apple is, and that ho-mo boyfriend of hers. If I remove this shirt, will ya tell me?" Eyonna responded by kicking out again, and he just laughed. "Yonna, Yonna, Yonna. It don't look like you're sayin' yes ta me. You see, Eyonna, that's what your problem is. You always playin' tough. You always wuz the strong-minded one. The powerful black sista that ain't take no shorts. Well, that shit ain't gon' help you here tonight. Not in Kentucky it ain't."

Eyonna had made eye contact with Sam twice, and she could see that he was showing some concern for the way she was being treated. Therefore, whenever Zachary threatened her with bodily harm, she would cry a little harder. It had gotten to the point where she was lying stretched out on the dingy carpet, rolling her head back and forth with her eyes in the back of her head.

Sam went to check on her, but Zachary snatched him back. "What the fuck you doin'?"

"I'm sayin', that's a lady," Sam answered. "If you gon' kill her, then do it. But like I said before, I ain't down wit torturing no women."

Zachary snatched his pistol from the floor and jumped to his feet. "What the fuck you doin'? Don't go gettin' stupid on me the minute you get to Kentucky," he yelled. The two men were standing chest to chest, as Eyonna lay stretched out on the floor at their feet.

Sam sneered, "I thought we came down here to take care of business. I ain't come down here fo' this shit!"

Zachary appeared embarrassed. He shamefully dropped his head into his hand and then he took a deep breath. Then he exhaled and said, "I'm sorry - you right. I must be losing my fuckin' mind. This shit got me stressed out down here." He then extended his hand to shake Sam's hand.

The two men shook hands, and then Zachary pulled him closer to his body, and fired a single shot into Sam's stomach. The dying man awkwardly grabbed Zachary by his waist, and then slowly slid down his legs. His eyes and mouth were wide open as he clung onto Zachary's front pockets, almost pulling him to the floor. Zachary snatched away, and Sam dropped to his knees.

Zachary sneered, "Dumb ass."

Sam was clutching the wound, and Eyonna took advantage of the distraction to make a run for it. She pushed the door open with her shoulder and dashed down the stairs, and though Zachary tried to grab her, she was too fast for him. He glanced at Sam, who was bleeding profusely on the ground, and then he looked toward the open door. He was about to shoot Sam again to make sure that he was dead, but he didn't want Eyonna to get away - so he took off after her instead.

§

Apple was hysterically crying as she and Chuck raced back to the trailer-park, praying that they'd find Eyonna alive and well. Apple was practically pulling her hair out, and Chuck kept trying to assure her that everything would turn out well.

"I jus' can't believe that ya'll would be doin' all this crazy shit," she sobbed.

Chuck sighed, "It wuz to protect you Apple, that's all."

"And what makes you so sure that Zachary is down here?"

"'Cause, like I told you before, me and her had a argument, and I felt I couldn't trust her. So I came back down here and I threw some grapes on the ground in front of the trailer door, an' I hid some underneath the doormat."

"So what? Why you do that?"

"So when I came down here to check on the traila, the flour wuz still smooth n'shit, but the grapes wuz all smashed up."

"So, maybe the mailman smashed'em."

"The mailbox is on the curb, Apple."

"Oh."

"He don't have no reason to come up to the front door. Plus he delivers the mail early in the mornin', anyway."

Apple sucked her teeth and dropped her head back into her hand.

"So now what? You think you can talk to'em and he'll jus' let Eyonna go?" Chuck asked.

"My head is so fucked up right now, Chuck. An' I told you what I thought about all this before we even came down here."

"What, we should call the cops?"

"Yeah!"

"Nah, fuck that. If we call the cops, then Zachary might mention my name... an' I don't want that. They'll fuck aroun' an' maybe connect me to Tone's murder, n'shit."

"So what, you didn't actually kill'em."

"Nah, you crazy. Then the A.T.F. is gon' get involved."

Apple rolled her eyes and slapped her thighs.

"Listen, if you can jus' persuade him to let her go, then we'll be jus' fine. A'ight?" Chuck was grasping at straws.

"Chuck, if Zachary came down here from New York, ain't no persuading him. We should jus' call the cops an' get this shit ova wit."

§

They were now nearing number 808, and Chuck quickly drove past it when he saw that there were no lights on. "Dey in there! Dey in there!" he excitedly whispered, "Dey in there, Apple. I always make sure ta leave the lights on!"

"Yeah I see, I see. It's darka then a muthafucka in there too. But I don't care. I jus' wanna get her outta there."

"So, what'chu wanna do."

"I don't know."

"We gotta do sump'n 'fore dey kill her."

Eyonna and Apple were the best of friends, and Chuck knew it. He knew that Apple would never forgive him if he turned his back on her and kept going. He could never look Apple in her eyes and tell her that he loved her if he didn't at least try to save her friend.

In a flash Chuck heard Mr. Ray's voice in his head. He remembered the long talks they'd had about thinking big and not ending up in jail. Then his mother's face flashed across his mind, and the dreadful dream she'd told him about. And last but not least he thought about the necklace his dad had given him, and the promises that he had made to him. That's when he said, "Fuck it!" He made a sharp U-turn and sped back down the dark street towards 808 - and as soon as he got near it, Eyonna came running toward the car from out of nowhere. Chuck smashed on the brakes, the back tires screamed, and Apple had to put her hands on the dashboard so her face wouldn't hit the windshield. Eyonna was so scared that she ran right past the car. Zachary was on her heels, and when Apple spotted them she jumped out of the car screaming her friend's name.

Meanwhile back at number 808, Sam was struggling to stay alive, and although he was rapidly loosing blood, he was still able to make it to his feet. Sam was weak and his pistol felt like a 50-pound dumbbell in his frail hand, but he didn't care. The little bit of life that remained in his body was reserved for killing Zachary, and this was evident as he floundered down the rickety stairs. Blood trickled from Sam's nose until his white T-shirt was half red, and when he spotted Zachary he staggered towards him.

When Chuck caught sight of the wounded man, he feverishly started screaming Apple's name. He reached under his seat for his pistol, but when he raised his head to open the car door, bullets had already started flying. Off in the distance, approaching police cars looked like disco lights racing down the highway, and when the gunshots finally stopped, Sam was dead.

Chuck fired his last bullet at Zachary as he chased him

through the high grass, but when he saw Apple lying helplessly on the ground, he dropped his pistol and stopped dead in his tracks. Chuck stood and stared at Apple as Zachary made his way across the highway back to the motel, jumped into his car and drove off.

The evening dew had soaked through Apple's clothes, and strings of dead grass clung to her small body. At first Chuck didn't even know if she was dead or alive - but just the sight of her stretched out like that on the ground was enough to make his legs weak. He stopped a few feet from where she was lying, dropped to his knees, and started crying. He banged his fists on the ground, wildly screaming, "No! No Apple, Nooo! I didn't want this, Apple... God, NOOOOO!"

Eyonna rushed to Apple's aid. She kneeled down beside her, and put her ear as close as she could to Apple's mouth to hear what she was saying, but all she could hear was Apple's desperate panting. Neighbors peeped from their windows as additional police cars raced to the scene, and a helicopter hovered above them with a spotlight so bright that it made the trailer-park look like a stadium during a night game.

Chuck crawled over to the girls and stood above them whimpering Apple's name. When Apple took her final breath, her eyes rolled to the back of her head and her mouth dropped open, and Eyonna started screaming.

Chuck bitterly snatched Eyonna away and sat down next to Apple in the wet grass. He pulled her lifeless body across his thighs, then swung her arm around his neck as if she were embracing him. Their chests were pressed together, her head dangled over his forearm, and he rocked her back and forth, hoping to coax life back into her body. "Baby wake up, we gotta go home," he softly whispered. "We gotta get outta here."

He would have stayed out there the entire night, gently brushing the hair away from her face, but once the police had enough backup they called out to him, demanding that he put his hands up were they could be seen. Chuck ignored the officers, and they continued to shout at him. The policemen were well trained, but they were also scared, and they didn't to misjudge a crazed man who seemed capable of almost anything. The scene was now chaotic, with medical units and a couple of news vans stationed behind the police blockades.

Twenty or more officers had their pistols aimed at Chuck's head, with their elbows locked and their fingers on the triggers.

"DROP YOUR GUN," an officer demanded. He spoke with a southern accent, and it was obvious that he wanted to go home alive that night. "PUT YOUR HANDS WHERE WE CAN SEE THEM!" He insisted again.

"MISTER, DO NOT MOVE," another officer added, "DROP YOUR GUN AND MOVE AWAY!"

Chuck paid the police no mind. He closed Apple's eyelids, and then he wiped the tears from the corners of her eyes. "My baby is gone," he whispered. He kissed her forehead again, then slowly laid her head onto the wet grass. He clumsily got to his feet, and the wind from the helicopter blades made him look intoxicated. He wiped his own eyes, then snatched his pager from his waist, and pointing it towards the policemen, and he ran directly at them.

Chapter 34:

A tall, dark bottle of vintage scotch sat on Mr. Allen's counter. He had received it as a housewarming gift when he and Mr. Ray moved into the new barbershop and he vowed not to open it until his next birthday, which was three weeks away. The joke going around the barbershop that Saturday afternoon was a bet that one of the customers had made with him as soon as he noticed the bottle. The customer was a sharp, quick-witted senior citizen who had more hair on his face than on his head. When he went to sit in Mr. Allen's chair, he started joking with him.

Mr. Allen snatched up the large bottle, tapped the bottom of it and playfully said, "Stop lookin' at my scotch, and no you can't have none."

"Hell, I don't drink no more," the customer answered, "You heard what I said jus' a minute ago. You ain't gon' let it sit there for long. I guarantee you that bottle won't be here next week when I come in here."

The shop full of patrons looked on and laughed as the two men traded lighthearted humor back and forth. Once they shook hands confirming their bet, the laugher faded.

Everyone was making small talk when another customer

held up the newspaper that he had folded underneath his arm. "Ya see this?" he asked aloud in disbelief. He slapped the newspaper with the back of his hand causing it to unfold. There was Eyonna's mug shot next to a larger photo of her dressed in bright orange prison fatigues. She was standing before the judge with her hands chained behind her back, her hair all over her face, and her serial number across her chest in bold black letters. "I hear dey only gon' give this girl down in Kentucky five years," he continued.

"You mean that girl from aroun' here?" Mr. Allen answered without looking up. Hearing about the tragedy was old news but everybody in the neighborhood still talked about it because it had hit so close to home.

"Nah, I'm talkin' about down in Kentucky."

"Yeah, we know," Mr. Allen quickly said.

"Ya'll knew them?" another man asked.

"We mos' certainly did," Mr. Ray confidently said. "Knew all of 'em. I knew that girl when she was a little baby, out here playin'."

Once Mr. Ray started talking, the shop was completely quiet and all of the customers were looking up at him like a story-teller around a campfire. They felt since Mr. Ray knew Chuck so well, he would have a first-hand account of what actually happened.

"They only sentenced her to five years?" the customer asked. He then began to quote the newspaper article aloud. "They said she was the mastermind behind everythin'."

"The state of Kentucky don't play," Mr. Allen noted. He was shamelessly shaking his head back and forth with his mouth twisted up. "But dey probably ain't give that girl a lotta' time 'cause dey felt bad for shootin' Chuck so many times."

"Yeah, that's a damn shame," a customer said. "They shot 'em 32 times and the boy didn't even have a gun."

"He did have a gun!" Someone yelled.

"They thought he had a gun," the customer yelled back.

"The cops said dey thought the boy had a gun. But dey

always seein' sump'n," Mr. Ray harshly answered. "We knew all of them kids." Mr. Ray was now pointing out the window. "But when I seen him talkin' to my nephew that day I knew it was only a matter of time before sump'n like this was gon' happen. I tried ta tell'em, ain't no shortcuts in life."

"Yeah?"

"Yes sir, it hurt me to my heart when I heard the news," Mr. Ray was still shaking his head with a somber look on his face. "But it killed his mama when she found out what happened."

"They some racist bastards down there in Kentucky," the customer loudly said, which cause a ruckus. Now they were all talking at the same time like barbershop lawyers.

§

A month later Mr. Ray was well settled in his new place, the news about Chuck, Eyonna and Apple had died down, and it seemed the streets were quieter without Zachary in New York.

Then one Wednesday night Mr. Ray was closing up the shop by himself only because Mr. Allen had left early. It was a slow day so he didn't feel like sitting around watching television.

It was daily routine for Mr. Ray to make sure the shop was clean before he locked the doors, then he pulled down the steel gates that covered the barbershop's window.

While he was locking the gates, people walked by telling him to have a good night and to get home safe. He had just finished closing the last lock on the gate when out of the corner of his eye, he spotted a figure lurking in the dark. Mr. Ray quickly dropped the small bag he was holding and he reached for his pistol. The dark figure quickly pleaded with him not to shoot. The only thing that stopped him was the voice that he knew so well.

"It's me, uncle," Zachary anxiously said and it was clear to see that he was in bad shaped because he was not sharply dressed as usual. He had grown a full beard, his pants were wrinkled and he smelled horrible.

"What the hell is wrong wit you?" Mr. Ray asked with his face in a knot. He really didn't care what Zachary's problem was but he was surprised to see him looking so disreputable.

Zachary went on to tell Mr. Ray that he was on the run and he was unable to get a good night's sleep. "The police tryin' to accuse me of murda', uncle. I ain't kill nobody, Uncle Ray."

"Shhhit…I doubt that," Mr. Ray sternly said. "We seen the papers, but what the hell you want me to do? I can't do shit for you, Zachary. When I tried to talkin' to you, you didn't wanna nut'n I had to say."

"They tryin' ta say I killed somebody," Zachary cried again as he tugged on Mr. Ray's sleeve. "I ain't kill nobody. Everybody I know is turnin' dey back on me an' now I ain't got nowhere to go. I ain't kill nobody, Uncle Ray."

"I doubt that."

"Please uncle, don't turn ya back on me now."

"Boy, listen to me," Mr. Ray said as he snatched his arm away. "I know the cops lookin' for you. Them agents came aroun' here wit'cha picture and I told 'em the truth. I told 'em I don't give two shits about you Zachary and when they find you, the streets of New York will be a betta' place."

Zachary cried, "Na uncle, I ain't do shit man! Jus' hear me out?"

Mr. Ray stood there for a moment listening to Zachary's story and it looked as if he was beginning to feel sorry for him. "So what'chu want me to do?"

"Jus' let me stay in the shop for the night?" Zachary begged and Mr. Ray stepped back and looked at him like he was crazy. "I ain't got nowhere else to go."

When Mr. Ray told him "no" for the final time, he began to

walk off, leaving Zachary to stand alone.

Zachary quickly ran behind Mr. Ray and grabbed him by his arm again. Mr. Ray stopped short and stared at Zachary's hand. Zachary was now coldly staring at Mr. Ray as the two men stood there for a moment.

Mr. Ray suddenly had a change of heart. He started thinking about all of the hard times he had with Zachary but on the other hand, he thought "this is my sister's baby."   "I'll let you stay in the shop for tonight and tonight only," Mr. Ray said, "but ya gotta be out first thing in the mornin'."

"Thank you, Uncle Ray. Thank you."

Mr. Ray began to undo the locks on the gates and after he turned on the lights in the back of the shop, he showed Zachary the refrigerator. Once he made sure that Zachary was comfortable the two men started talking and then they hugged like long-lost brothers. Zachary felt strange because they had not shared a moment like this in years, but he was happy to know that he had someone to talk to.

After Mr. Ray told Zachary that he would be by early in the morning, he left the shop.

Twelve minutes later the barbershop was swarming with federal agents. Most of them were dressed in T-shirts, jeans and the only things that separated them from the average pedestrian walking the streets were their bulletproof vests.

Mr. Ray had purposely left he pistol on the counter where Zachary could see it, knowing that he would reach for it when the police knocked on the door.

The agents burst in the shop with their guns drawn and Zachary tried using the thick barbershop chairs as cover but he didn't stand a chance. Soon as they saw Zachary with a gun they started shooting. Shards of glass flew in a heap of gray smoke and once he realized that he didn't stand a chance against those agents he fled to the back of the shop and tried to jump out of the bathroom window. He was shot so many times in the back and in his ass that night that the bullets broke his hip bone. Zachary fell back and died with one foot hanging out of the window and upside down with his head nearly hitting the toilet seat.

Mr. Ray stood across the street behind the police barricade, only hoping that the business didn't go up in smoke again but on the other hand, he didn't have to put up with Zachary's bullshit any more.

The end

Other books by
The Great Persuader includes

Corner Stores
In The Middle Of The Block

by **by BLUE**

www.Poetryisalive.com

For information about special discount
for bulk purchase please contact

The Great Persuader©
P.O. Box 1100 New York N.Y. 10030

Greatpersuader@Hotmail.com